THE SMILE OF THE BOUGAINVILLEA

DURAI R

INFINIDATUM PRESS

A novel of migration and becoming

ISBN: 979-8-9935232-6-2 (Hardcover)

ISBN: 979-8-9935232-5-5 (Paperback)

ISBN: 979-8-9935232-4-8 (Ebook)

Library of Congress Control Number: 2025925513

First Edition: December 15, 2025

Published by Infinidatum Press LLC, USA

❀ Formatted with Vellum

For those who left home.

For those who are still searching for where they belong. For those who have learned to bloom in unexpected places.

"I don't know what I expected. Something different than this."

Heard at Heathrow, Terminal 5

PREFACE

This novel concerns lives lived provisionally.

The narrator grows up in a government township in Neyveli, leaves for Chennai, then Dubai, and later London. Across these moves, he forms relationships that quietly and unevenly shape him. Some are chosen; others arise through circumstance. Their effects do not announce themselves at the time but accumulate gradually, often unnoticed, until they become unavoidable.

Rather than tracing an apparent rise or fall, the novel focuses on the middle years—periods shaped less by decisive events than by habits that are formed and maintained. It follows a man who builds a stable life by postponing specific questions, convinced that clarity will come later, when there is more time or less at stake.

The story is told through therapy, with the narrator recalling his past through memory rather than in chronological order. These recollections are partial and shaped by distance. They are attentive to what was said, what was done, and what remained unspoken.

This is not a story of arrival or redemption. It is concerned instead with the quiet negotiations that define adulthood: choices that seem minor when made, compromises that appear reasonable until they become irreversible, and the ways people learn to live with the lives they have built.

AUTHOR'S NOTE

This novel is a work of fiction. Its characters are composite, its timelines adjusted, and certain scenes imagined. Some events are wholly fictional.

These choices were made not to obscure truth, but to render it more clearly, in service of narrative and emotional coherence rather than strict factual sequence.

Migration resists simple explanation. It is neither only an act of courage nor a single, irretrievable loss. Much of what it demands is negotiated quietly, without language. Its consequences are often felt long before they are fully understood.

PROLOGUE

*J*anani sits in Dr Claire Hammond's consulting room.

Claire is in her early fifties, with short grey hair and rimless glasses that soften her gaze rather than shield it. She waits without interrupting.

"I don't know if I'm imagining it," Janani says finally. "Or if this is what divorce looks like."

Claire nods. "Tell me what you're noticing."

Janani lifts her teacup, then sets it down untouched. "He switches. Mid-sentence. His accent changes. His posture. It's like he becomes someone else."

"How long has this been happening?"

"I noticed it during the marriage. I thought it was stress. Work. The visa." She hesitates. "I told myself it was temporary."

Claire writes something. "What else?"

"Blankness," Janani says. "He'll look at me as if he's looking through me. Not unkindly. Just... absent. And his voice—sometimes it's his. Sometimes it's this corporate version. Perfect. Polished. Empty."

"Does he seem aware of it?"

11

Janani shakes her head. "No. That's the worst part. He doesn't know it's happening. When I mention it, he looks at me like I'm inventing it."

Claire leans forward slightly. "And you?"

"I feel like I'm talking to someone who keeps leaving the room while staying seated."

A pause.

"Can you help him?" Janani asks.

"I can," Claire says carefully. "But only if he wants help. He has to come here himself."

"He won't," Janani says. "If I suggest it, he'll think I'm trying to fix him. Or manage him."

"Then how do you imagine this happening?"

Janani is quiet for a long moment. "There's someone else. Someone he trusts."

Later that evening, she finds Amir's number.

She tells him what she has noticed—the switching, the distance, the way Dev seems to be receding from his own life.

"He won't hear it from me," she says. "But he might hear it from you."

Amir doesn't answer immediately.

Finally, he says, "I'll try. But he has to choose it."

"I know," Janani says. "I just need someone to try."

Back in the consulting room, Claire listens.

"You're asking me to see him as a favour to you."

"Yes," Janani says. "I know it's unusual."

"You're separated."

"Yes."

"And yet?"

Janani exhales. "He's the children's father."

Claire considers this. "I'll see him," she says. "If he comes."

"Thank you."

Claire adds gently, "This isn't your responsibility anymore."

Janani stands. She nods, once.

"I know," she says.

She pauses at the door.

"Not yet."

PART I
ROOTS & RESTLESSNESS

Where leaving feels like the only honest choice

THE BEAUTIFUL
PAST AND THE CARD

That afternoon, Janani sat in a café near Regent's Canal, grading papers between lectures.

The university had offered her a part-time teaching role in literature, not in marketing copy. She needed it now, needed the income.

She'd woken at five, made breakfast for the children, packed their lunches, dropped them at school, rushed to campus, taught two classes, and held office hours.

The papers were from her first-year literature class, all essays on The God of Small Things. Some were good, most were adequate, and a few were brilliant—those reminded her why she wanted to teach, why she had declined the job twice before, and why she finally accepted it this time.

She reread the same paragraph, pen hovering, and she hadn't taken a full breath in minutes. She'd marked three papers. Seventeen remained. The stack felt endless.

The café was quiet in the mid-afternoon lull between lunch and the evening rush. She'd chosen a table by the window overlooking the canal. The still water reflected the grey October sky, the clouds, and the branches lining the towpath.

A few mallards drifted past, their green heads catching the light, creating small ripples. On the opposite bank, a pair of moorhens sat close together, their red-and-yellow beaks bright against the dark water.

She watched them move in harmony, aware of each other without needing to look. One shifted, the other adjusted. Small movements, almost imperceptible. They occupied the same space, perfectly attuned.

She took a sip of tea and returned her attention to the papers. The words blurred. She rubbed her eyes and pressed her fingertips against her temples. A headache was forming, the kind that began behind the eyes and spread slowly.

* * *

SHE REMEMBERED Valentine's Day three years ago.

He came home with pink roses, her favourite, and for once hadn't checked his phone. He cooked, played music, and pulled her into the kitchen like they were nineteen again. The curry smelled of cardamom and cinnamon. He'd slightly burn the onions, as he always did, and she'd laugh and say it was perfect.

She'd reciprocated. Breakfast in bed. Small notes around the flat. Calls during lunch to say she loved him, the accumulation of small things that made something real.

Birthdays, too. Not expensive gifts, but thoughtfulness. A walk, a picnic, something that showed he'd been thinking of her. The time he planned a day trip to Brighton, packed sandwiches, a blanket, and a book he thought she'd like. They sat on the pebbled beach, watching the waves, not saying much, just being together.

She recalled another drive, from Bethnal Green to Hackney Marshes on a late autumn afternoon, the sky turning gold, orange, pink. They'd been talking and laughing, unguarded. The radio played softly. The sun sat low, casting long shadows across the road.

Then they saw it, a murmuration. Hundreds, maybe thousands of birds moving together, forming shapes in the sky. A heart. A wave. A spiral dissolving and reforming. Each bird knows precisely where to be, how to move.

Dev had pulled over and jumped out, his face lit up like a child's. He stood watching, then pulled out his phone and began typing, eyes still on the birds, fingers moving quickly, urgently, as if the words would vanish if he missed them.

When he finished, he turned to her, eyes bright.

"Listen," he said, and read a poem about the murmuration and them.

> *In the hush before evening*
> *Your hand finds mine,*
> *Love isn't loud. It gathers slowly...*

She knew the rest by heart.

"I love you," he said. "This is how I feel. This is what we are. A murmuration. Moving together."

Tears filled her eyes. They stood there until the light faded, until the birds settled, until the sky darkened. She'd saved that poem, printed it, framed it, and hung it in their bedroom.

It was now in a storage box, sealed with tape.

She looked back at the papers but couldn't focus. Her mind remained in the past, with the man who had written that poem. The man who had been present. Who had noticed things? Who had seen her?

She glanced at the clock. Twenty minutes. Enough time to finish two more papers if she concentrated. But focus felt impossible.

She gathered the papers, stuffed them into her bag, paid at the counter, and stepped outside.

* * *

THE CANAL WAS STILL. The moorhens were gone. The water reflected nothing now, only the grey sky.

She walked to her car, sat with the key in the ignition without turning it. The engine would start. The children would be waiting.

But for a moment, she stayed there, then started the engine.

* * *

JANANI STOPPED at the florist on the corner of Camden Road without meaning to.

The door chimed softly as she stepped inside. The air was cool and damp, heavy with the smell of cut stems and earth. Buckets lined the walls, tulips just opening, chrysanthemums already past their best, lilies still tight and green. Water pooled on the floor near the sink, darkening the concrete.

A woman stood behind the counter, trimming rose stems with practised efficiency. The scissors made a clean, decisive sound each time they closed.

Janani drifted toward the window display. Bouquets were arranged in loose clusters, not symmetrical, some flowers leaning into others, some already shedding petals. A few pale pink roses lay apart, their outer petals bruised, edges curling inward.

She reached out and touched one, lightly. The petal was cooler than she expected, almost waxy. It left a faint moisture on her fingertip.

"How long do they last?" she asked, not looking up.

"Depends where you put them," the woman said. "Heat kills them faster. Direct sun too."

Janani nodded. She turned the rose slightly and noticed a brown mark near the stem, where the florist's fingers must have held it earlier, a small, human imprint.

"I'll take just one," she said.

The woman wrapped it in plain brown paper, folded it neatly, and secured it with a thin piece of twine. No ribbon.

Outside, the October air felt sharper. Janani tucked the flower under her arm and walked toward the car. The stem brushed against her coat with each step.

At a red light, she rested the rose on the passenger seat. The car smelled faintly of paper and an unfamiliar green odour. When the light changed, she drove on, careful not to let it slide.

* * *

JANANI REACHED the school gates ten minutes early and sat in the car with the engine off. The playground was already loud. Children ran in uneven bursts, jackets half-zipped, backpacks swinging low enough to knock their legs. Teachers stood in clusters, watching without intervening unless they had to.

She watched for her children the way she always did—scanning faces, then more slowly, her eyes trained to notice hesitation before recognition.

Her son came out first. He walked rather than ran, shoulders already slumped, as if the day had been heavier than he expected.

He looked up, saw the car, and raised one hand in a gesture that wasn't quite a wave. Her daughter followed, stopping to tie a shoelace that didn't need tying, delaying the moment of leaving.

They climbed into the back seat.

"How was school?" Janani asked.

"Fine," her son said.

Her daughter didn't answer. She pressed her forehead briefly against the window, leaving a faint mark that fogged and then cleared.

Janani started the car.

They drove in silence for a few minutes before her daughter spoke.

"Why doesn't Appa come to pick up anymore?"

Janani kept her eyes on the road. "He's busy with work."

"He was busy before, too," her daughter said.

Janani nodded once. She didn't correct her.

At a traffic light, her son leaned forward between the seats. "He used to tell jokes," he said. "Remember? Bad ones."

"Yes," Janani said. "I remember."

21

"He doesn't do that now," her son said. "When he talks, it's like he's talking to someone else."

Janani felt something tighten just behind her ribs. She adjusted the rearview mirror, buying herself a second.

"He's tired," she said.

Her daughter turned toward her. "You're tired too."

Janani smiled, careful. "Everyone is tired sometimes."

At home, backpacks were dropped in the hallway. Shoes were kicked off unevenly. The house filled with noise—cups clinking, drawers opening, the scrape of chairs against tile.

Janani stood at the kitchen counter, slicing apples, the knife moving with practised precision. The children sat at the table, arguing quietly about whose turn it was to choose a snack.

Her son watched her hands.

"You always cut them the same way," he said.

She looked down. She did—thin slices, uniform, arranged without thinking.

"Does it matter?" she asked.

He shrugged. "No. Just noticed."

They ate. Homework followed. Janani moved between rooms, answering questions, correcting spelling, and reminding them to sit correctly.

She did all of it efficiently, as if competence itself could keep things from unravelling. Later, after the children had showered and put on pyjamas, her daughter climbed into Janani's bed without asking.

She curled against her, small and warm, already halfway asleep.

"Will Appa read to us tonight?" she asked, eyes closed.

"Not tonight," Janani said.

"Tomorrow?" Janani didn't answer immediately.

Her daughter opened one eye.

"You don't know." Janani stroked her hair.

"No," she said softly.

"I don't know."

When her daughter finally slept, Janani lay awake, staring at the ceiling. The day replayed itself in fragments—questions she had answered too easily, silences she had filled out of habit.

She thought of how often she chose calm. Usually, she deferred. How natural it had become to smooth things over before they caught. She wondered when that had stopped being patience and become something else.

Then, she filled a glass with water and set the rose on the kitchen counter. It leaned slightly to one side, unsupported. A petal loosened and fell, landing near the sink.

She left it there.

* * *

AMIR CALLED me to his flat.

I hadn't heard from him in weeks. The invitation was unusual. Formal. Tense. Not the usual casual message, not a pub invite. This was serious.

He opened the door, and I saw immediately that something was wrong. His expression was set, his hands clenched, shoulders tight. I'd never seen him like that, not in all the years we'd been friends. Not in Dubai. Not in London. He was always the one who joked, who lightened the mood. Not today.

"Come in."

His flat was tidy, but uneasiness lingered in the air. He didn't offer tea or ask how I was. He stood there, watching me, as if deciding how to proceed.

"Sit."

I sat on the sofa. He stayed standing. It felt like an intervention.

"Dev, we've been friends a long time. I've been watching you. I see what's happening."

"I don't know what you're talking about."

"Dr Claire Hammond," he said, pulling a card from his pocket. White cardstock. Simple typeface. An address in Hackney.

He didn't look like a man making a suggestion.

"I don't need this."

"I'm not asking. I'm telling you. It's time."

"Time for what?"

"To get help. To stop pretending you're fine."

"That's not true."

"It is. I'm tired of watching you disappear."

He left the room, returned with a phone, and held it out.

"Call. Now."

I saw fear in his eyes. Not concerned. Fear. As if this were the last chance to reach me.

I took the phone. Dialled and made the appointment. When I handed it back, he only nodded.

The card stayed in my hand. I slipped it into my pocket.

* * *

THAT EVENING, I walked to Claire's clinic.

The building was unassuming, a converted Victorian house in Hackney. Inside, the waiting room was small, warmly lit. A plant stood in the corner. Magazines lay neatly arranged. Everything felt intentional, considered.

I sat, trembling.

I could leave. No one would know. But I stayed.

A door opened. A woman with short grey hair and kind eyes stepped out.

"Dev?"

"Yes."

"I'm Claire. Come in."

Her office overlooked a small garden. Two chairs. Books on trauma line the walls.

I sat. The chair felt solid, grounding.

She waited. Didn't rush. Didn't fill the space. The silence held.

"Why are you here?" she asked.

"Amir made me come."

"Did he? Or did you choose to come?"

I didn't answer. I wasn't sure.

"Tell me about yourself."

I tried. The words sounded flat, scripted, facts without weight.

She waited.

"How do your days usually start?"

"I wake up. Go to work."

"And when you're alone?"

"I sit."

"Just sit?"

"Yes."

"And?"

"And I wait," I said. "Like something is supposed to happen."

She didn't interrupt.

* * *

THE FOLLOWING WEEK, I came back.

"Are you ready to tell me your story?" she asked.

I looked at my hands.

"I don't know where to begin."

"Start where it makes sense to you."

I looked out the window. Rain streaked the glass. October light faded.

Where to begin, when the only pattern was leaving.

"This wasn't the first time I left," I said.

The words were there, somewhere. Distant. As if they belonged to someone else.

THE FLOWER THAT
DIDN'T ASK QUESTIONS

*T*hen I began: "Neyveli, my birthplace. A lignite mining town where dust settled before memory did."

* * *

THE BOUGAINVILLEA GREW outside our government quarters without anyone planting it, bright pink blooms returning year after year in the Neyveli heat, too vivid for a coal town, too alive against the grey dust that settled on everything. The colour always looked almost artificial, as if someone had painted it on and forgotten to stop.

My mother tried to tame it once. She cut back the branches that reached toward our windows, careful but firm, as if discipline could make a plant behave. Within weeks, it came back, wilder, more determined, its thorns catching the light the way small truths do when you try not to look at them. The flowers remained that impossible pink, the kind that shouldn't exist in a mining township, yet there they were, defying expectation, defying soot, refusing to be muted.

Neyveli was a government township built around lignite mines. Planned streets. Identical white quarters for engineers and mining officials, arranged in a grid that spoke of bureaucratic order. In the distance, the plant dominated the skyline, chimneys releasing smoke that turned the evening into burnt orange and amber.

The air carried the mineral tang of coal dust, the acrid scent of lignite, and something else, a metallic sharpness that lingered on the tongue. My father worked there. So did most of the men in our colony. They returned each evening with coal dust embedded under their fingernails, their hair powdered grey, their shirts smelling faintly of heat and machinery.

The bougainvillea didn't care. It bloomed anyway, defiant, persistent.

My mother watered it every evening after the worst of the heat broke, when the sky began to shift from orange to purple. She would stand at the edge of the verandah with a steel tumbler, pouring water at the roots, talking to it as if it could hear her. I watched from my window with my homework spread on the desk and wondered why she bothered. The plant would bloom whether she watered it or not.

But she did it anyway. Every evening.

Thara lived three houses down, in the blue building with the broken gate. She was two years younger than me and, in our colony, that meant she could walk in without knocking, call my mother "Aunty," and ask, as if she owned the place, "I'm making coffee, do you want some?"

Yet when she arrived, I either ceased to exist or became the common enemy.

She and my mother formed alliances instantly. If I even mentioned computers, they would unite, two women with the same tone, to lecture me on how technology was rotting my brain.

They'd sit in the verandah with their coffee, talking. If I walked past, they'd pause, look at me, and continue as if I were furniture that had started moving. I'd hear my name. My marks. My future. Their voices carried through the house, creating a soundtrack of expectation, of being known.

* * *

THE ENGINEERING COLLEGE took me to Thiruchirapalli.

Four years in a hostel room shared with three others. Computer Science, because it was the promising path, because it led to good jobs, because it sounded like an answer.

I wrote letters to Thara on inland letters, thin blue pre-stamped sheets that folded into their own envelopes. I told her about college, about the hostel, about my roommates, about small humiliations and small victories I couldn't tell anyone else.

Thara wrote back.

Her letters were shorter. She wrote about her own college in Pondicherry, about new friends, new routines, a life that was slowly becoming hers.

* * *

TWO YEARS BEFORE COLLEGE, 12th standard.

I was in 12th, drowning in entrance exam preparation. Thara was in 10th, facing board exams. Our futures hung on those scores, mine on engineering entrance results, hers on the first set of marks that people would treat like a verdict.

I'd promised her I'd collect all the question papers for her subjects.

I kept forgetting.

One afternoon, her voice cut through the house from the front room. "Where is that idiot, aunty?"

The words were sharp enough to travel.

Footsteps in the hallway. My door swung open.

She stood there, hands on her hips, face flushed, eyes bright with anger, her whole body tense as if she'd been holding it in for weeks.

"Idiot. Two months I've been waiting."

"I have them somewhere."

"Somewhere?" She grabbed a pillow and threw it at me. It hit my chest, soft, but her hand shook as she released it.

My mother appeared in the doorway holding coffee. "Thara." She extended the tumbler.

Thara's entire demeanour shifted. "Thank you, aunty," she said, sweet and polite, only for my mother. Never for me. I got the real Thara.

My mother's eyes moved to me. "Where are the question papers, Dev?"

Betrayal, that my mother always sided with Thara, that she believed Thara's anger more than my panic.

I started pulling papers from different stacks: mathematics buried under entrance exam tests, physics behind novels, question papers scattered everywhere, disorganised, as if my room itself had been studying.

"That's not everything," Thara said. "What about Tamil? Social Studies?"

"You said science subjects."

"I said all subjects." Her voice rose, sharper now.

My mother set down her cup with a decisive clink. "Dev. Get her all the question papers. All subjects. By tomorrow."

"Yes, Amma."

Thara finished her coffee, still glaring. Tomorrow. All subjects. The sentence landed like law.

The next day, I showed up at her house with a folder. Everything she'd asked for. Every subject. Every paper I could find, as if paper could undo time.

She opened the door and snatched it from my hands. "About time."

Then she made a face, scrunched her nose, stuck out her tongue slightly, the way she did when she wanted to punish me and forgive me at the same time.

The door closed.

I stood there grinning like an idiot.

* * *

BACK TO COLLEGE, four years later.

College passed in letters and visits. Thara wrote about missing me. I wrote back about missing her. Distance felt manageable when it had an end date, when you could say: two years, and one, then soon. She still had time left; I still had time left. The ceremonies were formal; the futures were uncertain.

But I was still the boy from Neyveli.

* * *

ONE EVENING in my third year, I was walking back to the hostel after classes. The sky was turning crimson, the sun dropping behind buildings, painting everything in red and orange and gold. The air was still, the day's heat finally loosening its grip.

I was thinking about exams, assignments, the future that felt both close and impossibly distant, and I saw it.

A murmuration.

Hundreds of birds moving as one, a living cloud against the golden evening. They shifted and turned and folded into themselves, shaping the sky into something that seemed impossible: a wave, and a spiral, then a heart, dissolving, reforming, always moving, always together.

I stopped. Just stood there. Breath caught in my throat.

They moved like a single organism, something beyond individual will, beyond individual choice, as if togetherness itself had a physics.

I watched until the light thinned, until the sky darkened, until it was only me in the middle of campus, standing still after witnessing something that felt like magic.

* * *

I STARTED SPENDING hours at internet cafés, watching videos of Dubai, London, and Singapore.

The cafés were dark, small, and crowded. The computers were slow. Connections unreliable. The video is grainy.

But I watched anyway for hours.

* * *

DURING ONE OF my holiday visits home from engineering college, I told Thara to meet me at the Indian Coffee House.

"Somewhere no one will recognise us."

To our parents, we were childhood friends. In the colony, that was safe. But outside, when two teenagers meet in public, people would talk. Talk could become consequences.

The coffee house became our sanctuary.

I claimed a corner table obscured by a pillar, creating a small pocket of privacy inside a public room. The lights were dim, the ceiling fans turning slowly, blades making a hypnotic rhythm. Photographs lined the walls, political leaders, literary figures, their faces watching like silent witnesses. The air carried the scent of filter coffee and fried snacks.

When she sat down across from me, I forgot how to breathe.

She wore a plain cotton saree, pale yellow, warm against her brown skin. The fabric caught the window light softly. Her hair was tied low, gathered into a loose bun threaded with fresh jasmine, the white flowers bright against her dark hair. The fragrance was subtle but present, like a thought you couldn't shake.

She didn't look dressed up.

She looked composed. Serene. As if she had found her place, her peace, herself.

"What?" she asked, smiling slightly.

"You look beautiful."

Her smile widened. "You can't say things like that here. Someone might hear."

She reached across the table and traced a pattern on my palm. Her fingertip was electric. The touch sent a current through me, making me aware of every breath, of this moment, of her, of us.

We ordered filter coffee, strong and sweet.

When it came, she closed her eyes on the first sip as if tasting something sacred. The coffee arrived in the stainless steel tumbler and davara, the traditional South Indian way. The tumbler was hot to the touch, the coffee dark and aromatic, the foam on top a testament to the person who'd made it.

"I'm always happy when I'm with you," she said. "Even when I'm terrified we'll get caught."

She leaned forward, voice dropping. "I want to hold your hand where people can see. Walk down the main street in Neyveli with you beside me, not ten paces apart. I want, " Her eyes met mine with an intensity that made me forget to breathe. ", not to have to hide that I love you."

"Don't," I said. "Not when we're hiding. When you say it, I want it to be somewhere we don't have to whisper."

We sat there for two hours, hands linked, talking about our colleges, what we were learning, the lives we were building apart from each other.

The conversation flowed easily, as if we'd been saving words for this, saving moments, keeping the feeling of being fully seen.

"Do you think about what comes after?" she asked.

"Sometimes. A job somewhere. Perhaps Chennai. Perhaps Bangalore. I'm uncertain yet."

Not here. Not a question.

* * *

WE DIDN'T WALK BACK TOGETHER at first.

Not until the street thinned and the noise dropped away, until the shops gave way to houses and the open ground came into view. The neem tree stood where it always had, its branches barely moving in the evening air.

She stopped there.

"You don't have to walk me all the way," she said.

"I know."

Neither of us moved.

After a moment, she reached for my hand. Not quickly. Not as if she were afraid I'd pull away. Her fingers rested against mine, light enough that I could have pretended it was accidental.

I didn't close my hand around hers immediately. I waited. I don't know why, perhaps because everything between us felt like it required confirmation.

When I did, her thumb traced the inside of my palm, slowly, as if she were learning it. The gesture unsettled me more than anything she'd said all afternoon.

"If someone sees—" she began.

"No one is looking," I said, although I wasn't sure.

We stood there longer than needed. No kiss. No urgency. Just the quiet realisation that something had crossed a line it couldn't come back from.

When she stepped away, she did so carefully, as if she were giving something back rather than pulling it away.

That night, lying awake, I realised I had already learned how intimacy begins—quietly, before you recognise it for what it is.

* * *

ONE EVENING during one of my visits home from Chennai, Thara asked me to come to her house.

The house was quiet.

We sat in her room. The walls were covered with books, Tamil novels, English classics, and poetry collections.

Stories she'd written were tucked into notebooks, hidden in drawers. She was always writing, always creating.

"I want to read you something," she said.

She pulled out a notebook, the cover worn from handling, pages filled with her careful script. Her handwriting was neat and deliberate, each letter formed with intention, beautiful in its precision, the way she was. She found what she wanted and looked at me. Her hands trembled slightly, as if she were offering something vulnerable.

"It's a short story," she said. "About a girl who lives in a small town. Who dreams of something more. Who writes letters to herself, pretending they're from someone else. Someone who sees her."

She began reading.

Her voice was soft, careful, each word chosen, each sentence crafted. The story held longing and dreams, and that space between who you are and who you want to be, the letters bridging the gap.

I listened, not only to the words but to her: how she held the notebook, how she breathed between sentences, how she had made a world out of what she couldn't say aloud.

When she finished, she studied me, waiting, the notebook still in her hands.

"That's beautiful," I said. "How do you write. How do you see things? How do you understand people?"

"You think so?"

"I know so. You're an excellent writer. You should write more. You should share this. Please send it to Tamil weeklies. They'd publish this."

Her smile came bright and sudden, as if I'd given her something she didn't know she was allowed to have. "You think so?"

"I think so. You're talented."

She laughed softly. "You're being silly."

"I'm not. I'm being honest. You should let people read them. You should let people see what you can do."

Her gaze locked with mine, eyes bright with gratitude. "Thank you," she said. "That means everything."

"It's the truth."

She closed the notebook and held it to her chest as if it were precious. "I'll think about it," she said. "About sending it."

"You should."

She smiled again, that same bright smile.

"I will," she said. "Because you believe in me. Because you see me."

"You can," I said. "You absolutely can."

* * *

35

ONE WEEKEND DURING COLLEGE BREAK, I went to Pichavaram with my friends, Ravi, Saravanan, and Alvin. We'd planned it for weeks, saving money from part-time jobs, borrowing a friend's car, and packing food for the day.

Pichavaram was a mangrove forest near Chidambaram, one of the largest in India. The backwaters stretched for kilometres, a labyrinth of channels cutting through mangroves, roots creating a network above and below the water. We hired a boat, a small wooden thing that sat low in the water.

The water was still, reflecting the sky, the mangroves, everything doubled.

The mangroves looked ancient, their roots like gnarled fingers reaching into the water, a forest existing half on land, half in water. The air was thick with salt and mud, decay and growth.

We spent the day exploring, getting lost in channels, finding our way back, laughing when we realised we'd been going in circles. Ravi tried to catch fish with his hands. Saravanan fell into the water trying to climb a mangrove root. Alvin, the sensible one, watched and laughed at the rest of us.

When I got back to Neyveli that evening, I went straight to Thara's house.

She was in her room writing. I knocked on her window, and she came out.

I told her about it, about the mangroves, their roots like a network of veins; about the water reflecting everything; about channels that seemed endless; about the feeling of being in a place that existed between land and sea, between fresh and salt water.

I got carried away. I started describing details: the light filtering through mangrove leaves; the boat sliding through channels with the water making almost no sound; the canopy overhead, branches inter-locking into a green tunnel; the whole place feeling timeless, as if it had existed that way for centuries.

"What are you doing?" I asked.

"Taking notes." She didn't look up. "Your description. The way you're narrating it. I'm going to use this in my story."

I stopped. "You're going to use my narration?"

"Yes." She looked up, eyes bright, excited. "How do you describe things. How do you see them? It's different. It's good."

I laughed. "That would be one of your worst products."

She smiled, knowing. "I know how to protect my writing quality. I'll take what works. I'll make it better. I'll make it mine. But your voice, how you see things, that's what I want to capture."

* * *

WE SAT under the neem tree at the edge of the open ground.

The neem tree was old, trunk gnarled and weathered, branches spreading wide to make a canopy of shade. The sun was turning everything gold, light filtering through leaves, casting dappled patterns on the ground, on our faces, on the space between us. The air was still, the heat of the day finally breaking, evening bringing a slight breeze.

"Do you think there's a universe where we don't have to hide?" she asked.

"Probably," I said. "Somewhere out there, there's a version of us that can walk down the street holding hands."

She reached for my hand. Her fingers were warm.

"I'm terrified," she said. "Of how much I feel. Of not knowing what happens next."

"I love you."

Her hand tightened around mine. "I know," she said. "I love you too."

* * *

CHENNAI.

My first job was at InfoBridge Solutions in Chennai. Contract work for American banks. The work was tedious and repetitive. I wrote code that tested other people's code.

But I learned. I learned to debug production issues at 2 a.m.

37

My mother kept asking when I would look for a suitable girl. On weekends, I kept watching videos of San Francisco, London, and Dubai on the internet in internet cafés. The routine calcified: work, weekends, visits home. The same questions. The same answers.

I visited Neyveli on weekends. Thara graduated a year later, moved back home, and worked as an engineer at a small firm in the township. We met at the coffee house or under the neem tree. We talked.

* * *

DUBAI APPEARED in an email three years into my job in Chennai.

A recruitment firm was hiring for tech consulting positions in the UAE. They needed engineers with three to four years of experience in enterprise systems. The salary was more than ten times what I was making in Chennai. Company-provided accommodation. Medical insurance. Annual flight home.

I printed the job description at an internet café and read it three times.

When I told Thara, we were at our coffeehouse. Afternoon light filtered through the windows, casting long shadows across worn wooden tables. The smell of filter coffee and fried snacks hung in the air, familiar, comforting.

I'd carried the printout in my bag for a week before showing it to anyone. I'd folded it carefully, kept it in my wallet, pulled it out to read again when I was alone. The words felt like a promise. The salary felt like freedom.

I slid it across the table.

She looked at the page and at me. Her expression didn't change, but her eyes did. A small distance opened, something closed, something retreated.

"You're going to apply." Not a question. A statement. A fact she had already accepted.

"I can't say."

"Yes, you do."

Silence. The kind that fills a room and makes you aware of breath and heartbeat and time passing, each second bringing you closer to leaving, to ending.

"It's a good opportunity," I said.

"I know," she said. "It is. But that doesn't make it easier. It doesn't make it hurt less. It doesn't make it okay."

"It's two, three years. Save money. Get international experience."

"That's what everyone says who leaves," she said, voice steady but sharp underneath. "Two years become five. Five becomes ten. You don't come back. You don't come back because you can't, because you've changed, because you've become someone else. The person who left no longer exists. They're gone. If you come back at all."

"So you think I shouldn't apply?"

She stirred her coffee without looking at me. Her hands were steady. "I think you're going to apply whether I think you should or not."

* * *

"If you leave, you won't come back," my mother said.

We were sitting in the verandah on a Sunday evening. I had come home for the weekend, ostensibly to visit, to tell them about Dubai. I had shown her the job posting and the salary expectations.

"I will," I said. "For two, three years. Save some money. Learn from working abroad."

"No." She didn't raise her voice. She didn't need to. "Once you leave, you won't come back. You'll be stuck between."

"That's not, "

"Do you love Thara?" she asked.

I stared at her.

"Why are you asking? I'm not sure."

"Then what are you doing?" she said. "If you love her, talk to her. I can see you both like each other. You work in Chennai. Have a family life here. Settle. Don't love someone and say nothing, leaving them without asking. That's not bravery."

My jaw tightened.

"Your father and I have a good life," my mother continued. "You have a life."

Then she flinched, as if she'd revealed too much.

"It's not the life I want," she added.

"And what life do you want?" she asked.

"I want to be part of something bigger than a town," I said. "Somewhere I'm evaluated on what I can do, not who I'm related to."

"And what would it mean," she asked, "to be known so thoroughly?"

"It would be suffocating," I said, and even as I said it, I heard how ungrateful it sounded.

"What's suffocating about it?"

I couldn't answer cleanly. I tried anyway. "Maybe it's not wrong."

She said nothing.

Finally, she spoke, quieter. "No. It's not wrong. It's human. But it costs things. People you leave."

"I know," I said. "And I'm choosing to pay that cost."

She didn't answer. She didn't look at me.

"You have to choose one thing," she said at last. "One place. One person. Your father and I chose this town."

"Maybe that's the difference between us."

She turned to face me then. "Yes," she said. "That's exactly the difference. And it will cost you more than you understand."

* * *

I STOPPED and looked at Claire.

"That's how I left," I said.

Claire was quiet.

"I was twenty-two," I said. "I thought I was choosing freedom."

I looked at my hands.

"At the time, it felt easier," I continued.

"To leave without explaining.

To not have to face what I was doing."

Claire nodded once. "And how does that feel now?"

"Different," I said.

"Now it feels like avoidance."

By the time Janani and I married, I had already been abroad for nearly a decade.

Enough time that the paperwork felt more permanent than promises.

DEPARTURE IS A QUIET ACT

J was five minutes late.

The Tube had been delayed.

I sat down.

Claire waited. She didn't check her watch. She didn't comment on the time. She rested her hands loosely in her lap and let the moment settle.

"I've been thinking about what you asked," I said. "About what I avoided. About Thara."

"And?" she said.

"I'm not sure I can answer it directly yet. But I can tell you what happened next. How I left."

She nodded once. "Go ahead."

* * *

I HAD SUBMITTED applications to companies in Dubai and Abu Dhabi. Then I waited.

The waiting became its own routine.

I checked my email before work, again at lunch, again at night, each time preparing myself for nothing.

The inbox refreshed. My chest tightened. I told myself that meant nothing.

That Saturday evening, I met Thara under the neem tree.

It was the same place we had met for years. The ground beneath it was worn smooth from footsteps. The leaves filtered the late light into shifting patches that moved across her face as the breeze stirred.

We talked about ordinary things. She was in a trainee position at a manufacturing company. My work in Chennai. Updates we exchanged carefully, the way people do when they are trying to keep something steady that is already moving.

Come with me.

The words formed. They reached my mouth. They stayed there.

She looked at me. "What?"

"Nothing," I said. "Just thinking."

"About?"

"Dubai. The applications."

She nodded slowly, as if she had already placed that information somewhere inside herself. "I'll figure it out," she said.

Then she looked away.

The email arrived on a Tuesday morning.

The offer was clear.

The start date. The salary. The logistics lay out neatly, as if order itself could make the decision easier.

I read the email twice before telling her.

By the time I spoke, I'd already chosen which parts to translate.

I went to see her that evening.

We sat under the neem tree once more. Neither of us spoke for a long time. The sun lowered itself, and the sky shifted from pale gold to pink and then to something more profound. It felt too beautiful, the light too generous for what I had to say.

"I got the job," I said.

She didn't react. She didn't ask questions. "When do you leave?"

"Two weeks."

She let that sit.

"Are you going to ask me to come?" she said.

The question landed cleanly between us.

I hesitated. "Would you?" I said. "If I asked?"

She turned to face me fully. "Ask and find out."

"Come with me," I said.

She made a slight sound, not quite a laugh, not quite a sigh. "No."

"Why not?"

"Because you're asking incorrectly." She looked into my eyes. "You're asking as if this is a test. As if the answer will reveal something about yourself."

"That's not what I mean."

"It is what you're doing." Her voice stayed steady, but something underneath it tightened. "You don't want me there."

"That's not, "

"You want Dubai. You want the job." She paused and continued, choosing her words carefully. "You want to know what it feels like to be free. To make choices without carrying anyone else with you."

I didn't speak.

"My family is here," she said. "My job has started. My life began here, among people who know me. Who sees me?" She took a breath. "And even if none of that were true, you're not asking because you can't imagine your life without me."

She watched my face as if waiting for something to change.

"You're asking because you think you should," she said. "Because leaving without asking would make you look worse than you already do. But you decided when you applied. Maybe even before. When you started reading job listings in cities I'd never seen. When you began imagining a life that didn't include me."

Defensiveness rose, quick and sharp.

"So what do you want me to do?" I said. "Not go? Stay here and always wonder?"

"I want you to stop acting like this is hard for you."

Her eyes filled. She didn't wipe them away.

"I love you," I said.

"I know." She looked past me, at the ground beneath the tree.

"I'm sorry."

She didn't answer.

After a while, she stood. She adjusted her dupatta, smoothing it as if the moment required order.

She walked away.

I stayed under the neem tree until the light faded.

* * *

LAST WEEK in Neyveli passed as if each day were a task to be completed.

My mother cleaned my room every morning, even though nothing had changed. After breakfast, she would close the door, open the wardrobe, refold clothes, and move the hangers.

"Amma, I'm taking two bags," I said. "I can't carry all this."

"I know," she said, without looking up. "But it should be clean."

There was no arguing with that.

My father said nothing about my leaving for three days.

On Wednesday evening, he came into my room and sat on the edge of the bed.

"Why are you leaving?" he asked.

"For the job."

"Don't lie to me."

"I can't stay here," I said. "I can't live the life you lived."

He studied me for a long time.

"You think my life wasn't enough."

"That's not, "

"Yes, it is."

He stood, paused at the doorway.

"One day you'll realise," he said, "the problem was never Neyveli."

The latch clicked shut.

For an hour, I stared at my half-packed suitcase.

* * *

THARA CAME to our house on Friday.

My mother offered tea. Thara accepted. They spoke carefully, choosing safe topics. Work. Teaching. The weather.

When my mother left us alone, Thara said, "Walk with me."

We walked to the open ground at the edge of the street. No one was there. It was too hot. The sun was still intense.

We stopped under the neem tree.

"I need you to answer something honestly," she said. "Did you ever consider staying?"

"Of course I did."

"Did you consider it," she said, "or did you keep me waiting while you planned your exit?"

I opened my mouth. She didn't wait.

"That's your answer."

"I loved you."

"That's not love," she said. "That's nostalgia."

The word stayed between us.

"I thought if you asked, I might say yes," she said. "I might leave everything."

"I didn't want to make you give up everything."

"Deciding for me again."

"Don't, "

"Don't explain." Her voice held. "Please don't make it easier."

We stood there in the heat.

"I'm leaving," I said.

"Yes," she said. "You are."

She turned away.

I went back to the house. My mother was cooking. She glanced at my face and said nothing.

In my room, I picked up my phone.

I didn't call.

* * *

I WROTE TO HER ONCE. Not immediately.

Months later, when Chennai had started to feel routine, and Neyveli had receded into something manageable.

The message wasn't long. It wasn't dramatic.

It said nothing I hadn't already said before.

I told her I hoped she was well. That work was settling.

That I still thought of the neem tree sometimes, though I didn't explain why.

I read it twice and recognised its careful avoidance of an apology and a promise.

I didn't send it. I closed the laptop and went to sleep.

The next morning, the draft was still there. That evening, it wasn't. I told myself that was restraint.

I didn't yet know how often I would mistake it for something else.

* * *

BACK IN CHENNAI, I returned to work.

I completed tasks. I handed things over. My manager reminded me to stay focused until I left.

I nodded.

I wasn't.

* * *

THURSDAY NIGHT, I picked up my phone.

I put it down.

I picked it up again.

I put it down again.

* * *

SATURDAY WAS PACKING.

Two bags.

My mother repacked everything I touched.

She cooked as if food could last years.

Outside, the bougainvillea bloomed against the white wall.

* * *

CHENNAI AIRPORT. 4:30 a.m.

My parents came with me.

My mother held my hand. My father drove.

At security, my father shook my hand.

My mother cried.

I didn't look back.

* * *

ON THE PLANE, I sat by the window.

Below, the ground receded.

Somewhere, my mother would water the plants that evening.

Somewhere, Thara would be living a life that no longer included me.

I closed my eyes.

I stopped talking.

"I left," I said. "Without asking. Without choosing."

Claire stayed quiet.

"And after?" she asked.

"I went to Dubai," I said. "Started the job."

"And Thara?"

"We didn't talk."

"Why?"

"It was easier."

She let the silence settle.

"And now?" she asked.

"Now I wonder what would have happened if I'd asked her to come."

Claire nodded once. "We'll come back to that."

She glanced at the clock.

"Next week," she said, "we'll talk about Dubai."

PART II
PROVISIONAL LIVES

Where ambition feels like love

A DIFFERENT KIND OF SILENCE

I arrived early. Sat in the waiting room and flipped through a magazine I didn't really read.

When Claire opened the door, I was already standing.

"You're early."

"Couldn't focus at work."

She nodded and led me in. I sat and stared at the books lining the walls.

"Dubai," she said, not a question, a statement.

"Yes," I said. "Dubai."

* * *

THE COLD HIT FIRST.

The airport's air conditioning was set so aggressively that my skin tightened, and goosebumps formed on my arms even through my shirt. It felt wrong, my body bracing as if it were winter, while outside, behind the glass, heat awaited.

When I stepped through the sliding doors, the heat hit me—not gentle, but a heavy force that made breathing harder. It was May, early morning, but already brutal, with air shimmering and distant views untrustworthy.

Glass walls and ceilings surrounded me, reflections multiplying on polished surfaces. I saw multiple versions of myself in the floor, panels, and doorways: a young man with a suitcase, a wrinkled shirt, trying to look calm. All I owned was in one bag.

The airport stretched ahead, fluorescent, immense, filled with people moving with purpose, as if the city itself had trained them. Everyone seemed to know where they were going.

I stood in the arrivals hall after 6 a.m., holding my suitcase. The shirt my mother ironed two days earlier had wrinkled on the flight, feeling wrong against my skin. The air smelled of cleaning products and jet fuel.

At immigration, the officer barely looked at my face.

He scanned my passport, stamped a page, and slid it back without comment. The sound of the stamp landed heavier than it should have.

I stood there for a moment longer than necessary, waiting for a question that didn't come.

He turned to the next person.

Outside, the heat blurred the edges of everything. Even the glass towers in the distance wavered slightly, as if the skyline were a mirage you had to earn.

The company had arranged a taxi. A Pakistani driver met me at the curb and reached for my suitcase.

"First time in Dubai?" he asked.

"Yes. First time."

"You will like it here. Clean city. Very safe. Good money for you, yes?" He loaded my bag into the boot.

"Tamil Nadu," I said. "Small town called Neyveli."

"Ah. Good place. Many Tamil people here."

We drove towards Dubai Marina, the taxi's air conditioning providing a steady coolness, a relief that made my shoulders relax. The roads were wide, highways stretching in neat lines, bordered by towers rising from the sand as though the desert had chosen to build upward. Cranes dotted the skyline.

The apartment building materialised as we entered the Marina, a sleek tower among other sleek towers, glass and stone and polished confidence.

My flat was on the fourteenth floor. One bedroom. A balcony that overlooked a panorama of yachts bobbing in turquoise water, with the marina glowing in a shade that didn't seem real to me yet. The building was new: marble floors polished to a mirror finish, and a lobby that faintly smelt of air freshener and money.

An older, crisp-uniformed security guard stood when I entered the apartment.

The door opened to a furnished emptiness: a bed, a desk, a sofa. Beige and functional. Clean. Austere. A place designed for someone to pass through without leaving marks.

I set my suitcase down in the middle of the living room and stood there for a moment, not moving.

I had never lived alone before. Even in Chennai, I'd shared space, roommates, noise, people in the next bed turning in their sleep, somebody always cooking something in the corridor. Even solitude had company.

I unpacked methodically: three pairs of jeans, six T-shirts, dress shoes that pinched my feet, books I'd bought and never read. The apartment smelled of fresh paint and new carpet. The air felt too cold on my skin.

At the bottom of the suitcase, wrapped in one of my mother's old sarees, I found a photograph of my mother and father standing in front of our house in Neyveli. The bougainvillea vine was visible behind them, blooming pink and defiant against the white wall. That first night, I couldn't sleep.

The apartment was too quiet, not peaceful quiet, but the kind that made every sound echo: the hum of the air conditioning, distant traffic, the sound of my own breathing too loud, too immediate, too real. The temperature was wrong; the air conditioning was set too high. The bed was too soft. The pillows felt unfamiliar.

At 3 a.m., I gave up and stood on the balcony.

Yachts sat lit like toys in the marina. Across the water, glowing windows revealed lives in glass towers, each with an unknown story. The warm, humid air mixed salt and exhaust, while the marina water reflected city lights in broken lines.

There was no one to account for me. No one is waiting. No sound behind me that belonged to anyone else.

Her name crossed my mind, uninvited.

Thara.

Later, I would hear through a mutual friend that she'd published a short story in a Tamil weekly. That she'd kept writing. That she'd found her voice.

My first morning, I awoke to the call to prayer echoing across the city, something I'd heard before in India, but never quite like this. Amplified, resonating from minarets, weaving through glass and concrete. A reminder that I was somewhere fundamentally different.

I made instant coffee, hot water and powder, because I hadn't thought to buy a coffee maker. I dressed in the khakis and button-down shirt my mother had ironed.

The office was located in DIFC, Dubai International Financial Centre, a district that felt like a city within a city. The building had thirty-two storeys. The elevator moved so quickly my ears popped. When the doors opened on the twenty-eighth floor, I was halted by the view: floor-to-ceiling windows, downtown sprawled below, and the Burj Khalifa puncturing the sky like a needle.

* * *

THE PROJECT LASTED SIX MONTHS. Then nine. Then longer than planned.

I learned the rhythm of late nights—conference calls timed for other continents, meals eaten standing, the city outside the office windows darkening and brightening again without him noticing.

I became reliable. The kind of person managers trusted not to panic.

At night, I returned to the apartment and sat on the sofa without turning on the lights. The marina glowed outside, reflections breaking and reforming on the water.

I opened his laptop. Closed it.

Some nights, I typed Thara's name into the search bar and stopped there.

Once, I drafted an email.

I think about you.

I deleted it.

Another night:

I don't know how to explain what I did.

Deleted.

I told myself it was better this way. Cleaner. Less disruptive.

On weekends, colleagues invited me out. I declined politely. I needed rest, I said.

What I needed was predictability.

One evening, a power outage briefly darkened the apartment. The air conditioning stopped. The silence was immediate and complete.

I stood in the dark, heart racing, realising how much I depended on controlled noise. When the lights returned, I sat down and laughed quietly at myself.

* * *

BY MY SECOND year at TechConsult, Dubai's startup scene was impossible to ignore, pitch nights, networking drinks, people talking in compressed language about funding, traction and scale as if those words could replace sleep.

I'd been promoted to senior developer six months earlier. Prerna, my colleague, someone I'd worked with on multiple projects, noticed the way my life had narrowed.

After a weekly review meeting, she said, "You need to get out more."

"I exist outside of work," I said.

"When's the last time you did something that wasn't work or sleep?"

I couldn't remember.

"There's a tech meetup Friday night," she said.

"I don't build things," I said. Not for myself. Not like that.

"Exactly," she said. "Which is why you need to see what it looks like."

* * *

PRERNA DRAGGED me to a bar near the Emirates Towers.

"You need to meet people outside work," she said, like she was assigning me a task.

The bar was high up, one of those rooms designed to make you feel both powerful and insignificant. When the elevator doors opened, the noise hit first: music, voices, the clink of glasses. Noise that made you feel alive, that made you feel included even if you weren't.

Floor-to-ceiling windows framed the city, Sheikh Zayed Road lit in streams, the skyline stacked in glass, the Burj Khalifa visible in the distance like a declaration. The view was spectacular. A view that made you feel small.

I stood at the bar, ordered a drink, and watched the crowd.

* * *

I WAS STILL at the bar when I saw her.

She stood by the windows, downtown behind her, a group gathered around her, yet she still appeared separate, vivid and immediate. Not aloof. Not trying. Just… different.

She was speaking animatedly, her gestures purposeful. People leaned in to listen. I watched her hands as she explained something, shaping concepts in the air, fingers precise, movements confident. She looked completely at ease.

When she laughed, it wasn't polite or performative. It came from somewhere deep, like her body couldn't help it.

"That's Maya Krishnan," Prerna said. "Founder of a logistics optimisation startup. Indian-Irish. Route optimisation for last-mile delivery. She raised a seed round from London VCs."

"You know her?"

"I interviewed with her last year," Prerna said. "Didn't take it. Too much risk. But she's impressive."

As the evening thinned out, Maya ended up beside me at the bar. Not by accident. She'd noticed me watching.

"You're the one Prerna brought," she said. Not a question. An observation.

"How did you?"

"She told me she was dragging someone from her consulting firm." She held out her hand. "I'm Maya."

"Dev."

"Prerna says you're good," she said. "Technically solid."

"Possibly."

"Possibly?" She smiled slightly. "That's already an answer, isn't it?"

She took a sip of her drink and studied me with dark, intelligent eyes that didn't soften into politeness.

"What are you doing here?" she asked.

"To see what it looks like when people build things for themselves."

"And what do you see?"

I looked around: the ambition, the energy, the easy talk of risk, the way people used certainty like perfume.

She checked her phone. "I need to leave. Early flight." And, as if she were bored by my caution, she said, "But you should work for yourself."

"I can't, "

"Of course you can," she said. "You're choosing not to." She picked up her bag and slung it over her shoulder. "If you ever want to talk about why you're choosing that, tell Prerna."

She left.

* * *

I MESSAGED Prerna the next day. Asked for Maya's contact.

I wrote to Maya.

She replied: "Tuesday, 8 a.m. Brew & Bean. Marina Walk."

* * *

TUESDAY MORNINGS BEFORE WORK, the same café, the same table if it was free. One meeting became two, and three. We never talked about what it was. That seemed to matter.

I went in, telling myself it was technical. Curiosity. Exposure. Nothing more.

* * *

I CAME BACK to the room and settled into the chair again.

"You were talking about someone you met," Claire said. "About meeting for coffee."

"Yes," I said. "Six weeks. Every week."

"What were you doing during those meetings?"

"Talking," I said. "About her company. About the product. Technical stuff."

"What weren't you talking about?"

I paused. "Salary. Benefits. Start dates."

"Why not?"

"It didn't come up."

Claire didn't move. "Did you avoid bringing it up? Or did it genuinely not come up?"

I thought about those conversations, what I'd asked, what I hadn't.

"I think…" I said. "I avoided it."

"What were you avoiding by not asking about compensation or visas?"

The answer was there, immediate, but saying it felt like admitting something I'd built my life around.

"Dev?"

Claire watched me for a moment. "You stayed in the part of the conversation where nothing had to change," she said.

"Safe," I said. "Easier."

* * *

EACH MEETING FOLLOWED the same rhythm. Maya would talk about what she was building and the role she thought I'd be perfect for. I would respond with technical questions, architecture, scaling, edge cases, anything that let me stay engaged without stepping into the part where a decision had to be made.

By the fourth coffee, she'd had enough.

"You're wasting my time," she said bluntly. She set down her cup with a sharp click. "You're not going to take the job. You've made that clear without saying it.

You ask technical questions, you seem interested,

"What were you avoiding by not asking about compensation or visas?"

I saw the form before I saw Maya again—the one that would have required names, dates, declarations. I'd chosen silence because it didn't need handwriting.

I opened my mouth to protest.

Instead, I heard myself say, "I'm sorry."

She stood and gathered her bag. "Don't be sorry," she said. "Be honest next time someone offers you something. It saves everyone time."

She left.

That night, late, I wrote: You were right. I'm sorry I wasted your time.

Work, apartment, sleep, the days blurred, the same routine, as a seam had loosened.

She replied within minutes.

Coffee Friday? Same place. I'll give you one more chance to stop being boring.

* * *

THAT FRIDAY, she didn't waste time.

"I'm not recruiting you anymore," Maya said, getting straight to it. "You've made it clear you're staying at TechConsult. So let me be blunt: why did you reach out?"

I thought about it. The question had been following me for days.

"I'm not sure," I said. "Your question bothered me."

"Which one?"

"About what I want," I said. "Not what's safe. What I want."

I looked at her. The words felt exposed as I said them.

"I've been making decisions based on what's safe for so long," I said, "I'm not sure I know what I want anymore."

She stirred her coffee slowly, watching me. "And?"

"I still don't know," I said. "But I'm tired of pretending the answer doesn't matter."

Something tightened behind my eyes, the way it does when I realise I've been avoiding a thought too long. Something I couldn't fully name, but couldn't ignore either.

"That's the first honest thing you've said to me," she said.

She leaned back. "Alright. New deal. No job talk. No recruitment. But I'm launching something that's probably going to fail, and everyone around me either wants funding or wants to tell me why it won't work." She paused. "You're the first person in months who's asked me actual questions about the product instead of the cap table."

"What kind of questions?" I asked.

"Technical ones," she said. "Whether the algorithm scales. Whether the assumptions are stupid. Stuff that matters." Her mouth twitched. "Most investors can't code. Most engineers won't push back."

"You did both," she said. "So here's my offer: I buy you coffee once a week. You tell me when my technical decisions are stupid. No job offer. No pressure. Honest feedback."

"Why would you want that?" I asked.

Her gaze held mine, direct, candid.

"Because I'm running a logistics startup in Dubai as a woman," she said, "and I'm surrounded by men who either underestimate me or want something from me." She didn't soften it. "You treated me as an engineer first."

She exhaled lightly, as if that admission cost her something.

"That's rare," she said. "I'd like to keep talking to someone who doesn't have an agenda."

"I'm not sure about logistics," I said.

"You know systems," she said. "That's enough."

MAYA WAS ALREADY STANDING when I arrived.

Not seated. Not settled. Standing with her phone in one hand, bag on her shoulder, scanning the room as if the café were a temporary inconvenience.

"You're late," she said, checking her watch.

"I'm on time," I said.

"You're on consulting time," she said. "Which is late in startup terms."

She sat down, then immediately stood again to wave at the barista.

"Flat white. Oat milk. Extra shot. If they mess it up, I'm drinking it anyway."

She finally sat.

"You have thirty minutes," she said.

"That's generous."

"I have a board call at nine, a supplier who thinks 'urgent' is a personality trait, and a flight tonight." She smiled slightly. "So yes. Generous."

I ordered coffee. Regular. Nothing complicated.

"You always order like you don't want to be noticed," she said.

"I don't want to be noticed."

"That's obvious," she said. "But you're sitting with me, which suggests a contradiction."

She leaned forward. "So. What are we doing today?"

"Talking," I said.

"About?"

"Whatever you want."

She laughed once. Not loud. Sharp. "No. That's not how this works. If you let me talk, I'll fill the space, and you'll leave thinking you participated."

"That sounds efficient."

"For me," she said. "Not for you."

She pulled out her laptop, opened it, and closed it again.

"I changed the routing logic," she said. "Tell me why it's wrong."

I thought for a moment. "It assumes drivers behave rationally."

"They don't?"

"They do," I said. "Until they don't. Then everything breaks."

She oversaw me. "You like edge cases."

"They're honest," I said.

She nodded. "Good answer."

Her phone buzzed. She ignored it.

"You know," she said, "most men I meet here try to impress me."

"Am I failing?"

"Yes," she said. "Which is refreshing."

She stood suddenly. "Walk with me."

We walked toward the Marina. She walked fast. I adjusted.

"Do you ever feel like you're late to your own life?" she asked.

"That's an odd question to ask while walking this fast."

She smiled. "Answer it anyway."

"Yes," I said. "Often."

She nodded as if that confirmed something.

"Time's up," she said. "Same time next week?"

"You're busy."

She shrugged. "So are you. You pretend you're not."

* * *

WE KEPT MEETING. No one suggested stopping. No one suggested changing anything. By the time the heat finally broke and evenings cooled, we'd been meeting for months.

* * *

WE STAYED LONGER than usual that evening.

The café emptied around us, chairs stacking, the espresso machine hissing as it cooled. Neither of us mentioned leaving. The space felt ours temporarily.

She took my notebook from the table without asking, flipping through pages of diagrams and half-formed thoughts.

"You think on paper," she said.

"I think out loud," I said. "Paper is safer."

She smiled and stopped, studying me with the same precision she brought to her work.

"You know," she said, "most men don't sit this close without trying to turn it into something."

I hadn't noticed how close we were until she said it. Our knees were nearly touching. The awareness sharpened the air between us.

"I'm not most men," I said.

"No," she said. "That's obvious."

She didn't move away. Neither did I.

For a moment, it felt possible—leaning in, misreading the silence, letting proximity become permission. The thought arrived fully formed and stayed where it was.

Instead, she stood.

"We should go," she said, already reaching for her coat.

Outside, the night air cut cleanly between us. Whatever might have happened remained untested, intact.

Later, I understood that restraint had been the most honest thing we shared.

* * *

SOMETIMES I CAUGHT issues in what she was building. More often than not, I pointed out a flaw and watched her nod, already moving on to the next step.

Other times, she let me talk until I reached the conclusion she'd arrived at hours earlier. Two months into this rhythm, she showed me something different.

She pulled out her phone and scrolled through photos.

"This is what I'm building," she said. "Not the logistics platform. The other thing."

Iceland.

Volcanic landscapes. Black sand beaches. Waterfalls cutting through rock. And aurora photos, green light folding across a dark sky.

"I want to go there," she said. "See the Northern Lights. In winter, when they actually show up." She smiled at her own precision. "Before I get too busy with this company ever to leave Dubai."

"You've never been?"

"No," she said. "I've spent the last five years building. First one company, and this one. No time for vacations." She looked at the images again. "But Iceland... something about it. Fire and ice. Contradictions that make sense."

"It looks beautiful," I said.

"It does." She put her phone away. "Maybe this year. If the Series A closes. If everything works out."

"If," I said.

"Always if," she said, smiling like she hated that word. "That's the problem with building. You're always waiting for the next milestone. The next round. The next success. And life keeps happening around you while you're waiting."

"What if you went anyway?" I asked. "Not next year. This year. Even for a week."

"I can't," she said automatically. "The team needs me. Investors need updates. Product needs everything."

"What if it doesn't?" I interrupted. "What if you went for a week and the world didn't end?"

She studied me. "That's risky talk for someone who's been avoiding risks."

"Maybe I'm tired of avoiding them," I said.

"Are you?" She leaned forward slightly. "Because if you are... I might have a proposition."

* * *

NOT LONG AFTER THAT, the rhythm changed again.

One morning, she said, "Can we not talk about work today?"

"You're the one who always brings it up," I said.

"I know," she said. "But I'm exhausted. The Series A pitch is next week, and I've been living inside spreadsheets for a month." She looked at me. "I need to think about something else. Something that's not work. Something that's me."

Then, quieter, as she surprised herself: "Us."

"Like what?" I asked.

"Books," she said. "You mentioned you read. What are you reading?"

I thought about it, and the question exposed me.

When had I last read something that wasn't technical? That wasn't work? When had I last read something for pleasure, for myself?

I looked down at my cup. The coffee had gone cold.

"I don't remember," I said. "I haven't read anything in a while. Not for pleasure. Not for me."

"That's sad," she said.

"Is it?"

"Yeah," she said. "Because reading is one of the few things that's only for you."

We talked for two hours, about books, about growing up between countries, about the particular loneliness of being good at something. The café's background chatter faded until it felt distant and unimportant.

When we finally left, it was dark. Neither of us had noticed. We'd forgotten time. We'd forgotten work. We'd forgotten everything else.

The evening air was cooler than the café, a relief against my skin.

"Good different or bad different?" she asked.

"I'm not sure yet," I said.

She looked at me directly. "Want to get dinner next week instead of coffee?"

The question was simple. Direct. She wanted more, wanted to continue.

"Yes," I said. "I'd like that."

"Good," she said. "Because I want to keep talking."

* * *

DINNER TURNED INTO WALKING. Walking turned into standing on her balcony at 2 a.m., the city below us still awake. We talked about Dublin and Neyveli. About work. About what it costs to be good at something.

Three months after that first night when Prerna dragged me to the bar, I was at Maya's apartment helping her debug an algorithm that wasn't scaling.

She was barefoot, wearing an old Trinity College Dublin T-shirt, hair pulled back, focused on her laptop screen.

"I'm scared of this," she said suddenly, not looking up. "I'm excellent at building companies. I'm terrible at building relationships. I have a track record of choosing work over people."

"So why are you here?" I asked.

She smiled, small, honest. "That's what scares me. For the first time, I'm choosing to be somewhere else."

I reached across and found her hand.

"That's not how my brain works," I said.

"I know," she said. "But maybe that's okay."

She stood and led me to the edge of the balcony. Dubai spread out below, lights, towers, motion, the city performing itself.

"See that?" she said. "That's what I understand. But this is different." She turned back to me. "Letting someone see you when you're not in control."

"You're doing it right now," I said.

"I am," she said. "That's terrifying."

She kept her eyes on me. "I know this probably won't work. You and me. Different paths, different timelines." She paused, as if she hated the sentence and had to say it anyway. "But right now, I want you here anyway."

"That's dangerous," I said.

"Why?"

"Because when you let someone see you this way, you start to want them." My voice came out quieter than I expected. "And wanting something you know you can't have is the worst kind of pain."

She was quiet for a long moment.

Then: "Stay tonight. Not... not that way." She swallowed. "Stay. Talk. Be here."

We sat on her sofa with the city lights spread out below us. We talked in low voices, algorithms, ambitions, the loneliness of being good at something, the loneliness of always having to be in control.

At some point, she fell asleep with her head against my shoulder.

* * *

I PAUSED.

"The loneliness. Then Maya. Her intensity. Her brilliance."

Claire stayed quiet for a beat, listening.

"I notice something," she said finally. "When you talk about Thara, you describe stability. When you talk about Maya, you describe intensity."

I swallowed. "Thara was steady," I said. "Maya wasn't."

"What happened with Maya?" Claire asked. "How did that relationship end?"

I was quiet.

"She left," I said.

Claire nodded once. "We'll continue next week. Tell me more about what happened in Dubai after Maya left."

TEMPORARY STATUS

I walked into the session carrying my laptop bag and set it down beside the chair.

"Rough week?" Claire asked.

"Work," I said. "Always work."

She watched me the way she always did, calm, not pushing, waiting for the words to find their own shape.

* * *

MY VISA RENEWAL came through on a Tuesday. The email arrived at 9:47 a.m.

I saw the subject line, clicked, read the first sentence, and felt the relief move through me in a quick, quiet wave. Not joy. Not excitement. Just something unclenching, something easing enough for me to keep breathing.

That evening, Maya asked me what I'd do.

"It renewed," I said. "Got the email this morning."

She didn't look up from her food. "That's not what I asked."

"What did you ask?"

"What would you have done if it didn't renew?"

I shrugged. "Found another job."

She finally looked at me then. Not angry. Not disappointed. Just precise.

"Would you have left Dubai?"

"The honest answer is complicated," I said.

"Complicated how?"

I didn't answer. I couldn't. The truth was there, but it didn't want to be spoken.

Maya went back to her food as if she'd made her point and didn't need to press harder.

* * *

IN MID-AUGUST, I stopped counting what was hers and August in Dubai. Nightly temperatures stay above forty, pressing against your skin like relentless force, slowing you without noticing you've surrendered. The city empties as people retreat indoors, leaving the streets to delivery riders, guards, cleaners, workers moving through the heat like swimmers, each step and breath slowed by density.

I took a week of vacation, something I rarely do.

Maya invited me to her office. "Come see what I've built."

Her startup occupied a floor in Dubai Internet City. The building was new enough to still smell faintly of paint and fresh plaster, with a chemical sharpness beneath the sheen of glass and confidence.

The office was controlled chaos. An open floor plan. Standing desks arranged in clusters. Whiteboards filled with diagrams that looked like maps of invisible cities. Sticky notes everywhere, little flags marking problems, ideas and deadlines. Air conditioning set to Arctic, making the office feel like a refuge from the heat outside.

And in the middle of it all was Maya, moving between desks with a kind of authority that didn't require permission.

"Dev! You came!"

She hugged me in front of her entire team, unselfconscious, unguarded, as if affection was just another form of truth.

She demonstrated the product: optimisation for logistics firms, routing and dispatch, algorithms that cut delivery times and fuel expenses. She discussed in terms of systems, inputs, constraints, edges, and exceptions.

"It's beautiful," I said.

She smiled as if she'd been waiting to hear that exact word.

That night, after everyone left, we stayed.

The office transformed. Chaos became quiet. The building's hum softened. The city outside kept shimmering, but inside it felt like a sealed room, just us and the work.

She showed me the investor deck: the metrics, the growth curve bending upward. Emails from VCs, some encouraging, some dismissive, some cruel in their politeness.

"It's terrifying," she said. "Some days I think I'm mad. Some days I think I'm going to pull this off."

"Why do you do it?" I asked.

Her eyes found mine and held. "Because I have to. Because every time someone tells me it can't be done, my resolve crystallises."

She closed the laptop and leaned back.

"You know what the hardest part is?" she said. "It's not rejection. I can handle rejection. It's how they frame it."

She spoke slowly, like she was choosing words that wouldn't let her down.

"They don't say, 'We don't invest in women founders.' Instead, they say, 'We're looking for teams with proven exits,' or 'We need someone with more experience,' or 'The market isn't ready for this.' And you are left wondering: is this about my metrics, or is it because I'm a woman, I'm Indian, and I don't have a Stanford MBA?

"Does it matter?" I asked.

She didn't answer right away.

"It matters because you start rehearsing two versions of yourself," she said. "The one you are, and the one that gets nodded at."

"You start performing and trying to be less yourself and more of what they expect. You bring a male co-founder into meetings even when you don't need one, because you know they'll take you more seriously. You dress differently. Speak differently. Make yourself smaller, less threatening, more palatable."

She looked out at the skyline as if she could see the meetings hovering in the air.

"And even then, they'll ask questions they'd never ask a man," she said. "'How do you plan to balance this with family?' 'Are you planning to have children?' 'Who runs the company when you're on maternity leave?' As if men don't have families. As if building a company isn't already total."

She paused, then said, quieter, more exposed:

"I'm not asking for special treatment. I'm asking to be evaluated on the same metrics. My unit economics are better than half the male-led startups they fund. My retention is higher. My burn is lower." She gave a sharp, humourless laugh. "But they'll still pass, and they'll frame it as a business decision, not bias."

She turned back to me.

"Perhaps it is business," she said. "Perhaps I'm just not good enough. But I've sat in enough pitch meetings to know the difference. I've watched male founders with worse metrics get term sheets. I've watched them raise money on vision alone, while I'm asked to prove traction, prove fit, prove I can execute."

"Is that why you're so driven?" I asked. "To prove them wrong?"

"No." Her answer was immediate. "I'm driven because I'm good at this. Because I see problems worth solving. Because I can build something that matters. The proving them wrong is just a side effect."

She exhaled, as if the truth tired her.

"But it's exhausting," she said. "Being twice as good to get half the recognition. Justifying your existence in every meeting. Performing competence instead of just being competent." She shook her head. "And the worst part? If I succeed, they'll say it's because I'm a woman. Because of diversity. Because of quotas. They'll never say it's because I executed flawlessly."

Then she opened the laptop again, like action was the only antidote to despair.

"But I'm going to do it anyway," she said. "Not to make a point. Not to prove anyone wrong. Because this is what I'm good at. Because this is what I want to build."

She'd been showing me her latest algorithm when she stopped.

"What?" I asked.

She was looking at me.

"I've been trying not to do this," she said.

"Do what?"

"Notice how much I like having you here," she said. "How are you the only person who doesn't look bored when I talk about Dijkstra's algorithm?"

I smiled. "I wasn't bored."

She tilted her head, daring me to be honest.

"I was wondering if you realise you do this thing with your hands when you're excited," I said.

"What thing?"

"You shape the air," I said. "Like you're building the idea in front of you."

She stared at me for a beat, as if she hadn't known she was visible like that.

"It's captivating," I said.

She froze, then closed her laptop with deliberate slowness. She stood. Walked around the desk.

"You're dangerous," she said.

"Me?" I said. "You're the one building a company from scratch."

"Exactly," she said. "I have a plan. I've always had a plan."

"Is that so terrible?"

"Yes." Then, instantly: "No."

She laughed, then caught herself.

"I spent four years in Dublin with someone who wanted me to want less," she said.

I smiled, and before I could stop myself, I said, "That's not what you sound like when you're trying to be composed."

"Stop that," she said.

"Stop what?"

"Looking at me like I'm not terrifying."

"You are terrifying," I said.

She touched my face, lightly, like she didn't trust herself.

"I don't do this," she said. "I don't let people in. I don't have time for wanting someone."

"We don't have to define it tonight," I said.

"That's the problem." Her voice tightened. "I want to define it. But I can't. That's new. I don't like not knowing."

I moved to stand beside her.

"What if we exist in the not-knowing for a while?" I said. "No plans. No definitions."

"What?" she said, almost offended.

"Late nights," I said. "Algorithms. Coffee at 2 a.m. because neither of us can sleep."

She watched me as if assessing risk.

"That's a terrible strategy."

"I know."

"High risk. Undefined outcomes."

"Reckless."

"I hate reckless."

"I know that too."

Then she smiled, small, genuine, as if she'd surprised herself.

"Okay?" she said.

"Okay," I said. "Whatever this catastrophe is going to be."

"That's romantic."

"I'm not romantic," she said. Then, a beat later: "I'm pragmatic. And pragmatically speaking, you're the most interesting problem I've encountered."

"I'm a problem?"

"The best kind."

We stood at the window for a long time, watching Dubai shimmer beneath us. At some moment, her hand found mine. Her grip was firm, almost urgent.

* * *

WE BEGAN to move in a pattern: her place, my place, coffee, work, late nights that turned into mornings before we admitted what we were doing.

Maya and I spent the better part of a year entangled.

Her apartment was in a less glamorous area, quieter, less spectacular, filled with bookshelves instead of furniture. The sofa became our space, where we sat for hours talking and working, arguing gently over decisions that mattered, laughing at the absurdity of how easily two people could become a habit.

* * *

I RETURNED to the room and sat back in the chair.

"Dev," Claire said, "you've been talking for a while. How are you feeling right now?"

I stopped, looked at her, and shook my head.

"What's happening?" I asked.

"I can see it," I said. "But it's like my hands weren't there."

"Someone else?"

"A version of me that doesn't exist anymore."

"How does that feel?" she asked.

I was quiet. "Strange," I said. "Like it happened to someone I know, but not me."

"We can stop if you need to."

"No," I said. "I want to continue."

* * *

ONE EVENING, Maya looked away from her laptop and stared out the window. The city sprawled below, lights stretching to the horizon.

"This is dangerous," she said. "Not you. Us."

"We don't have to figure it out tonight," I said.

"Actually, we do," she said. "I need you to understand what this is."

She turned to face me, serious in a way that felt like discipline.

"I like you, Dev," she said. "I want this connection. But I need you to know: I'm not looking for someone to build a life with right now. I'm building a company. That comes first." She didn't apologise for it. "And I can't predict where Singapore will take me, or where your visa situation will take you."

She held my gaze.

"I know that right now this matters to me," she said. "You matter to me. And I want it deliberately. This conversation. This understanding."

"It's clear," I said.

She exhaled, relieved.

"And I'm not asking for guarantees," she said. "I'm not promising you a shape for this. I'm telling you what's true right now." She held my gaze. "And right now, I want it."

She smiled. "Good. We both know what this is."

During the day, we moved in separate worlds.

She was raising, building, and performing certainty.

My work was going well. Senior architect now, leading a team of five developers, trusted, relied on, stable in a way that felt like safety and also like a cage.

* * *

I PAUSED.

Claire waited.

"You're describing two separate lives," she said. "Hers and yours. How did that feel?"

I searched for the honest word and found the easiest one.

"Normal," I said. "Maybe."

"And how did that work?" she asked.

"It just did," I said. "We were together, but we had our own work."

"What happened when those goals conflicted?"

I thought about it, about Maya's company, about Singapore, about my visa, and the answer rose like a wall in my throat.

Claire didn't rush me.

"Try," she said.

"Safe," I said finally. "Separate. Like we could both have what we wanted."

"And did that work?" she asked.

I didn't answer.

THREE WEEKS before Maya's funding deadline, I stayed up past midnight helping her with the investor deck. She'd exaggerated her retention forecast. I advised her to dial it back to a more credible figure, one she could confidently defend in front of a room full of sceptics.

I heard my own voice then, and it sounded wrong, flatter, more distant, like it belonged to someone else.

Maya didn't notice. But I did.

My mother's birthday came and went. I remembered it, delayed calling, then forgot. By the time I sent a late text, the weekend had already been taken up with a trip to Hatta with Maya.

But the evenings were ours.

We sat on her balcony. She talked about building something that could not be dismissed. About creating jobs. About proving, quietly, relentlessly, that Indian women belonged in rooms designed to exclude them.

One evening, she stopped.

"I'm thinking about someone," she said. "An ex."

Words failed me. I waited.

"A man in Dublin," she said. "Before I came to Dubai. We were together for four years. He was good. Kind. Wanted to marry me, build a life." She looked at the railing, fingers tightening around her mug. "I loved him. But if I stayed, I would spend my life resenting him. He kept asking me to choose him over myself."

"Why are you telling me this?" I asked.

"I'm not afraid of commitment," she said. "I'm afraid of the kind that makes you smaller. I think." She paused. "I'd have married him, and then, five years later, I'd probably hate him for it. Or maybe I'd hate myself. I don't know. So I left. To figure out who I was first."

"Do you regret it?"

"No," she said. "I don't think so." Then, more softly: "I'm telling you this because… I'm trying to warn you. Or maybe I'm trying to convince myself." She looked at the skyline. "I'm not going back to being someone's supporting character. I'm the protagonist of my own story. At least, that's what I tell myself."

SEPTEMBER ARRIVED.

Maya chartered a boat for an evening. We left the marina at five, the skyline shrinking behind us—champagne on ice.

We sat on the deck as the boat moved away from shore. She was quiet for a long time.

The sun began to drop. The sky went vermillion, then bruised into indigo. We sat together on cushions, close enough to feel each other's warmth. Her hand found mine, grip firm.

After a while, she propped herself on one elbow, eyes bright with mischief.

I laughed.

"Come on," she said, clearing her throat, adopting a formal posture.

"Alright," I said, matching her tone. "Madam, I find your proposal most intriguing. Though I confess the celestial display above us renders such linguistic artifice rather superfluous."

Her eyes lit up.

"I had a friend who loved period dramas," I said. "We watched a lot of plays and films. You pick things up."

"Fie!" she said, trying not to smile. "'Rustic charm.' How devastatingly tepid."

I shifted closer.

"My grandmother taught me," I said. "She loved Austen and Trollope."

I took her hand with exaggerated formality. "Then permit me to cultivate further. I confess myself quite overcome by the lady's presence, her beauty, her intellect."

She went still.

"I endeavour," I continued, "to improve upon acquaintance."

"You succeed," she said, squeezing my hand. "Though I prefer you without the performance."

* * *

LATER, wrapped in a blanket against the night breeze, I shifted to look at her.

"Northern Lights in winter," she said. "A place where the light behaves differently." Then, as if she were forcing courage into her mouth: "I want us to go. December. After my funding closes."

I opened my mouth, but she cut in quickly.

"It won't fix anything," she said. "Iceland won't solve visas or companies or the fact that we're on different timelines. But we could have one place that's ours."

She lifted her head to look at me.

"Yes," I said.

She settled closer. The boat rocked.

Eventually, she fell asleep with her head against my shoulder. I stayed awake longer, watching the sky.

* * *

A FEW NIGHTS LATER, I woke to find her side of the bed empty.

I found her on the balcony, wrapped in a blanket, staring down at the city. The lights stretched to the horizon, but she wasn't really seeing them.

"Maya?"

She didn't turn. "I can't sleep."

I sat beside her. The night air was cool.

"What's wrong?"

She was quiet for a long time.

"Talk to me," I said.

"I'm wondering if this is it," she said finally. "If this is what my life is. Work. More work."

"You're feeling it now," I said.

"Am I?" She looked at me. "Or am I too exhausted to perform being okay?"

"What do you want?"

"That's the problem." She pulled the blanket tighter. "I know what I want professionally. I know what I want for the company. But personally?" She shook her head. "I don't know. I'm good at building things. I'm terrible at knowing what I want from life beyond the next milestone."

"That's nothing."

"It's not everything either," she said. "I'm scared, Dev, not of failing. I know how to fail. I'm scared of succeeding and realising I've built the wrong life. That I've optimised for all the wrong things."

"You have me," I said.

"Do I?" She held my gaze. "Or do you have a version of me that exists between work calls and investor meetings?"

I reached for her hand.

"Sometimes I think I'm a collection of ambitions and anxieties," she said. "That there's no actual person underneath. Just drive. Need."

"That's not true," I said.

"How do you know?" Her voice was small. "I don't even know. I've been performing competence for so long, I can't distinguish what's real from what's performance."

We sat in silence, city lights below, stars above.

"You're real," I said finally. "This is real. Right now."

She leaned against me.

* * *

REALITY ARRIVED ON A SUNDAY MORNING.

I walked to Maya's flat with breakfast — pastries from her favourite bakery and coffee from her preferred café. I'd woken early and made the effort, thinking about what she'd want. A gesture that told her I was thinking of her.

She opened the door already dressed, laptop bag on her shoulder. Ready to leave. Ready to work.

"Oh," she said. "I didn't realise you were coming."

"It's Sunday," I said. "I thought we could have breakfast."

"I can't," she said. "I have to work."

"On Sunday?"

"Especially Sunday." She glanced at her phone. "We're in crunch mode for the Series A close. This matters."

I followed her inside. She moved quickly, packing her laptop, checking messages, and already somewhere else.

"How long will you be?" I asked.

"All day," she said. "Probably."

I reached for her hand.

"I know," she said. "I'm sorry. But this is important."

"More important than us?"

Her expression sharpened.

"Than spending time together," I clarified, and hated how needy it sounded.

"You knew what I was building when you got involved," she said. "You knew the company came first. You knew what this was."

"I do," I said. "But we had that perfect night on a yacht where you talked about Iceland and home, and now three weeks later, you can't spare a Sunday morning?"

Maya set down her bag.

"Is it enough or not?" she asked, very quietly. "Me. This. What can I give you?" She held my gaze without blinking. "Because I told you from the beginning, the company comes first."

Silence.

She started zipping her bag.

I started to protest, but she cut me off.

"No, it's fine," she said, tight and controlled. "You're right. I'm always choosing work."

I crossed the room and pulled her into my arms.

She resisted, then broke, laughing once, wet against my shirt.

"I didn't say you're not enough," I said.

"But you thought it," she whispered. "And you're not wrong. I know how to build companies."

"We built this, too," I said. "Badly. Together."

She laughed again, softer. "Most relationships are."

She pulled back. "I know."

Then, as if she were forcing herself to do it: "Come back tonight. Around eight. I'll make time."

"Okay," I said.

She looked at me, fierce. "Don't give up on me yet. I'm trying, yeah? To be here."

"I know you are," I said.

After she left, I sat in her apartment eating the pastries alone.

The silence was different, not empty, not dramatic. Just quiet.

The pastries were still warm, but they tasted different.

I washed the plate, put it away, looked around her apartment, her books, her plants, the evidence of a life built around a mission.

Then I walked back to my own place. The city was waking up.

* * *

BY NOVEMBER, we were both at inflexion points: my contract renewal and Maya's Series A grind toward legal close.

* * *

ONE AFTERNOON, Maya's phone rang during lunch. She glanced at the screen.

It rang again. Same number.

"You can take that," I said.

"I don't want to."

The phone rang a third time. She stared at it.

Then she answered.

"Hi, Mum." Her voice changed, smaller. "No, I'm not too busy. I'm at lunch."

She listened for a long time, free hand gripping her coffee cup.

The café's chatter faded.

"Mum, I know you're disappointed," she said. "But I told you, I can't come for Christmas. The Series A closes in January. I need to be here."

Another pause. Longer.

I shifted to stand, to give her privacy. She caught my wrist and held it.

"I'm not choosing work over family," she said, voice tight. "I'm creating something that matters. Why can't you understand that?"

She looked away.

"Siobhan has two kids and a husband in Cork," she said. "She's done everything you wanted. But I can't be her."

Silence.

Her jaw tightened.

"I love you too," she said finally. "I'll try to come in the spring."

She hung up and set the phone face down.

She stared at nothing.

I reached for her hand, but my fingers felt numb, as if they weren't quite connected to me. I pulled back, flexed them. Sensation returned in waves.

"You okay?" I asked.

"My sister had her second baby three weeks ago," she said. "I haven't met him yet. My mother thinks I'm selfish. My father stopped asking when I'm coming home."

She swallowed.

"They wanted me to be a doctor. Marry an Irish boy. Live in Cork. Have Sunday dinners. And instead I'm in Dubai building a logistics startup they don't understand, dating an Indian engineer they've never met."

"Do you regret it?" I asked.

"Every single day," she said, too fast, then caught herself. "Not the company. I don't regret the company. But I regret that I can't be both. The daughter they want and the person I am."

"What did you say?" I asked.

"Nothing wrong," she said. "I didn't say, 'You raised someone who couldn't be small.' I didn't say, 'This is who I am.' I said I'd try to visit at Christmas."

She opened her photo app and showed me a picture: an older woman holding a newborn, smiling at the camera.

"I want to be there," she said. "I do. But if I go, I come back, and the round collapses. Someone else captures the market. Twenty people lose their jobs." She set the phone down. "So I chose the company. Every time."

"You could go for a weekend," I said.

"I could," she said. "But I'd be physically there and mentally elsewhere. Checking emails at dinner. Taking calls during the baby's christening. My mother would see it."

She finished her coffee.

"I don't know how to be good at both," she said. "I've tried. When I was with Sean in Dublin, I worked so hard to be the good Irish girl who wanted a ring and a mortgage in Cork. And I was miserable. Now I'm exactly who I want to be. And I'm still miserable."

"Maybe there's no version where everyone's happy," I said.

"I know that," she said. "Intellectually, I know. But it doesn't stop me lying awake at three a.m. wondering if I'm making the biggest mistake of my life."

She shook her head. "Sorry. I don't usually... this isn't your problem."

"It's not a problem," I said. "It's you."

She smiled slightly.

"Actually, you are more interesting," I said.

She reached across the table and found my hand.

"Don't let me disappear into the company completely," she said.

"If you see me becoming the CEO who can't take calls from her mother, tell me."

"I will," I said.

* * *

LATER, at the same café, we sat in silence for ten minutes, both of us staring into our cups.

"Come work with me," she said finally. The words came out flat, as if she'd already lost the argument in her head.

"I can't," I said. "You know I can't."

"Why not?"

"My visa is through TechConsult," I said. "If I leave, I have thirty days to sort it."

"I'll sponsor you," she said. "I'll make you CTO."

"Your company is early," I said. "You need capital, not expensive hires."

"A good business decision," she said, almost bitterly. "You're smart. You're experienced."

"I can't focus if I'm terrified about my visa status," I said.

She didn't speak.

Some doors were open to her: Irish passport, mobility, permanence. Other doors were barred to me. The imbalance sat between us like a third person.

A woman at the table in the following photo laughed at something on her phone.

"So this is it?" Maya's voice was low, almost a whisper. "This is where we end? All those conversations, those late nights... this is it?"

"Probably," I said.

Then I corrected myself.

"Because I'm terrified," I said. "Because you're willing to burn everything down for your dream, risk everything on something that might not work, and I'm still trying to keep my head above water."

She reached across the table and took both my hands in hers, grip firm, urgent.

"Listen to me," she said. "You are as brave as I am. More, maybe." Her eyes were direct. "You left India at twenty-two with nothing but a suitcase and a job offer. You built a career in Dubai, a place that treats you like you're temporary. You survived visa precarity, workplace politics, the constant awareness that one mistake could end everything." She exhaled. "That's bravery, Dev. Or maybe it's survival."

"But that's different," I said. "That was survival. This is choosing to risk what I've built."

"And what's the alternative?" she asked. "You stay at TechConsult, safe, and then what? In two years, you're still there. In five years, you're still there. Building other people's products, following other people's vision, is safe but stuck."

She paused, then said the part that felt like a door closing.

"And if I expand to London or Singapore, you're right. I won't ask you to follow. I can't."

"So you're already planning our ending."

"No," she said. "I'm trying to be honest about what's possible. I'm not planning an ending." A beat. "Or maybe I am. I'm accepting that this might not have a forever and choosing it anyway."

She squeezed my hands again.

"That's what I'm asking you to do," she said. "Not plan for forever. Choose now. Choose this."

"Realistic," I said, pulling my hands away, "is another word for protecting yourself."

"No," she said, soft now. "Realistic is another word for afraid, I think. And you're allowed to be afraid."

I looked at her, the woman who'd built a company from nothing, who'd risked everything.

"I'm sorry," I said.

She nodded. Let go of my hands. Picked up her cup. Drank. Set it down.

* * *

AFTER THAT, I went to the office early, stayed late, volunteered for projects no one else wanted.

I started using work the way some people use prayer, something I could repeat until the day held together.

The routine filled the days, the weeks.

My studio smelled of stale laundry and instant coffee. I stopped opening the curtains. The room stayed dark.

I didn't call Maya. The silence between us felt permanent, necessary, like we'd both made our choices and it was better to leave it clean than to drag it out.

Dubai felt smaller. The Marina towers that had once seemed impressive now felt like glass boxes. The expat community that had once felt welcoming now felt temporary, everyone counting down to their next move, their next contract, their next exit.

I was counting down too.

I buried myself in projects, took on extra assignments, and worked late every night. The office became refuge, routine became anchor, work became identity.

I'd come home to an empty apartment, order takeaway, eat in front of the television, and fall asleep on the sofa. Wake up. Repeat.

One evening, walking through the Marina after another late night, I passed restaurants full of people laughing, talking, living. I walked past them, invisible.

I saw a couple holding hands across a table.

For a moment, I thought it was Maya.

I kept walking.

I'd made my choice. I'd chosen stability. The visa. The job.

* * *

I SAW her name months later.

An article shared in a group chat. A funding announcement. Her company is expanding into Europe—a photograph of her standing beside a screen, mid-gesture, unmistakably herself.

I read the article once. Then again, more slowly.

Nothing in it surprised me. The language was confident. Decisive. There was no mention of the early doubts she'd spoken about over coffee, no trace of the hesitations she'd allowed herself only in private.

I didn't message her. I didn't need to.

I closed the article and returned to my work. For the rest of the day, I noticed how often I avoided decisions that would have required explanation.

* * *

I PAUSED.

"That's how it ended," I said. "I chose," I stopped.

Claire's voice came gently. "What do you think you chose?"

I was quiet for a long time.

"Safety felt organised," I said. "Like I could list the steps. Maya felt like stepping off the marked path and pretending it was still a plan."

"What happens in your body when you think about choosing safety?"

"Tightness," I said. "In my chest."

"Good," she said. "You're noticing. That tightness, what do you think it's telling you?"

"I can't say," I said.

"Think about it," she said. "What was the difference between choosing safety and choosing Maya?"

"Safety felt controlled," I said. "Predictable. Maya felt… risky."

"And which did you choose?"

"The visa," I said. "The job." I looked down at my hands. "The small, careful life I knew how to keep."

"What do you think you were really choosing?" Claire asked. "Safety, or fear?"

I didn't answer at first.

Then: "I chose what felt safe."

"And what did that cost you?"

The answer came before I could soften it.

"Her," I said. "Us."

"And what did choosing safety give you?"

"Stability," I said. "Predictability."

"Was it worth it?" Claire asked.

I looked away.

"At the time," I said. "Perhaps."

Claire nodded once, as if she were marking a point on a map.

"We'll continue next week," she said.

THE MACHINERY OF SURVIVAL

Claire was writing in her notebook when I entered. She looked up.

"You've been quiet about London again," she said.

"Again?"

She nodded. "You keep coming close to it," she said. "Then you move away."

I considered that. "It's complicated."

"You've said that before," she said gently. "What's different today?"

"I'm still living there," I said. "I think that makes it harder to see."

"What happens if you stay with it a little longer?"

I didn't answer.

"And what happens if you stop protecting it?" she asked.

I was quiet. "A lot of things," I said. "Good ones. Bad ones."

She waited.

"Let's start small," she said. "When London comes up, what's the first image, not the story, just the image?"

I thought about it. About London. About what had happened there.

Claire didn't interrupt.

* * *

SIX MONTHS AFTER MAYA LEFT, TechConsult called me into a meeting. I was twenty-six, four years in Dubai. The city had become familiar. My manager and the regional director sat across from me.

"We're expanding our London office. We need senior engineers who understand our systems. You've been with us for four years now."

London. Not Singapore, not India.

"It would be an intra-company transfer. We'd handle the visa."

"I'll do it."

"You don't want time to think about it?"

"No. I'll do it."

Thirty seconds. My future is decided.

* * *

I DIDN'T CALL MAYA. The silence between us was permanent, necessary. I'd made my choice. She'd made hers. Better to leave it clean than to drag it out.

Packing took one afternoon. Four years in Dubai, and everything fit into three suitcases. The apartment looked like a place no one expected to return to. I stood in the middle of the living room, the balcony doors open, listening to Dubai's sounds for the last time: construction, traffic, the call to prayer in the distance.

I walked through each room: the bedroom where I'd slept for four years, the kitchen where I'd made instant coffee every morning, the balcony where I'd stood watching the Marina, wondering if this was it, if this was what I'd left Neyveli for.

The morning of my flight, I walked to the Marina one last time: the yachts, the glass towers, people who walked with an ease I'd never quite learned. I'd never felt as if I owned any of it: borrowed space, borrowed time, four years, reduced to three suitcases. I tried not to count what hadn't come with me.

When TechConsult sent the visa application paperwork, I flew back to India to submit it.

The forms asked for every country I'd visited, every job I'd held.

I slowed down, not because I didn't know the answers, but because writing them made the years feel final.

The consulate waiting room smelled of disinfectant and old paper, the air-conditioned air stale and recirculated. Fluorescent lights hummed overhead, their harsh white light making everything look washed out, unreal. I sat in a plastic chair, its surface cold and hard against my back.

The woman at the counter looked at my Dubai residency visa. "Work transfer." My palms were damp. I wiped them on my trousers. She stamped something. I read it as days, not weeks, counting them the way you count breaths.

Neyveli was smaller, almost claustrophobic, the streets narrower, the government quarters more cramped. My mother had repainted the house and had new curtains in the front room. The vine had grown wilder, its branches reaching further, its pink flowers more abundant.

Tears in my mother's eyes when she saw me. "Three weeks. Maybe four."

"And then London?"

"Yes."

The visa application took weeks. The days in Neyveli stretched long.

* * *

THE FLIGHT to London was thirteen hours. I slept badly, drifting in and out, watched three movies, ate the aeroplane food, and stared at the flight map on the screen.

* * *

WHEN WE LANDED AT HEATHROW, it was raining, persistent, damp rain that seeps into everything, that makes you feel the weight of water in your clothes, in your hair, in the very air you breathe.

Not the dramatic rain of monsoons that arrives with thunder and leaves with sunshine. Not the brief, intense rain of Dubai that evaporates before it touches the ground.

This was London rain, patient and unrelenting, rain that didn't announce itself, just stayed. Leaden skies hung low overhead, and biting air wrapped around me the moment I stepped onto the jet bridge, the smell of wet pavement and jet fuel mixing with something else, something metallic and cold.

I'd been in the air for thirteen hours. My internal clock was still on Dubai time. My muscles ached from sitting, and my eyes felt dry from the recycled air. But I was here. London.

Immigration took forty minutes.

I kept my passport open to the photo page, as if familiarity might count for something.

I kept my passport open to the photo page, rehearsing my name. The air smelled of cleaning products and stale breath, the fluorescent lights overhead flickering slightly, their hum a constant background noise.

The officer, when I finally reached him, flipped through my passport: Dubai residency, Indian citizenship, UK work visa. Three countries stamped into my passport. None of them felt settled. The counter was cold under my hands.

Purpose of visit?

Work transfer. Starting a new role with TechConsult. Intra-company transfer.

How long are you planning to stay? Indefinite. The visas are for five years.

He stamped the page and slid my passport back. That was it. Again. I walked away, my palms still sweaty.

I arrived on a Tuesday with two suitcases. Collected them from baggage reclaim and wheeled them through customs. Bought a Tube

ticket from a machine. Piccadilly Line to Central London, then transferred to the Metropolitan Line.

The journey lasted two hours. I watched London pass by outside the
window, with industrial areas giving way to suburbs, then proper suburbs
with rows of identical houses, and finally Uxbridge, the end of the line.
By the time I arrived, the rain had stopped, but the sky remained heavy.

* * *

UXBRIDGE STATION on the Metropolitan Line. Deep in the suburbs,
the terminus was a place where everyone arrived exhausted and left
quickly. I stepped off the train onto a platform that felt quieter, less
crowded, and more modest than King's Cross.

The station carried the scent of diesel and damp concrete, that
particular London smell of underground spaces and perpetual moisture. The October air was cold in a way Dubai's heat never was, a
penetrating chill that carried moisture, seeping through my thin
jacket, finding every gap in my defences. My body hadn't adjusted.
My skin still expected the dry heat of the Gulf.

I followed the signs toward the exit, dragging my suitcases
behind me. The wheels caught on the gaps between platform tiles,
forcing me to lift them. My arms ached. Four years of life condensed
into three suitcases.

Outside, the sky was the colour of slate. Not grey, but slate,
specific. A sky that promised rain but hadn't delivered yet. The
streets were narrow, unlike Dubai's wide highways, unlike Neyveli's
planned grid.

My flat was a studio above an Indian takeaway, a place that only
became home because I had no other choice. Seven hundred and fifty
pounds a month for a room barely big enough to turn around in, with
a bed against one wall, a small kitchenette against another, and a
window overlooking a car park, its tarmac shimmering with rain.

The smell of curry and fried food drifted up through the floor-
boards, especially in the evenings when the restaurant below was

busy, the scent of onions frying, of spices toasting, of oil heating, creating an olfactory bridge to a home that felt increasingly distant.

It should have been comforting and familiar, the smell of home, but it wasn't home. It was another reminder that I was somewhere else, working to find home in the scent of food that wasn't quite the food I remembered, with the flavours slightly different.

I unpacked the same clothes I'd brought from Dubai, the same photograph of my mother.

The first morning, my alarm went off at 6:47 AM. London's cold was different from Dubai's dry heat. Damp, seeping through the single-glazed window, made the room feel perpetually chilly, no matter how high I turned up the heating. I made instant coffee, dressed in layers.

8:02 AM, Metropolitan Line towards Aldgate, the train is already packed with commuters. The tube in the morning becomes a lesson in contained proximity, bodies pressed together, everyone slightly holding their breath, upholding the unspoken agreement of shared space without interaction. No one spoke. Eye contact was avoided. We existed together but separately, each person in their own bubble of headphones and phones.

The fintech firm occupied three floors in Canary Wharf. This building looked as if it had been designed to intimidate, glass and steel, its architecture speaking of corporate power and financial might, its reflective surfaces creating a mirror of the city around it.

Open-plan offices that seemed to stretch endlessly, rows of desks where people stared at screens displaying algorithms that transferred money across borders within microseconds, the numbers flickering, transactions accumulating, wealth being created and destroyed in the space between heartbeats. The air was filtered, temperature-controlled, creating an environment that made you forget about weather, about time.

My team consisted of eight people. Seven were white British, all privately educated, speaking in accents I still had to concentrate to follow. One was Indian. Rajesh, from Mumbai, who had been in

London for five years and had perfected the art of code-switching so seamlessly you'd never know English wasn't his first language.

We didn't discuss race. We didn't talk about anything personal, really. We worked twelve hours a day, sometimes more, building systems that would make someone else rich while we earned salaries that felt substantial but somehow never quite felt enough. The silence between us was tacit, an unspoken agreement to keep our distance.

The routine had become second nature. Work, then the tube, then the flat, then repeat.

My team was friendly enough. Amir, a British-Pakistani developer from Birmingham, had been the first to reach out; James, reticent and Welsh.

We'd exchange pleasantries at the coffee machine. Small talk about the weather, the project deadlines, and the Tube delays.

I'd learned to navigate London, to exist in it, to survive in it. But I hadn't learned to live in it.

Weekends were the hardest. The city would come alive, people out and about, families together, friends meeting. I'd stay in my flat, work on side projects, and watch television.

Then one Friday, after a year of this polite distance, Amir stopped by my desk.

"We're going to the pub. You coming?" I hesitated.

"It can wait till Monday. Come on. You can't spend every Friday night alone."

I went.

Friday evenings became a ritual. Pubs near the Thames, warm beer, fish and chips. Amir taught me about football. We went to Old Trafford, and I became a casual United fan. Alex organised cultural trips: Stonehenge, Bath, and the Globe Theatre.

One evening, Amir took me to a pub by the Thames. Warm beer, fish and chips. We talked about work, London, and the things we missed from home. The conversation was relaxed, familiar.

* * *

THE FOLLOWING WEEK, Amir called me on a Saturday morning. "You doing anything today?"

"Not really. Why?"

"I'm going to Borough Market. Want to come? I'm cooking for my mum's birthday next week."

I hesitated. Going out. On a Saturday. With someone. Spending time with someone and being social.

"Sure. Why not?"

We met at London Bridge Station and walked to Borough Market together. The market was crowded, lively, and bustling with people. Stalls sold cheese, bread, fish, vegetables, and spices. The aroma of coffee and fresh bread filled the air.

Amir knew the vendors. Greeted them by name. Asked about their families and made conversation.

"You come here often?"

"Every Saturday. It's my routine. My ritual."

We walked through the market. The air was thick with the smells of cardamom and cinnamon from spice stalls, the sharp tang of fresh fish, and the earthy scent of vegetables. Amir bought ingredients, his hands moving with purpose as he selected tomatoes, onions, and fresh herbs. I watched. Learned. "This is what he did every week," he said. "Not in big moments. In small ones, in routines, in rituals, in showing up."

We left the market. Walked back to the station, the city around us.

Life happening. People living. "Thanks for today."

"Anytime. But next time, you're cooking."

* * *

ICELAND. Three friends from work, a week in March. We'd planned it for months, saved up, booked flights, and rented a camper van. The Ring Road, the whole thing.

The surreal landscape featured black-sand beaches, glaciers, geysers, and waterfalls emerging from nowhere. We travelled through snow-covered fields, past giant-sculpted mountains, and small villages with vivid, brightly painted houses standing out against winter's white and grey.

But it was the northern lights that I'd been waiting for. We'd checked forecasts, driven to remote spots away from light pollution, stood in the cold for hours, our breath visible in the air, our hands numb despite gloves. And then, on the third night, they appeared.

Green and purple hues dancing across the sky, shifting and moving, alive. For a moment, everything else vanished. The work stress, visa worries, the constant performance — all of it disappeared. All that remained was this: the sky, the lights, the cold air, the silence.

Maya once mentioned Iceland, months before we broke up. "I've always wanted to see the northern lights," she said. "There's something about them. About standing under that sky, watching something bigger than yourself." She had planned a trip, with the same Ring Road route we're now following.

Under those lights, her words echoed in my mind. She desired this, planned for it, but never saw it. Not guilt or regret, but a realisation I was here, witnessing her wish fulfilled while she wasn't. I was present; she was not. The only difference was a person I knew in Dubai, a chapter now closed.

The lights moved again, forming fresh patterns. I grabbed my phone and snapped a picture. Not for social media, not to share. Just to capture the moment.

* * *

A FEW MONTHS after returning from Iceland, back in London, the routine settled in: work, flat, the same patterns.

South Asian Professionals Network Diwali Celebration & Networking Evening Saturday, 7 PM.

By Saturday afternoon, I was lying on my floor looking at the ceiling.

I had nothing better to do.

At 6:45 PM, I was still on the floor. At 6:50 PM, I stood up and showered.

At 7:15 PM, I was on the tube to Walthamstow.

* * *

I MET Janani at a South Asian community event in East London.

I never attended these things. I had spent years working to be invisible, to blend into the grey efficiency of London life.

But I went.

The event was held at a community centre in Walthamstow. The room was filled with the aroma of cardamom and cumin, sambar and coconut chutney, creating an olfactory map of South India. Each spice served as a reminder of home, of distance, and of the places we had left behind.

Bollywood music crackled from old speakers, the sound tinny but familiar, with the rhythms and melodies forming a soundtrack for a community gathering. Cheap streamers in saffron, white, and green made it look like a school gymnasium; the decorations conveyed celebration and community.

The room was full of people speaking Tamil, Telugu, and Malayalam. I was about to leave when she appeared.

She stood near the door, speaking rapidly in Tamil to someone. Her back was turned to me, but her posture, movements, and gestures drew my attention. She was completely absorbed in the conversation—leaning in, listening, and responding—something I hadn't experienced in months.

Then she turned, and I saw her face.

She wore a pale green handloom cotton saree, soft and airy, the shade resting between mint and sage. The fabric had a natural texture and effortless drape typical of handloom cotton, falling into relaxed, graceful pleats. Her pallu was drawn loosely over her shoulder, unpinned.

But it wasn't just her appearance. It was how she moved—her effortless physicality, leaning against the doorframe, gesturing widely, occupying space without hesitation. Her presence was whole, open. Her hands moved when she spoke, expressive and natural, as if she weren't performing.

She was lively, speaking rapidly in Tamil, but her Tamil sounded different — clipped and lacking the fluidity of someone who had grown up speaking it daily. She would pause mid-sentence, searching for words, then switch effortlessly to English, her London accent clear. The switch was smooth and natural, as if both languages were equally at home in her.

Laughing: "Sorry, I don't know the Tamil word for 'dissertation'. My parents tried."

Tamil for family talk, English for everything else, both languages occupying the same breath. The ease of it, the naturalness.

I couldn't look away. Something in her reminded me of home, of Neyveli, of the vine that bloomed without asking, persistent and defiant. But there was also something new, something London, something that spoke of a life built intentionally, chosen with care.

When the conversation ended, she moved and nearly walked into me. I was still staring. I'd been watching her. Listening to her. Noticing

her.

"Oh, sorry!" Then, looking at my plate: "Did you try the kothu roti?"

"Not yet."

"You should. It's the only reason I come to these things. Well, that and my mum makes me."

Sri Lankan Tamil heritage. British accent. The combination felt familiar. Comforting.

I'm Janani.

I'm Dev.

Let me guess, software engineer? How did you know?

Every Indian bloke at these things is either a software engineer, a doctor, or lying about being a software engineer.

I laughed. First time I'd laughed at one of these gatherings. First time my shoulders had dropped.

What about you?

Digital marketing—mainly strategy. I work for a fintech company in Canary Wharf, leading campaigns for European expansion. I had planned to become a teacher, specialising in literature—proper books, not marketing copy. I had a place at UCL for an MA in Education.

What happened?

Student loans, my parents' mortgage, the sensible choice. Turns out I'm great at helping people move money around and pretending it's innovative. That's what I do.

Canary Wharf? I work there too. TechConsult. "Good grief." She laughed, and the heaviness lifted. "Probably."

She paused, then asked: "Are you here alone?"

"I'm alone."

"Me too. Easier that way."

Someone called her name from across the room. "That's my mum. I should go say hello to people."

"You too."

She walked away, and I stayed for another twenty minutes out of politeness.

The event continued around me. People were talking, laughing, eating, and connecting, but I wasn't connecting. I was still thinking about her.

I walked out into the London evening.

* * *

I STEPPED into the launderette on Mare Street because the rain had come down harder than I expected.

The bell above the door rang once and then fell silent. Inside, the air was warm and thick with the scent of detergent. Machines lined the walls, white and scuffed, their round windows fogged over. Water shifted inside them in a steady rhythm, a dull sound that filled the room without demanding anything from me.

I stood near the door for a moment. Rain dripped from the edge of my jacket onto the tiled floor. No one looked up.

An older woman sat near the back, folding clothes and smoothing each piece before stacking it. A man in a hooded jumper leaned against a machine, scrolling through his phone. His foot tapped against the floor, slightly out of time with the washers.

I walked to an empty chair by the window and sat. The plastic was still warm. I rested my hands on my thighs and watched the machines turn.

A child's sock clung to the glass of one washer, tumbling and sticking, tumbling and sticking again. I followed it until the motion slowed and stopped.

Rain streaked the window in uneven lines. Outside, buses passed in red blurs, distorted by water. People moved quickly with umbrellas angled forward, heads down, leaning into the weather.

A machine beeped sharply. The woman stood, opened the door of her washer, and a cloud of steam escaped. She reached inside and lifted the clothes against her chest without hesitation.

I checked my phone, no new messages.

I slid it back into my pocket.

The scent of detergent lingered on my jacket, clean yet unfamiliar. I zipped it up, stood, and made my way to the door. As I opened it, the cold rushed in, sharp against my face.

Outside, the rain had eased into a gentle mist. I stepped back onto the pavement and continued walking, the sound of the machines still faintly accompanying me.

* * *

I RETURNED TO THE CHAIR. The afternoon light had shifted. Claire was still holding her pen.

"That's how I met her," I said. "At a community event."

She waited.

"She was calm," I added. "Where Maya was fire. Consistent where Thara was hopeful."

Claire looked up. "You're talking about her in relation to other people"

"I think I'm trying to understand her," I said. "Or maybe understand why she fit."

"And what do you notice about yourself in that moment?" she asked.

I thought about it.

"I'm not in the picture," I said finally.

She didn't respond immediately.

"When you think about London now," she said, "where do you feel it in your body?"\

I waited for something to appear.

"I don't," I said. "That's what worries me."

Claire set her pen down.

"We'll stay with that," she said.

PART III
MORAL WEATHER

Where survival replaces desire

THE PAUSE BEFORE FALLING

I sat down and rubbed my hands together. The room was cold.

"You stopped mid-sentence last week."

"Did I?"

"When you were talking about London."

"I remember."

Claire didn't look down at her notes. "You remembered the stop. You didn't go back into what you were saying."

I thought about it. "It's hard, perhaps."

"What's hard about it?"

"It's complicated, perhaps."

"You've used 'hard' and 'complicated' before," Claire said. "What do those words keep you from naming?"

I didn't answer.

"When was the last time you were fully here?" Claire asked. "Not performing. Not disappearing, the disappearing we've been tracking."

I was quiet.

"Dev?"

"With Janani, perhaps," I said. "Early on. Or it felt like that at the time."

"Tell me what you mean by 'fully here,'" she said, precise. "Not the story yet. The sensation."

* * *

SHE WAS at Pret à Manger near Canary Wharf.

"Janani?"

Her face brightened. "Dev! The software engineer."

"Do you work around here?"

"25 Bank Street. You?"

"One Canada Square. We're practically neighbours."

"Sorry," she said, already stepping back. "I'd love to stay and chat, but I'm running late."

She rushed out, and the door swung shut behind her with the soft, impatient click of a place designed for people who never linger.

* * *

THE FOLLOWING WEEK, on Thursday afternoon.

I was on my laptop at one of the high tables near the window, reviewing code, trying to debug something that made no sense. She walked in, saw me, hesitated, just enough to decide.

"We have to stop meeting this way."

"About the engineer and the marketing person?"

She sat across from me. "Go ahead."

She ordered a coffee, came back, and pulled out her laptop. Before she opened it, she leaned forward.

"What are you working on?"

"Database optimisation. Boring."

"Everything's boring if you explain it badly," she said. "Go on then."

I explained it as searching through a filing cabinet versus using an index, the difference between brute force and finding a path that already exists.

"You're good at translation," she said. "Technical and human."

We worked in silence for a while, parallel screens, two lives pretending to be separate in the same square of light.

When she packed up, she didn't leave right away.

"I come here most Thursdays around this time."

"I might be," I said, and heard how careful it sounded.

"I hope you will be." Then, softer: "Dev? Next time, we should skip the laptops."

She left before I could respond, and my hands stayed where they were, as if they hadn't received the instruction to move.

* * *

IT BECAME A THING, Thursday afternoons at Pret. Sometimes we worked; sometimes we didn't. Sometimes we talked as if talking itself was the assignment.

"Why did you come to London?"

I shrugged. "Visa transfer."

"Do you like it here?"

"It's fine. Grey and cold."

She studied me, head tilted, as if she were listening for what I was not saying. "What do you mean?"

"You say it's fine," she said, "but you say it like you're convincing yourself."

"I don't know if I like anywhere," I said. "I exist in places."

"I get that," she said. "Sometimes I think we spend our whole lives translating ourselves. Tamil at home. British at work. Never quite belonging to either."

"Is that what you do?" she asked.

"Every single day," I said. "And I'm good at it. But it's exhausting, having to choose which parts of yourself to show depending on who's watching. At work, I'm professional, calm, competent, and British enough to be trusted. At home, I'm the daughter, Tamil

111

enough to be understood. And when I moved between them, something kept slipping."

I paused, listening to myself. The words landed easily, whether I believed it.

"So you understand what I mean."

"Better than you know."

She studied me, seeing something I didn't know I was showing. I was quiet.

"It's okay," she said. "You don't have to stop. Not yet. But maybe, eventually, you could try being."

"What if there's nothing there?" I asked. "What if there's no real me underneath all the performance?"

"Then we'll build one," she said. "Together." She said it like a plan, not a promise, and it landed in me with both comfort and a kind of fear I didn't name.

"My parents reckon I should move back home," she said, "find a nice Tamil boy to marry. Instead, I'm renting a flat in Bethnal Green."

"Living the dream," I said.

"Exactly," she said. "Their dream. Not mine."

She turned to face me, as if turning mattered.

One Thursday, she didn't show up. The routine had settled, Thursday sessions, the same chair, the same view, the same careful conversations.

I'd been waiting. Looking forward to it. Planning what I'd say, how I'd tell her about my week, how I'd ask about hers, how we'd talk and connect and be here.

The following Thursday, she was back.

"I come here deliberately now," she said, like she was claiming the habit. "So we're friends now?"

"I think so," I said, and the words felt oddly new.

"Brilliant," she said. "Because I was going to ask if you fancied getting a drink sometime. Proper drink."

She studied me, working to see if I was ready to be more than coffee, prepared to attempt it without hiding behind a screen.

* * *

THE PUB WAS CALLED The Bell. Dark wood worn smooth, low ceilings, the smell of beer and old carpet that held on to other people's conversations.

Friday evening. We found a corner table near the window. She ordered a pint of lager. I ordered the same.

"You don't like beer, do you?" she asked, watching my face.

"How can you tell?"

"You made the same expression my dad makes when he's working to be polite about something he hates."

"Wine," she said. "Or maybe a soft drink."

"Then get wine," she said, nodding at my glass. "Or a soft drink. Life's too short to drink things you don't like."

I returned the beer and ordered a glass of wine instead.

"Better?"

"Much better."

"Good," she said. "Because pretending to like things you don't is exhausting. And I'd rather know what you like."

"What if what I like is boring?"

"Then I'll learn to find boring interesting."

"So," she said, leaning in slightly, "tell me your story. How does someone from India end up at TechConsult?"

"Dubai first. Then London."

"Dubai," she said. "God, I hated visiting Dubai. So austere and sterile."

"And before Dubai?"

"Chennai. A small town in Tamil Nadu. Engineering college."

Bar snacks arrived. I reached for the peanuts.

"Want some mallatai?"

"What did you call it?"

"Mallatai." I caught myself. "Sorry. Peanuts. I forget sometimes."

"No, no," she said, delighted. "Mallatai. That's very specific. You're from Cuddalore, aren't you?"

I was surprised. "Close. I'm from Neyveli."

"Ah!" she said. "My dad's from Jaffna. He had a friend from Cuddalore who worked at the cement plant. He always said 'mallatai' instead of 'verkadalai.' My dad used to tease him about it."

"Your Tamil is better than you think."

"It's terrible," she said. "I can order food and talk to my grand-parents. But I answered my parents in English. Now I regret it."

"You haven't lost it," I said. "It's sleeping."

She looked at me. "It's true. You need someone to wake it up."

"And you're volunteering?"

"I could teach you," she said. "If you want."

"What would you teach me first?"

"Depends. What do you want to know?"

"How to flirt. How to argue. How to tell someone they're being ridiculous."

"Those are the same thing in Tamil."

She laughed, her shoulders loosening. "See? You're already a better company than all of my dates. They're usually terribly earnest, nice Tamil boys my mum approves of. They bang on about their careers and five-year plans."

"Please don't," I said, and she smiled.

She shifted closer.

We talked for three hours about London, work, and the language we carried from home. She told me about a brief dating situation that didn't work out, involving a controlling Tamil man. I shared with her my experiences of Dubai and the loneliness brought by visa precarity, where your future always hinges on paperwork.

Midway through our third drink, she leaned back, studying me.

"What?"

"You never ask me about my work," she said. "Not really. You ask what I do, but you don't ask why I'm doing it instead of teaching."

"Why are you doing it?"

"Because I'm good at it. Because it pays the mortgage. Because I can't afford to be a teacher." She took a sip. "But also because I'm angry. I'm angry that practicality won over what I wanted. And I'm excellent at turning that anger into strategy."

"Does it help?" I asked. "The anger?"

"Sometimes. Mostly, it exhausts me. But it's mine. I own it."

Around 9 p.m., the pub got crowded. Someone bumped our table. I reached to steady her beer.

We both froze.

"Sorry," I said. But I didn't move my hand.

"It's fine," she said. She didn't move hers either. Her hand turned over, palm up, offering the decision back to me.

"Is this okay?"

"Yeah."

"Good," she said. "Because I'm not subtle when I like someone."

"I'm okay with not subtle."

"I'm second-generation," she said. "My parents wanted me to marry a nice Tamil boy, get a job in finance, have children, and live in Surrey."

"Which two?"

"Tamil boy. Finance." Her fingers tightened around mine. "Are you disappointed?"

"No." Her eyes stayed steady, not asking me to react.

* * *

I PAUSED and looked at my hands.

"The first Saturday," I said. "After the drink, after we stopped pretending Pret was just a coincidence, we met at a café near Regent's Canal."

I arrived early, sat at a table by the window, and watched the water. Its surface rippled with the occasional narrowboat, light filtering through the plane trees.

"What comes up when you think about that memory?" Claire asked.

"I didn't feel split," I said. "I stayed."

"And how did that feel?"

115

"Peaceful, maybe. Calm. Like I was in the right place."

"What happened when you walked along the canal?"

"We walked. The water was still, a dark mirror reflecting the sky. The silence between us was easy. We talked about everything and nothing."

"Tell me about that conversation," Claire said, then refined it: "What was different in you while you were speaking?"

I was quiet. "It was different," I said. "I didn't have to check myself before speaking."

"What else do you remember?" Claire asked. "About being here with her, without the performance?"

"The second Saturday," I said. "Same café. She arrived on time and ordered tea instead of coffee. I noticed and asked about it. She said she was trying to cut back on caffeine."

I paused, surprised by how clearly I could see it.

"I wanted to know," I said. "I wanted to learn what she liked."

"And how did that feel? Wanting to know?"

"Different," I said. "I wanted to know things without deciding what they meant."

"What happened next?"

"We sat there for two hours. Talking, laughing, watching the canal, watching the city wake up."

She said it was nice, Saturday mornings, coffee, conversation, no pressure, no expectations.

"How does that feel?" Claire asked. "Being here without pressure?"

I was quiet. "Rare," I said. "Special. Important. And I was learning, learning to be here."

ONE EVENING, Janani suggested an Ethiopian restaurant in Camden. She'd read about it, wanted to try it, wanted to explore. I'd never had Ethiopian food before.

The restaurant was small and warm, walls covered in woven baskets and photographs of Addis Ababa. The owner was a woman in her fifties, her hair wrapped in bright fabric, her smile wide and welcoming. She greeted us as expected.

"Have you had Ethiopian food before?"

"No," I said. "Never."

"Me neither," Janani said. "But I've been wanting to try it. I love how London lets you eat the whole world. Ethiopian on Monday, Tamil on Tuesday, Nigerian on Wednesday. That's what I love about this city: access to all these different ways of being."

The owner brought a large platter covered with injera, which was spongy and tangy, made from grey teff flour with a crêpe-like, textured surface but thicker. On top were mounds of spiced stews: doro wat, rich with berbere and slow-cooked chicken; misir wat, with red lentils in a deep, earthy sauce.

"Eat with your hands," the owner instructed, her accent warm, musical. "That's how we do it in my country. No forks."

Janani's face lit up. She tore off a piece of injera, used it to scoop the doro wat. The berbere hit the back of my throat, warm, layered, not heat but depth: fenugreek, cardamom, coriander, chilli.

"This is incredible," Janani said, full of wonder. "How the injera soaks up the sauce. How the spices layer. It's like dosai, but different, sour, fermented."

I'd eaten with my hands before. Growing up in Tamil Nadu, it was natural—dosa, idli, rice mixed with sambar or rasam—using the right hand, thumb, and first two fingers, to mix and scoop. But watching Janani savour each bite, notice details, and connect it to what she knew, made me see it differently.

"The owner's name is Alem," Janani said, reading from a small card on the table. "She's been here twenty years. Came from Addis, opened this place, raised three kids. Can you imagine? Building a life here, bringing your food, your culture, sharing it with people who've never tasted it."

She tore off another piece of injera, scooped the misir wat, and closed her eyes.

"This is what I want," she said. "To explore. To try new things. To understand that there are many ways to live, to find meaning, to build a life. And London offers access to all of it—Ethiopian, Thai, Nigerian, right here."

I watched her. She appreciated the food, but also what it represented: connection, story, the world held in a single plate.

"You really love this, don't you?" I asked.

"Food?" she said. "Or exploring?"

"Both."

"Yes," she said. "I do. Food reveals a place, its people, and its culture. It connects you to something greater. Reminds you that we're all linked, even when we come from different places."

We finished the platter, every last bite. Janani asked Alem about spices, about fermentation, and about how long injera takes. Alem answered, warm-eyed and animated, two women from different continents, connected by curiosity and food.

"This is what I love about London," Janani said as we walked out.

* * *

ON THE THIRD SATURDAY, she suggested we cook together.

"Your flat or mine?"

"Yours," I said. "You have a proper kitchen."

Her flat in Bethnal Green had a small but functional kitchen: a gas stove, a proper oven, enough counter space for two people if they didn't move too much. She'd already been to the market. Vegetables in brown paper bags. Rice. Spices in small jars, each with a hand-written label in Tamil and English.

"What are we making?"

"Biryani," she said. "My mother's recipe. But we're doing it together."

She handed me an onion.

I took the knife and started cutting.

She watched. "That's not small," she said. "That's medium."

She took the knife and demonstrated. Quick, precise movements. Uniform pieces.

"Now you try."

I gave it a try. Mine were uneven, but she didn't step in. She allowed me to learn. She chopped tomatoes while I focused on the onion. We moved around each other in the tight space, finding our rhythm and knowing when to step back.

"You're getting better," she said after a few minutes.

"Liar."

"No," she said. "You're learning. That's what matters."

We cooked for two hours. The flat filled with spices, onions caramelising, rice steaming. She taught me when to add each spice, how to tell when the rice was done, and how to layer everything in the pot. I followed her instructions, asked questions, and felt myself staying present instead of drifting.

When it was finished, we sat on her floor, with biryani between us, eating with our hands, as she had learned from her mother, as I had learned from mine. It wasn't perfect, but it was good, and it was ours.

"This is nice," I said.

"What?" she asked. "The food?"

"This," I said. "Cooking together. Being here."

She looked at me. "I'm glad," she said, and I believed her.

* * *

ONE SATURDAY AFTERNOON, she suggested Westminster Abbey.

"I've never been," she said. "Can you believe it? Born in London. Lived here my whole life."

"I haven't either."

"Then let's go," she said. "Together."

We took the Tube to Westminster. The station was busy: tourists with maps, locals with purpose, everyone moving as if they had somewhere to be.

We walked into the square. Big Ben caught the afternoon light. The Houses of Parliament rose with Gothic spires. Westminster Abbey stood ancient and weathered, its scale designed to humble.

We bought tickets and walked inside.

The nave stretched out beneath vast, high vaulted ceilings like a stone forest. Stained glass cast prismatic light across floors worn smooth by centuries of footsteps. The air was cool and still, smelling of old stone and candle wax. It carried silence the way water bears weight, making you lower your voice without being asked.

We walked, our footsteps echoing. Names, memorials, tombs, dates, history arranged as a corridor.

Then I saw it. A name.

I stopped.

Newton, I said, quiet with recognition. I studied him in school, physics, mathematics, laws of motion, and gravity.

I moved closer and read the inscription. Janani followed, watching me as if she were observing something awakening.

I kept walking, reading. Then another.

Darwin, I said louder. Origin of Species. Evolution. Natural selection. I observed him, but I never imagined he would be here, buried in the same church as Newton.

I kept walking, faster.

James Clerk Maxwell. I stopped. Maxwell, I said, my voice rising. Electromagnetism. The equations that explained light and electricity. I memorised them. Solved them. But I never imagined he was here with all of them.

I kept moving, urgent now.

Michael Faraday. Faraday. Electricity, magnetism, experiments. I studied him, but I never imagined he was here.

I started half-running from tomb to tomb.

Lord Kelvin. Thermodynamics. Absolute zero. Rutherford. The nucleus. J.J. Thomson. The electron. The discovery.

My voice rose as I moved, breathless.

All these people, I said, almost overwhelmed, all these scientists, scholars, thinkers.

I studied them as names, as equations, as problems on paper. But here they were, lives. Bodies. Tombs. The fact of them.

Janani was watching me, steady.

"You're seeing them," she said. "Not names in books. Not equations. People."

I nodded. "I am," I said. "Not names. Not equations. People."

We stood there surrounded by history, centuries carved into stone and silence, and I sensed something shift inside me, though I couldn't name it.

* * *

I RETURNED to the room and sat back in the chair. The afternoon light had shifted gradually, almost imperceptibly — the sort of change you only notice when you stop everything else.

"Dev," Claire said, "you're describing the beginning of a relationship. How does it feel to remember this?"

I paused and looked at my hands, how they rested on my knees, how they had rested in other rooms where decisions were made without me speaking.

"What happens when you say 'I'm not sure'?" Claire asked. Then she narrowed it, like she always did. "Right before you go quiet, what's the first cue?"

The room felt like a space between places, temporary accommodation I'd learned to navigate: sit, answer, be coherent, don't spill.

"How does that feel?" Claire asked. "Watching yourself from the outside like that?"

I was quiet. "Nothing, perhaps," I said, and heard how familiar that answer was.

Claire didn't respond right away.

"Notice what happens when you say that," she said finally.

She let that sit, then added, quieter: "We can stay with it without forcing it."

* * *

THE FIRST TIME she came to my flat in Uxbridge, she stopped in the doorway.

"This is smaller than I imagined."

"It's a studio."

"I can see that," she said, walking through, taking it in, the single room, the mini-kitchen, the bed that doubled as seating.

"Two years," she said, more to herself than to me.

"And you've never unpacked fully, have you?" She gestured to the boxes in the corner.

"I never saw the point."

"Do you like living here?"

"It's functional."

"That's not what I asked."

I looked around: beige walls, generic furniture, view of identical buildings. "No," I said. "I don't like it. But it's cheap."

"You're settling for functional," she said. "Because functional doesn't ask for anything"

"But you're not leaving," she said. "You've been here two years."

I laughed despite myself.

"That's what I do," I said, and didn't know whether it was a joke or a confession.

She looked at the room again.

"You don't stay anywhere very long," she said.

"Is it?"

"Yes," she said. "Because you're more than functional."

I felt it low in my chest, brief and unfamiliar. I sat beside her.

"I'd paint the walls," she said. "Not beige. Something with colour. Proper curtains. Plants. I'd make it feel like a home."

"You'd make it yours."

"Yes," she said. "Because it is mine. Or yours. Wherever I am, that space is mine."

"Would you help me?" I asked.

"Of course," she said. "But only if you want to."

"I want to."

She smiled. "Then mean it."

"I'm not abandoning it," I said, and heard myself trying to sound certain.

"Prove it," she said.

So we did. That Saturday, we went to IKEA, plants, curtains, and throw pillows in colours that weren't beige. We spent the afternoon rearranging furniture and hanging curtains.

When we were done, the flat looked different. It didn't feel finished.

But it didn't feel borrowed either.

"Better?" she asked.

"Much better," I said, and meant it.

"That's the goal," she said, putting her arms around my waist. "I wasn't planning to run away."

"Weren't you?" she asked.

I didn't answer.

* * *

ABOUT EIGHT MONTHS into our relationship, I asked the question.

* * *

CLAIRE LEANED FORWARD.

"I can't say."

"Think about it," she said. "What made you ask? What was different? What was the pressure you were responding to?"

I was quiet.

"Dev," she said, not unkindly, "you're going quiet again. Where did you go?"

I blinked.

"That's okay," she said. "When we get close to the hinge moments, you disappear. We'll work on that. But notice it."

* * *

DURAI R

WE WERE WALKING along the Thames near Tower Bridge. It was early evening in late summer, with that perfect London light that makes the city look gentler than it actually is. The river was busy with tourists, joggers, and couples. Movement was everywhere.

"Where are we heading with this?" she asked, and stopped walking.

"This," she said. "Us. The relationship. Where are we heading?"

"I can't say," I said.

She studied my face.

The words came out more blunt than I intended. "I don't want to be in a relationship that's not serious. If we're serious, we have to discuss practical issues. You're British. I'm not. My visa is tied to my employer. How does this work?"

She sat on a bench overlooking the river. I sat beside her.

"You're right," she said finally.

"I'm not trying to pressure you," I said quickly.

"You're not," she said. "You're being honest. Which is good." She looked at me. "You're asking if this is going somewhere. If we're building toward something."

"Are you asking if I want to marry you?"

"I'm asking if marriage is something you're thinking about," she said. "With me."

The Thames moved past us, indifferent and steady.

Finally, she said, "I've thought about it. Marriage. Not in a fairy-tale way. More practically. We're compatible. We understand each other. We both want stability. You're kind, which is rarer than people think. You listen."

"That's practical," I said.

"It is," she said. "Because I've seen what happens when people marry for passion, and it burns out. My cousin married for love. Divorced two years later. My parents married because their families thought they'd be compatible."

"So what are you saying?"

"I'm saying we could create something good together," she said.

"Something sustainable. But there are practicalities—your visa, where we'd live, whether we'd have children."

"I know."

"I'm on a visa, Janani," I said. "There's nothing permanent about my situation here. I don't see you moving to India, and I don't expect that. I want to build a life here. I hope that can happen. But I don't want to be in a relationship for a visa."

She looked at me, steady.

"In the months we've been together," I said, "you've made my life beautiful. Your conversations, you're amazing. Strong. Self-made. I'm happy with you. But sometimes reality hits hard. Knowing my visa isn't permanent. Knowing I could have to leave."

I let the words settle, and the river kept moving as if it had heard them all before.

She gave a slight nod.

"Let me look into this," she said. "I have a friend in immigration law. Let me understand the actual options. The process."

"Okay," I said.

* * *

I PAUSED.

"That's how it started," I said.

Then I stopped.

"Then what?" Claire asked.

"Small silences," I said. "Becoming larger ones."

"Can you identify when that started?" she asked. "Not the conclusion, the first cue. The first change."

I thought about it. "No. I can't."

"What did you do instead of speaking?" Claire asked, sharper now. "Where did you go, work, sleep, screens, logic?"

"It happened gradually," I said. "Working late. Avoiding conflict. Retreating into my head."

Claire let the repetition stand, then placed the following question carefully.

125

"And what did it cost you," she asked, "to keep retreating?"
I was quiet.
She watched me, not as interpretation, but as attention.

WHEN THE SESSION FINISHED, I left Claire's office and stepped into the evening. The air was cool, filled with the scent of rain and damp earth, and for a moment I wasn't sure whether the wetness on my skin was due to the weather or memory.

THE FORM THAT CHANGES THE ROOM

*C*laire was already writing when I entered, but her movement was swifter this time. The pen didn't pause. The pen didn't linger. It moved as if she already knew where the sentence was heading.

"You said she made you more present," she said, without looking up. "And then you said you started disappearing."

I sat. The chair accepted my weight as it always had, but my body didn't settle as smoothly. My hands rested together, not quite clasped, as if waiting for instruction.

"It wasn't dramatic," I said. "There wasn't a moment where something broke."

Claire stopped writing. Not abruptly. Deliberately.

"Then tell me the first small thing," she said. "The first shift."

I looked down, not at the carpet this time, but at my shoes. Scuffed. Familiar. Objects that were still where I'd left them

"It was a form," I said.

She waited.

"Not the big one," I added. "Not the kind that changes your status. One of the small ones. A reminder. A compliance email."

That got her attention.

"How did it change the room?" she asked.

"It made the future loud," I said. "It stopped being background noise."

She nodded, neither encouraging nor surprised. Recognition. As if she'd seen this exact moment occur in different bodies, different offices, different relationships.

"What kind of future?" she asked.

"The conditional one," I said. "The one that always arrives with deadlines."

She wrote again, briefly.

"And before that email?" she asked. "Before the future got loud?"

* * *

JANANI LIKED SATURDAYS.

Not because they were relaxing. Because they were hers.

She regarded them as fixed points, not suggestions—something to plan around rather than fill in later. Saturday mornings meant Borough Market. Vegetables still carry soil. Bread wrapped in paper, warm enough to leave grease on your fingers. Purchases that presumed continuity.

We met at London Bridge. She always arrived already holding a coffee. Sometimes tea. She never asked what I wanted. She handed me a cup anyway, as if being looked after was normal.

"Eat something," she'd say.

"I'm fine."

She'd nod, unconvinced, and buy a pastry anyway. Almond croissant. Cardamom bun. Something she thought I'd need more than I admitted.

She tore it in half before handing it to me. Not ceremoniously. Just swiftly. As if this was what you did when you expected someone to stay.

The first time, I hesitated. It felt too intimate for morning. Too easy.

"You're thinking again," she said.

"I'm not."

She looked at the pastry, then at me. "You are. Eat."

So I did. Butter and sugar and warmth. Something that didn't ask for an explanation.

We walked leisurely along the river. Past tourists framing themselves against landmarks they'd already started to leave behind. For a few hours, I wasn't counting anything. Not days. Not renewals. Not exit strategies.

Being with her changed the tempo. The counting fell away.

I noticed it only afterwards. It didn't feel like work. It felt like relief.

She selected items that suggested future use: lemons, coriander, jars she'd need to reopen. I watched her and felt a fleeting, irrational envy, not of the food itself, but of the underlying assumption.

Then one Saturday, she didn't turn toward the stalls.

She guided us instead to a quieter edge of the market, where the noise thinned, and people stopped colliding, a place you could pause without being moved along.

She took out her phone.

"Don't panic," she said.

That alone made my chest tighten.

"I'm not," I said too quickly.

She angled the screen toward me.

A UKVI reminder. Generic. Impersonal. Written for thousands.

My body reacted anyway. Shoulders lifting before I noticed them doing it, breath shortening.

"I set this for you," she said. "I used your date."

The words blurred. Expiry. Eligibility. Evidence. A language I was tired of translating.

"You didn't have to," I said.

"I did," she said.

Not sharp. Just decided.

"I don't want you living on three-month horizons," she said.

"It's been fine."

"It hasn't," she said. "It's just been functional."

I hated the word coming from her mouth. She said it the way people do when they've stopped softening the edges.

"Indefinite Leave to Remain," she said. "And the partner route. We should understand what's real."

"We," I repeated, like the word itself needed checking.

"Yes," she said. "We."

The air shifted, not as if in argument, but like a room you believed you knew until a light suddenly came on somewhere you hadn't noticed.

"I'm not asking today," she said. "I'm showing you there's a clock."

Then, after a pause, as if deciding whether to include it:

"My mum keeps asking," she said. "Not dramatically. ... whether you're a life or a season."

I didn't like being described like the weather.

"I told her I don't do provisional," she said.

It landed and stayed there.

My instinct was to joke. To lower the temperature. Humour was another way of leaving.

But she didn't open space for it.

"I'm not trying to trap you," she said. "I'm trying to make sure I'm not the only one building."

I nodded. Nodding is easy. It looks like an agreement.

We went back into the market, bought vegetables, took the Tube, and ate lunch as if nothing had changed.

It didn't go away.

That evening, she opened her laptop.

"One appointment," she said. "Immigration solicitor. Consultation. No decisions."

"What day?"

"Wednesday. Late afternoon. I booked it."

I stared at the calendar block. A rectangle that assumed I could show up like a person whose life didn't require rehearsal.

"I have a meeting," I said.

She didn't respond immediately.

"A meeting," she repeated.

"It's important."

She looked up. Not angry. Tired. The tiredness that comes from carrying weight alone.

"Everything is important to you," she said. "Except the things that make you real."

"I'll reschedule," I said, meaning hers.

She closed the laptop.

"No," she said. "I'm not rescheduling my life around something you won't look at."

"It's not fear."

She nodded, the way you do when you've heard this before.

"I'm not asking for marriage," she said. "I'm asking you to show up."

That night, I told myself I would go.

I rehearsed it like a task. Leave early. Sit beside her. Be competent.

Wednesday arrived.

At 6:12, my phone buzzed.

I'm here.

At 6:15:

Dev?

At 6:27:

Okay. I'll do it alone.

I stared until the words became shapes.

At 6:30, I joined a call and spoke calmly about timelines and mitigation. People thanked me.

I left at 8:10.

At home, the flat smelled like nothing. Beige. Airless.

On the counter: a brown envelope. TechConsult letterhead.

Reminder: visa renewal documents are due.

I turned it face down.

My phone buzzed again.

We'll talk later.

Later. The word held everything I was good at avoiding.

* * *

Claire's pen had stopped.

"So the first shift," she said, "wasn't that you stopped loving her."

"No," I said. "It was that she asked me to be present. And I started managing it."

"And when you didn't show up?"

"She handled it."

Claire nodded.

"And what did you learn?"

I looked away.

"That I could keep disappearing," I said. "And things would still run."

"And what did that cost?"

The answer didn't want to be a sentence.

"It cost me," I said finally, "the part of myself that could stay."

Claire didn't rush to fill the quiet.

Outside, the city kept moving. Inside, I could feel those early Saturdays again, warm, ordinary, real, and the thin retreat already threaded through them.

Like a seam you don't notice until it splits.

CARE, NOT CHAOS

J arrived the following week and sat down without comment.

"You missed last session," Claire said.

"Yes."

"No explanation?"

"Work."

She nodded. Wrote something.

"What happened instead?" she asked.

I hesitated. "Nothing."

Claire looked up. "That's usually when something happens."

I didn't respond.

* * *

I NEARLY DIDN'T GO next week. I stood outside the building for ten minutes, watched people walk past, considered leaving, but I went up and sat in the chair.

"You're here," Claire said. "Barely."

"What's different today?"

"I don't know if I want to keep coming."

"Doing what?"

"Remembering. Reliving it all."

"You don't have to. But you're here. So something's keeping you here."

I was quiet. Then: "Janani. I need to finish telling you about Janani."

* * *

WE STARTED SEEING EACH OTHER.

Coffee on Saturday mornings. Walks along the canal. Cheap Thai restaurants in Bethnal Green where we'd order too much food and talk until the staff started stacking chairs.

The first time she came to my flat in Uxbridge, she stopped in the doorway.

"This is smaller than I imagined."

"It's a studio."

"I can see that." She walked through, taking it all in: the single room, the mini-kitchen, the bed that doubled as seating, the boxes stacked in the corner, the generic furniture, the beige walls, and the window that looked out onto a car park.

"Two years."

"And you've never unpacked fully, have you?" She gestured to the boxes stacked in the corner.

"I never saw the point."

"Do you like living here?"

"It's functional."

"That's not what I asked."

I looked around: the beige walls, the generic furniture, the view of other identical buildings, the smell of curry from the restaurant below, and the single-glazed window that let in the cold. No. I don't like it, but it's cheap.

"You're settling for functional." She sat on the bed. The mattress dipped under her weight.

"Because functional is safe. It doesn't require commitment."

"But you're not leaving. You've been here two years."

I laughed despite myself.

"That's what I do." She leaned back on her elbows.

I tried to think of something I'd done without a reason. Not because it was necessary, not because it was expected.

"I can't remember."

"Then maybe we should start." She smiled, small and genuine.

I was quiet. I'd spent a long time choosing what worked.

"I can't say."

"That's sad, Dev."

"Is it?"

"Yeah. Because you're more than functional." I sat beside her.

"I'd paint the walls. Not beige. Something with colour. I'd get proper curtains. Plants. I'd make it feel like home."

"You'd make it yours."

"Yes. Because it is mine. Or yours. Wherever I am, that space is mine."

"Would you help me?" I asked.

"Of course. But only if you want to."

"I want to."

She smiled.

"I'm not abandoning it."

"Prove it."

So we did. That Saturday, we went to IKEA. We bought plants, curtains, and throw pillows in colours that weren't beige. We spent the afternoon rearranging furniture and hanging curtains.

When we were done, the flat looked different. Not transformed, but less generic.

"Better?"

"Much better." I looked around. She put her arms around my waist. "I wasn't planning to run away."

"Weren't you?"

I didn't answer.

* * *

THE FOLLOWING WEEK, she invited me to meet her parents. They lived in a suburb of London, in a house with a garden, a place that spoke of permanence and roots.

I was nervous, more nervous than I had been in years, more anxious than I had been for job interviews, visa applications, or anything else. My palms were damp.

Her father opened the door, tall and serious—a man who commanded respect without needing to ask. He was taciturn, speaking only when necessary, but his presence filled the room. Her mother stood behind him, smaller and warmer, her eyes appraising me.

"Come in," her father said.

I followed them inside. The house was warm, lived-in, filled with photographs, evidence of a life well-lived. Janani's school photos. Her graduation pictures. Images of her with friends, with family.

We sat in the living room. Her mother brought tea, Indian tea, strong and sweet, just like my mother used to make it, how I'd grown up drinking it, familiar and comforting.

"So you're from Tamil Nadu," her father said. "Yes. Neyveli. A small town."

"I know it. Coal mining town. My cousin worked there for a while."

We discussed Tamil Nadu, London, work, and life. Careful conversation. The kind that fills the silence without exposing too much. The kind that indicates I'm observing you, deciding if you're trustworthy.

Janani sat next to me, her hand on my knee, a small gesture of support, of connection.

When we left, her mother hugged me, a genuine hug, the kind that says you're welcome, you're family.

"Take care of her," her father said, shaking my hand. "I will."

"See that you do."

I nodded.

* * *

ONE SUNDAY AFTERNOON, I went to her flat in Bethnal Green.

She had a small balcony, barely three feet wide, filled with potted plants: tomatoes, herbs, and a struggling lemon tree. In the corner, a rose bush in a terracotta pot, blooming deep red.

Her fingers brushed the leaves, the touch gentle, almost reverent. "This is Rosa. She's my favourite."

I met her friends the following week: Priya, Anjali, and Sarah. They had booked a table at a restaurant in Shoreditch, a place that served small plates and craft cocktails. I arrived early and sat at the bar.

When Janani arrived with her friends, they took one look at me and started whispering. I could see them assessing me, trying to work out if I was worth their friend's time. Janani introduced me. I shook hands.

Priya inquired about my work. Anjali asked where I was from. Sarah wanted to know how long I'd been in London. These are typical questions—kindly ones asked when people are trying to get to know you better.

I carefully measured each word. Yet I could feel myself shifting, my accent softening, my answers becoming more refined, more British. I noticed Janani watching me. She didn't say anything.

After dinner, walking back to the Tube, she said: "You were different with them."

"How?"

"Your voice. The way you answered. More formal. Like you were working to impress them."

"I was trying to make a good impression."

"You don't need to. They'd like you either way." I was quiet.

"Dev, you don't have to be perfect. You don't have to be what you think they want."

"What if you aren't enough?" She stopped. Turned to face me. I wanted to believe her.

* * *

ONE SUNDAY AFTERNOON, I went to her flat in Bethnal Green.

She had a small balcony, barely three feet wide, filled with potted plants. Tomatoes, herbs, a struggling lemon tree. And in the corner, a rose in a terracotta pot, blooming a deep red.

Her fingers lightly caressed the leaves, her touch gentle and almost reverent. "This is Rosa. She's my favourite."

"You named your rose plant?"

"Of course. I talk to her every morning. She responds better when I

do."

"Do they now?"

"They do." She knelt beside the pot, checking the soil. "I make my own compost. Kitchen scraps, coffee grounds, eggshells. Takes about three months to break down properly."

Her hands moved through the soil. She talked about the process, the patience it required.

"You're staring."

"Sorry."

"Don't be." She glanced at me with a small smile.

"I'm thinking you're brilliant."

"For making compost?" She laughed.

"No. For caring about things. Properly caring."

She stood up and brushed the soil off her hands. "Rosa's been with me for three years. She's survived two harsh winters and one bout of aphids."

"Three years is a long time for a rose plant."

"It is. But when you care for something properly, it survives." She looked at me directly, her expression careful and measured, as if she were setting a boundary without saying it, as if she were showing me something about how she operated and what she expected. "Plants, relationships. Same principle."

She picked up a small handful of finished compost, dark and crumbly. "I'm good."

"No, seriously. Touch it." She grasped my hand, turned it palm-up, and let the soil fall into it. "Feel how light it is? That's three months of decomposition."

The soil was warm from the sun, surprisingly yielding.

"Finished compost shouldn't smell. If it does, you've done it wrong." She was standing close now.

I raised my hand cautiously, sniffed. She was right. "See?" She was grinning now, pleased with herself.

I held the soil out to her. She stepped away, laughing. "Complicit in composting?"

"Exactly. Now you have to help me repot Rosa next spring."

"I don't know how to repot a rose."

"I'll teach you. It's not complicated." She wiped her hands on her jeans, leaving dark streaks.

Soil in my palm. Her jeans were streaked with dirt, her hair coming loose from its tie, her eyes bright with genuine enthusiasm.

I didn't forget it. Not the composting itself, but the way she cared. Entirely, completely, without apology. Nothing she touched seemed provisional.

I noticed the difference. I tried to commit fully to something, without holding back.

"You're staring again," she said, but she was smiling. "I'm learning."

"About composting?"

"About you. About how you do things."

She stepped closer, took the soil from my hand, and dropped it back into the pot. "Then watch closely because I don't do casual, Dev. Not with plants. Not with people."

"I understand."

"Do you?" She looked at me directly. "Because I've been hurt before. By people who wanted the convenience of me without the commitment."

"I'm not that way."

"Prove it. Not with words. With actions." I reached for her hand, pulled her closer. She kissed me. Soft, tentative, then deeper.

"That's a start," she whispered against my lips. "A start."

"Good. Because I expect more than that." I laughed.

We stood there on her balcony, surrounded by plants, and the city spread out below us.

"Janani," I said. "Yes?"

"I'm going to mess this up. I'm going to disappoint you. But I'm going to try not to."

"That's all I'm asking for. The working at it."

"I'll try."

She squeezed my hand. "I'll be here."

"Promise?"

"Promise."

I brushed a smudge of soil from her cheek. She went still.

"You had dirt on your face."

"I probably have dirt everywhere." But she didn't step back. "You do." I showed her my palm, still holding the compost. She took my hand and brushed the soil off into the pot.

We stood there on her cramped balcony, the late afternoon sun catching the red petals.

* * *

ONE FRIDAY EVENING, she called me. I was at the pub with James and Alex. Second pint, halfway through a conversation about football.

It was Janani.

"Dev, can you come to my flat? Tonight. It's urgent." My chest tightened.

"Come soon, please." She hung up.

I stood up, grabbed my jacket. What's happening?

Janani. She needs me. Something's wrong. Alex grinned.

It's not that way. She said it was urgent.

Sure she did, James said, smirking. Urgent, Alex added, laughing.

My face heated.

Look at him blushing! Alex said. You two are children.

And you're whipped, James said, still grinning. Their laughter followed me out the door.

* * *

THE FOLLOWING WEEK, I introduced Janani to Amir. We met at a pub in Shoreditch. Amir arrived first, already seated at a table with a pint in hand. When Janani and I walked in, he stood up and shook her hand.

"So you're the one who's been keeping Dev busy."

"I am."

"Good. He needs someone to keep him busy. Otherwise, he works.

All the time."

"I've noticed."

"Have you?" Amir looked at me.

We sat down. Ordered drinks. Talked about work, about life, about London, about everything. Easy conversation. Natural.

Amir asked Janani about her work. She talked about digital strategy, her team, and the projects she was working on. He listened, asked follow-up questions, and showed genuine interest.

"You're good at what you do," Amir said. "Thank you. I try."

"No, you don't try. You do. There's a difference." She smiled.

Amir turned to me.

"I didn't ask for your approval."

"You didn't have to. I'm giving it anyway." Janani laughed.

"He's alright. When he's not being annoying."

"I'm never annoying. I'm charming."

"You keep telling yourself that."

We stayed for two hours. Talking, laughing, getting to know each other, building something, creating something.

When we left, Amir pulled me aside.

"She's good for you. I can see it. You're different. More here."

"Am I?"

"Yeah. You are. Don't mess it up."

"I'll try not to."

"Good. Because I like her, and if you mess it up, I'm taking her side."

"Fair enough."

* * *

FRIDAY EVENING, I was at the pub with James and Alex. Second pint, halfway through a conversation about football, when my phone rang.

Janani.

"Dev, can you come to my flat? Tonight. It's urgent."

My chest tightened. "What's wrong?"

"Just come. Soon. Please."

She hung up.

I stood up, grabbed my jacket.

"What's happening?" James asked.

"Janani. She needs me. Something's wrong."

Alex grinned. "Janani? Oh my god, mate. You're getting busy."

"It's not like that. She said it was urgent."

"Sure she did," James said, smirking. "Urgent. Urgent."

"Urgent," Alex added, laughing.

My face heated. "Shut up."

"Look at him blushing!" Alex said. "Dev's got a girlfriend. Dev's leaving us for a girl."

"You two are children."

"And you're whipped," James said, still grinning. "Go on. Save your damsel."

I left, their laughter following me out the door.

The Tube took forever. I kept checking my phone. No messages. No missed calls. What if something happened? What if she was hurt? By the time I reached Bethnal Green, I was nearly running. I knocked. She opened the door in jeans and a t-shirt, hair down, glass of wine in hand.

Breathless: "You're okay." I asked.

"Of course I'm okay." She stepped aside, let me in.

Her flat was... exploding with clothes—dresses draped over the sofa, the chairs, the coffee table. Shopping bags are piled in the corner—a mountain of fabric in every colour.

"What is all this?"

Casually, sipping her wine: "Shopping."

"Shopping."

"Yes. I went to Oxford Street. Got a bit carried away."

I stared at her. "You called me here, urgently, for shopping?"

"I need an audience."

"An audience?"

"For my fashion show." She gestured grandly at the chaos. "You're my audience tonight."

"Janani, I thought something was wrong. I thought you were hurt. I left my

friends..."

"So am I not urgent then?" she interrupted, eyes sparkling with mischief.

"Am I not a priority for you?"

"That's not... You said it was urgent."

"It is urgent. I need to decide what to keep and what to return. That's urgent."

She handed me a glass of wine. "Sit. Drink. Enjoy the show."

"You're serious."

"Serious." She disappeared into her bedroom.

I sat on the sofa, moving three dresses to make space, still processing what was happening. She emerged a minute later in a black dress, elegant and straightforward, fitted at the waist. She walked toward me with exaggerated runway confidence, one foot in front of the other, hand on her hip.

"What do you think?"

"It's nice."

"Nice?" She frowned. "That's the best you can do? Nice?"

"It's nice?"

"Terrible audience." She turned toward the bedroom.

"You know," I called after her, "you don't have to hide in the bedroom. Your

audience is accommodating. You can change here."

She stopped in the doorway, turned back. "Accommodating?"

"Exceptionally accommodating."

She picked up a dress from the pile and threw it at my face. "Pervert."

But she didn't go into the bedroom. She changed right there, unselfconscious, watching my discomfort with evident. Reached for the blue dress, flowy and almost bohemian, and slipped it over her head.

I tried hard to look casual. Failed.

"Still accommodating?" she asked, smirking.

"Very."

She twirled. "This one?"

"Keep it."

"You didn't even look properly."

"I looked."

She disappeared into the bedroom for the third dress. This one was red, fitted, bold. She modelled it with exaggerated seriousness, asking my opinion, dismissing my answers.

"This one's too formal."

"You asked if it was formal."

"I know, but you should have said it wasn't."

For the fourth dress, she didn't bother with the bedroom at all. Changed right in front of me, unhurried. White, simple, understated. It suited her perfectly.

"Well?" she asked, standing there.

"That one. Definitely that one."

Satisfied, she changed back into her jeans and t-shirt, still comfortable with the whole performance.

"Thank you for the show. That was interesting."

"Interesting?"

"Fascinating."

She laughed, walked over, and jumped onto the sofa, landing half on top of me.

"You're ridiculous."

"You called me here for a fashion show."

"And you came." She wrapped her arms around me, pulled me close.

We stayed like that for a while, tangled together on her sofa, surrounded by dresses and shopping bags. Eventually, she put on a movie, something forgettable and background noise, and we fell asleep as that, her weight against me, legs intertwined.

I woke up around two in the morning, her flat dark except for the TV screen, her breathing soft and steady. I didn't move. Didn't want to wake her. Just stayed there, surrounded by the quiet comfort of her presence.

* * *

WE CALLED IT DATING, though neither of us put a label on it for weeks. One evening, she came to my flat in Uxbridge. First time she'd visited.

She arrived at 7 PM with a bag from the Thai place we liked. "I brought dinner. Your kitchen is terrifying."

"It's functional."

"It's the size of a cupboard." She set the food on the counter and looked around.

The sparse furniture. The single window overlooks the residential street. "You do live like a monk."

"It's calm. Quiet."

"It's lonely." She said it gently, not as criticism. "You could have something better. You make good money."

"I'm saving."

"For what?"

I did not answer.

She opened the wine I'd bought and poured two glasses. We sat on the sofa, closer than necessary in the small space. She'd changed out of her work clothes into jeans and a soft jumper that kept slipping off one shoulder.

"Can I ask you something?"

"Yeah."

"Why did you agree to get drinks with me that first time? At The Bell."

"Because I wanted to."

"That's not an answer." She turned to face me fully. "I'm asking because I need to know if this is real for you. Or if I'm just... convenient. Someone to pass time with."

"You're not convenient. You're..." I struggled for the right word. "You're the first person in London who doesn't feel like work."

"What do I feel like?"

"Like I can breathe."

She set down her wine glass. "Come here."

I leaned in. She reached up, touched my face.

"I'm going to kiss you now. And I need you to know: I'm not subtle. I don't do half-measures. So if you're not sure about this, about me, tell me now."

"I'm sure."

"Good."

She kissed me. Not tentatively. Fully, ardently, like she'd been thinking about this for weeks. Her hand moved to the back of my neck, her fingers in my hair, pulling me closer with quiet urgency. When she pulled back, we were both breathing harder, the air between us charged.

"Bed. Now."

We moved to the bedroom. The single mattress on the floor. She laughed when she saw it. "Monk-like."

"I can sleep on the couch if..."

"Stop talking."

She pulled me down beside her. We kissed for a long time, unhurried, exploring, each touch a question and an answer. Her hands found the hem of my shirt, slipped underneath, her palms warm against my skin. Her touch was confident, purposeful, tracing the contours of my back. No hesitation.

When I reached for her, she caught my wrist.

Breathless: "Not yet. I want to. God, I want to. But not yet."

"Alright."

"I need to be sure. About us. About this." She pressed her forehead to mine. "I never wanted to do casual sex. I can't. I can only go physical if I'm sure about the relationship."

I pulled back slightly to look at her. "I was in a physical relationship with another woman. Does that bother you? Now, or will it in the future?"

She thought about it. "I was about to be trapped in such a physical situation once with someone. But I couldn't go through with it because I wasn't sure about that relationship. So I understand it can happen."

She looked at me directly. "Answer is no. It doesn't bother me. But I want to clarify, for me, I can only be in when I'm certain. About the person. About us."

"I understand. And I'm willing to wait. Until you're certain."

"Promise?"

"Promise."

She exhaled, her shoulders relaxed. "Alright. Then we wait. Do this properly."

We lay there for a while, entwined, fully clothed but intimate in a different way. She curled against my side, palm pressed to my ribs, her warmth seeping into me. The room was quiet, except for our breathing and the distant rumble of trains; the world narrowed to this moment.

Eventually: "I should go. If I stay longer, I won't want to leave."

"You can stay."

"I know. That's the problem." She sat up and fixed her jumper. "Walk me to the station?"

Outside, it was cold. December air is sharp and clear. She took my hand as we walked.

"Thank you."

"For what?"

"For not pushing. For listening, I said "not yet." Most blokes would have..."

"I'm not most blokes."

"No." She laced her fingers through mine. "You're not."

At the station entrance, she kissed me again. Slower this time. Sweeter.

After that, we continued to meet, mostly at her flat in Bethnal Green. We grew more comfortable with each other. More physical, but still waiting and building toward something neither of us wanted to rush.

* * *

OUR FIRST ARGUMENT HAPPENED. The routine had settled. Sunday mornings at Borough Market. Evening walks.

It was about money. Not a big thing. Not really. But it mattered.

We'd gone to dinner. A nice restaurant. Not expensive, but nice. A place where you order wine, where you share starters, where you talk, a place that feels like a date.

When the bill came, I reached for it. She reached for it, too. Our hands touched. Both of us are pulling.

"I'll get it," I said. "No, I'll get it."

"I asked you out. I should pay."

"That's an outdated concept. We can split it."

"But I want to pay."

"Why?"

"Because that's how it's done. Where I'm from, the man pays."

"And where I'm from, we split the bill. Or take turns."

"But I want to pay. I want to treat you."

"And I want to pay my share. I want to be equal."

We sat there. Both of us holding the bill, of us pulling, of us insisting. "This is ridiculous," she said.

"I know. But I'm not letting go."

"Neither am I."

We sat there. Staring at each other. Both of us are stubborn, neither of us refusing to back down.

Finally, she laughed.

"I know. But I'm still not letting go."

"Fine. You pay this time. But next time, I pay. Or we split."

"Deal."

I paid. She let me. But I could see she wasn't happy about it. I could see she wanted to pay her share.

On the walk home, she was quiet. "Are you okay?"

"I'm fine. thinking."

"About what?"

"About us. About how we do things. About how we're different."

"We are different. That's okay."

"Is it? Because sometimes it doesn't feel okay. Sometimes it feels as if we're speaking different languages."

"We are from different worlds. But that doesn't mean we can't understand each other."

"How?"

"By talking. By listening, understanding, and compromising."

"And if we can't meet in the middle?"

"Then we'll figure it out. Together. We'll find a way." She stopped. Looked at me.

"We are. We need to work at it. We need to try."

"And if working at it isn't enough?"

"Then we'll know. But we won't know unless we try. Unless we work at it."

She was quiet. Then she nodded. "Okay."

We walked home, hand in hand.

* * *

A WEEK LATER, we had another conversation about cultural differences.

We were at her flat. Cooking. Making dinner. Together. Like we'd done before.

She was chopping vegetables. I was watching. Learning.

"In my family," she said, "we always eat together. Every meal. Breakfast, lunch, dinner. All of us. At the table."

"In mine too. But it was different. More formal."

"How?"

My father would sit at the head of the table. My mother would serve. We'd eat in silence. Mostly, unless my father asked questions. Then we'd answer. But we didn't talk. Not really.

"That sounds lonely."

"It was. Sometimes. But it was also safe. Predictable."

And in my family, we talked. All the time. About everything, about nothing. We laughed, argued, and debated. We disagreed. But we were together. We were here.

"That sounds nice."

"It was. But it was also chaotic. Unpredictable. I never knew what to expect. I never knew how to behave."

"So we're different."

"We are. But that's okay. We can learn from each other, find common ground, and create our own way. Our own traditions."

"Can we?"

"Yes. We can. We need to talk, to listen, to understand." She stopped chopping. Looked at me.

"Me too."

"Then let's do it. Let's create it. Together."

"Okay."

We went back to cooking, together, creating, building, making.

* * *

I PAUSED.

"Her acts of care were quiet, consistent, and unnoticed by me at the time. She worked to reach me."

"What did you do when she worked to reach you?"

I was quiet. "I'd work late, I suppose. Avoid conversations."

"What happens in your body as you think about avoiding those conversations?"

"Tightness, perhaps."

"Good. You're noticing. That tightness, what do you think it's telling you?"

"I can't say."

"Think about it. What were you doing when you withdrew? When you went quiet?"

"Withdrawing, perhaps. Instead of engaging."

"And how did that feel? Retreating into your head?"

"Easier, perhaps. At the time. But now..." I didn't finish. "Now?"

"Now it's harder to look away."

"How does that feel? Seeing it now?"

"I'm not sure. Maybe... regret. Sadness."

She paused, watching me more closely than before. "I can't explain why."

"Then that's what we'll work on. Next week."

I stepped out into the afternoon—the air smelt of exhaust fumes and coffee from the café down the road. My footsteps were soft on the pavement.

PART IV
LEGAL LIMBO

Where existence requires proof

THE VISA BETWEEN US

I arrived with coffee, set it on the floor beside my chair, didn't drink it.

"You look tired," Claire said.

"Haven't been sleeping well."

"Why?"

"Dreams. About things that happened."

"Tell me about them."

* * *

THE EMAIL from HR arrived on a Tuesday afternoon.

Subject: Tier 2 (General) Visa Renewal - Action Required Within 60 Days

I was thirty. Two years into the marriage. Two years in London. Sixty days. I read it twice.

I opened the attachment. Forms. Sponsor letter. Bank statements. A checkbox asked, "Have your circumstances changed since your last grant of leave?" The screen's light felt harsh against my eyes, and the text blurred slightly.

Six months. Her name sat in my throat. The checkbox stayed blank

I closed the laptop.

* * *

JANANI MADE decisions as casually as some people breathe, without stopping to explain them. She remembered I disliked coriander and ordered accordingly. She introduced me to her friends as Dev, not "the guy I'm seeing," Dev.

Her friends sounded like they were from London and carried their families in their phones. They had names such as Priya and Radha, but they spoke with London accents, worked in finance and consulting, and lived in nice flats in Zone 2.

First-generation, not second. My accent still had traces of Tamil Nadu.

"My mum keeps sending me biodata," one of them said at dinner one night.

"Mine too," Janani said.

Later, when we were alone: "We're arranged-adjacent, really. We met at a community event my mum dragged me to. You're Tamil, I'm Tamil. Our families approved quickly. All the cultural compatibility, the family vetting, the practical considerations."

* * *

FOR WEEKS, I considered the visa situation.

On the page, it appeared tidy. Stay on Tier 2, depending on your employer, linked to a job that could end my right to stay with a single notice of termination. Or marry Janani, switch to a spousal visa, create a route to settlement, but tie our relationship to immigration paperwork, turning it into evidence: photos, dates, shared bills. The route I was most hesitant to take. Heard stories of immigration marriages and their consequences. Little I know what is about to happen.

One other option existed. Tier 1 (Exceptional Talent). No employer sponsorship required. Freedom, in theory.

I spent three evenings researching, with only the blue light of my screen illuminating my flat, my eyes aching from the strain. You needed endorsement from Tech Nation.

Published research, conference speaking, open source contributions, industry recognition — a checklist of achievements that felt impossible, a bar set so high it might as well have been on another planet.

The requirements read like a list of things I'd never done, never considered doing, never had the opportunity to pursue because I'd been busy keeping my job, keeping my status, keeping quiet.

I reread the list. Nothing on it sounded like me. The word itself felt unfamiliar, as if it belonged to others—people who had different opportunities, different starting points, and different systems working in their favour.

I could start now to build a portfolio that might qualify in two or three years. Two or three years of uncertainty, living with the constant awareness that one mistake, one layoff, or one company restructuring could end everything.

Two or three years on a Tier 2 visa that expired in sixty days, with each renewal a negotiation, each application a gamble, and each approval temporary, conditional, and revocable.

I closed the laptop.

* * *

I CALLED her on a December evening. "Can we meet? Your place?"

Not a question but a statement: "I need to see you. Come now."

When I arrived at her Bethnal Green flat, she answered the door before I could knock. The flat was on the second floor of a converted Victorian house, its high ceilings and tall windows evoking a different era, when these buildings were single-family homes.

The corridor smelled of curry from the ground-floor flat, with the scent of cumin and turmeric, frying onions, and spices that evoked both home and distance.

She pulled me inside and kissed me, urgent, intentional, the door closing behind us.

When she pulled back, her eyes were fierce.

"I've been waiting for you to decide. But I'm done waiting, Dev. I want you. Not the visa solution. You."

"I do."

"Then stop hovering," she said. "Be in it with me."

"Let's do this." I looked at her directly. "Are you sure?"

"I'm sure. I'm not giving up this relationship because of a visa. I did that before."

She paused, then smiled, something real, her shoulders dropping.

"Then let's do it properly. Get engaged. Tell our parents."

"Right. Yeah, let's do it properly."

"We'll handle the visa process. Together."

I called my mother that evening. She answered on the third ring.

"Amma, I'm thinking of getting married."

Silence. In the background, a Tamil serial played.

"Her name is Janani. She's Tamil. Sri Lankan Tamil. Her parents are from Jaffna. She's British, born here."

"And you're telling me now?" Her voice tightened.

"I'm telling you because we want to come to India. For your blessings."

"You want to get married there? In London?" The disappointment was evident.

"Yes. But we want your blessing first. Her parents will meet us there, too. And I was hoping you and Appa could come to London for the wedding."

Another silence, longer this time.

"Yes. I'll arrange visitor visas. It takes a few weeks."

"How long would we stay?"

"Two weeks. Maybe three. Enough time for the wedding."

"Let me talk to your father. But Dev, bring her here first. Let us meet her."

"She is," I said firmly.

The smile was clear in her voice, a mother's gentle challenge.

* * *

I TOLD Janani about the conversation the following evening. She was cooking, her hands busy with onions and spices.

"Your mother wants to meet me?"

"She wants to make sure I'm not making a mistake."

She set down the knife. Turned off the stove.

Without hesitation: "No."

"Are you doing this for the visa?" The question was direct. "Because I need to know. Before we tell the families, are you marrying me because you love me? Or because I'm the British passport that solves your immigration problem?"

I flinched.

"It's a fair question." She folded her arms. "You never mentioned marriage until I brought up the spousal visa option. So tell me: if I weren't British, would you still be proposing this?"

I opened my mouth, then closed it.

"Probably not," I finally said.

That doesn't mean the visa isn't a factor," she finished. "Be honest. If I were on a work visa like you, would you be asking me to marry you right now? Or would you be doing what you did with Maya?"

The comparison to Maya stung.

"Was it? You had feelings for Maya. But when things got complicated..." She stopped.

"Because you're British."

Like I was reading from a script I'd memorised but didn't understand.

She laughed, but no humour in it. "That's not what I meant."

"Isn't it, though?" Her eyes were hard now. "Maya was Singapore," she said. "I'm here. Convenient."

"That's what it sounds like," she said. "Like I'm paperwork that kisses you back."

"You know that's not all you are. I'm not marrying you for your passport."

"Then tell me," she demanded. "Do you love me? Do you love me? Not the idea of me, what I represent, what I can give you. Me, Janani."

"I do love you. Maybe the visa made me realise it faster. But that doesn't make the feelings less real."

"Doesn't it?" She wiped her eyes. "How do you know you're not convincing yourself? How do you know you're not telling yourself what you need to hear? Because you need the visa. Because you need to stay. Because you can't go back."

I started to respond, but she carried on: "Could you find another British Tamil woman in London? How replaceable am I? If I weren't British, if I were on a work visa like you, would you still be here? Would you still be asking me to marry you? Or would you be doing what you did with Maya?"

"You're not."

I pulled her toward the counter and kissed her. Not gently. Trying to prove something I couldn't say and trying to show her, to make her believe.

She pulled back.

I chose you. Before the visa. After. I chose you, I said. "And I hated that I needed a deadline to say it. It made me honest about choosing something. Someone. Instead of just… leaving."

Her eyes stayed fixed on mine. Then her shoulders eased, the movement slow and intentional. The tension drained from her body. The hardness left her eyes. She looked at me, as if seeing something.

She reached across the table and took my hand. Her grip was firm.

I want to believe you. Or at least, I wish I did. I want to believe that you chose me, that you love me, that I'm not just a solution or a way out. I want to be someone you truly want.

"Then come to India with me. Meet my parents."

She was quiet for a moment, then nodded.
"Okay."

* * *

WE BOOKED FLIGHTS IN JANUARY.

Her mother called the day before we departed. The conversation was brief, covering questions about Neyveli, my family, and what to expect.

"Dev? We're trusting you with her. Don't make us regret it."

* * *

THAT EVENING, Janani came to my flat in Uxbridge.

Our suitcases were packed, passports ready on the kitchen counter.

The flight was at midnight.

She stood in the doorway, hesitant. I hadn't seen that before.

"Can I come in?"

"You don't have to ask."

She walked past me and set her bag down. I closed the door.

She faced me. Her hair was loose around her shoulders. She wore jeans and a plain grey jumper, nothing fancy.

"I've been thinking. About us. About what this trip means."

"Janani:"

"Let me finish." She stepped closer. "I'm going to meet your parents. They're going to think we're getting married. And we are. But I don't want to go to India without..."

She searched for words, the feeling ineffable, something she couldn't fully articulate.

"Without what?"

"Without knowing you're choosing me. Not the visa. Not the convenience."

I reached for her hand. "Then show me."

* * *

I PAUSED and looked at Claire. She was waiting, her notebook shut. The silence lingered longer than usual. The room's air felt still and heavy.

"What happened then?"

I smiled, shook my head slightly. "I'm going to skip that part."

"Tell me about skipping that part."

I thought about it.

"And what happens when you talk about intimate things? What happens in your body?"

"Warmth. In my palms. Like I'm remembering."

"That's good. You're noticing. You're feeling. That's different from before."

* * *

LATER, we lay together, the flat dark except for the streetlight coming through the window.

Her head rested on my chest, her hair spilling across my skin. She shifted slightly, settling deeper against me.

"That was:" she started, then stopped.

"What?"

"Worth waiting for." Her laugh was quiet, almost a whisper. "I'm not that traditional."

"NO. YOU'RE NOT." She traced lazy circles on my chest, her touch tender, unhurried.

I kissed the top of her head, breathing in the scent of her hair: shampoo and something else.

"Me too."

We lay there in the silence.

Eventually: "We should pack." But she didn't move.

"We're already packed."

"We should sleep."

"We should." Neither of us moved.

Outside, London continued. Cars passing.

* * *

THE FLIGHT to Chennai was overnight. Janani slept most of the way, her head on my shoulder. I stayed awake, watching the progress map on the screen. London to Dubai. Dubai to Chennai.

When we landed, the heat hit us as a wall. It was February in Chennai, thirty-two degrees, humid.

My parents were waiting at arrivals. Amma in a silk saree, Appa in his usual white shirt and veshti. They looked older than I remembered.

Amma's eyes went straight to Janani.

"Amma, Appa, this is Janani."

Janani folded her hands in a proper namaste. My mother's face softened.

"Welcome, welcome." Amma took Janani's hands. "How was the flight? You must be tired."

* * *

NEYVELI HADN'T CHANGED. Same streets but narrower. Identical TNEB colony houses.

My mother had prepared the guest room. New bedsheets. Flowers on the dresser. A small shrine in the corner with a lamp already lit.

"You rest," Amma said to Janani. "Dinner is at eight. Nothing fancy."

* * *

THAT FIRST DINNER WAS CAREFUL. Polite questions. Safe topics. Janani's work. London weather.

My father barely spoke. He ate methodically, watching Janani from the corner of his eye.

After dinner, when Janani excused herself to freshen up, Amma pulled me aside.

"She's lovely. Well-mannered. Good family background."

"I told you."

"But she's very British, Dev. Modern. Are you sure she'll adjust to our ways?"

"She doesn't need to adjust to our ways, Amma. We're building our own ways."

My mother frowned but said nothing.

* * *

THE NEXT FEW days were a blur of relatives. Aunts and uncles and cousins I hadn't seen in years. They came to meet Janani, to assess her.

Janani handled it perfectly. Wore sarees, which Amma lent her. Remembered everyone's names and relationships. Laughed at their jokes even when her Tamil wasn't good enough to understand.

But I could see the exhaustion in her eyes at night.

On the fourth day: "They're very interested in our wedding plans. Your aunt asked about our plans. Your cousin wanted to know if I'd move back to India eventually."

"I'm sorry. They don't mean:"

"I know. They're curious. It's fine." She lay back on the bed.

* * *

ON HER LAST MORNING, we woke early. Walked to the small park near the colony.

"Thank you for coming. I know this wasn't easy."

"Your parents are lovely. A bit overwhelming, but lovely." She held my hand tighter. "And I'm glad I came. I had to see this. Where are you from?"

"And?"

"And now I understand you better. The way you are about family."

We settled on a bench. The morning was still cool.

"I wish I didn't have to leave. But work:"

"I know. It's fine. I'll stay. Help with the visa applications."

"Two weeks?"

"Maybe three. Depends on the visa processing time."

"Don't change your mind whilst you're here. About us, about London."

"I won't."

"Promise?"

"Promise."

* * *

I TOOK her to the airport that afternoon. Chennai airport, departures.

At security, she hugged me tight.

"See you soon."

She withdrew, then turned around and walked through. She vanished from sight. I drove back to Neyveli.

* * *

THE HOUSE FELT EMPTIER without her. My parents resumed their routines. I spent my days assisting Appa with the visa applications, bank statements, and invitation letters.

Then, a week after Janani left, Thara showed up.

She came by one evening. Stood at the door in a yellow churidar, hair pulled back.

"Dev. I heard you were here."

I turned.

"Can we talk?"

My mother was watching from the kitchen window.

"Let's walk."

We walked towards the colony park. The evening was warm.

"I heard you're getting married," Thara said, an edge to her tone.

"Yes."

"From my mother. Who heard it from your mother? Apparently, everyone in the colony knew before I did."

I remained silent.

"You couldn't tell me yourself?" She stopped walking and faced me.

"I didn't think:"

"That's right. You didn't think." Her eyes were hard. "I'm married, Dev. My life moved on years ago. But we were friends once."

"We were."

"Then why did you treat me as a stranger? Someone who couldn't handle the news?"

I didn't answer right away. Behind her, I could see her mother standing at their gate.

"I'm sorry. You're right."

"Yes. You should have." She crossed her arms. "My mother was so worried about how I'd react. Kept apologising for telling me."

"That wasn't."

"I know what it was. Everyone still thinks of us as the couple that almost happened, the tragic what-if. But Dev, I have a life. A good life. My husband is wonderful."

"I'm glad."

"Are you? Because you've been avoiding me as if I'm going to fall apart at the news that you're getting married."

"I'm sorry," I said again. "You deserved better than hearing it through gossip."

Her expression softened slightly.

We started walking again, slower this time.

"Her name is Janani," I offered. "She's British. Sri Lankan Tamil. She was here last week."

"I heard. The whole colony talked about nothing else. The modern British girl in jeans."

"Barely. She left after a week."

"Smart woman." Thara glanced at me. "Is she good for you?"

I thought about the question. Not the answer I believed I should give. Not the answer I thought she wanted to hear. But the real answer, the honest answer that came from deep inside, from understanding, from being here.

"I think so. Yes. She makes me feel as if I matter, as if I'm seen, as if I'm understood, as if I'm loved."

"Good." Her voice was genuine.

We reached the park entrance. She stopped, turned to face me.

"I should get back. I have things to do."

"I'll tell you. I'll be honest."

"Good." She turned to go, then looked back. "I hope so," I said.

She dipped her chin once, then walked back towards her house. She stopped at her mother, who was still standing at the gate, clearly anxious.

Her mother looked relieved.

I walked back to my own house.

* * *

THE VISA APPROVALS ARRIVED. My parents could come to the UK for three weeks, enough time for the wedding and a quick visit. I had stopped checking the mail daily and stopped expecting it.

I booked our flights, helped them pack, and answered their questions about London weather, British customs, and what to bring as gifts for Janani's parents.

My mother spent days deciding what to bring: sarees for Janani, spices for cooking, photographs of the family, a small Ganesha statue — things that would make Janani feel welcome and part of the family.

"Will she like these?" my mother asked, holding up a saree.

"She'll love them."

"Are you sure? What if she doesn't like the colour? What if it's not her style?"

"She'll love them because you chose them. Because you thought of her."

My mother smiled.

"She knows. She'll know even more when she meets you."

In the morning, we left for Chennai airport. My mother stood outside the house for a long moment.

"Last time you left, we didn't know when you'd come back. This time you're taking us with you."

"This time is different."

"Yes," she agreed.

At the airport, my father kept checking and rechecking the tickets. My mother smoothed her sarees in the suitcase, folding and refolding them. They had never been on a plane before, nor had they left India. Never been so far from Neyveli.

When we boarded, they settled close, holding hands during take-off. The plane lifted off, the ground receded, the city vanished, the country vanished. The continent disappeared.

But they held hands. They held each other. They held on.

London appeared through the window as we descended — the Thames, bridges, and the sprawling city I had made my home.

Janani was waiting at arrivals. She saw us through the crowd and waved. Her face was bright.

My parents walked with me. The airport was vast, the crowds were intense, and the noise was deafening. The pace was hurried. Everything felt different; it was all new.

But they followed me. They trusted me. They stayed close.

"Amma, Appa. Welcome to London."

Janani stepped forward and folded her hands in namaste.

The gesture was traditional, respectful. She respected them.

My mother's eyes filled with tears. She pulled Janani into a tight, warm hug.

"We're here for the wedding. To give our blessings. To see you both start your life together."

The words were simple, direct. They said everything.

We stepped out into the damp London afternoon, the air heavy with moisture, together. The four of us: my parents, Janani, and me.

* * *

I PAUSED.

"The visa between us. Career instability. Missed moments. Arguments that dissolved into silence instead of resolution."

"Why does silence feel safer than speaking?"

I thought about it. "Speaking means being seen and being known. Silence means I can hide. Perform."

"What happens in your body when you think about being seen? About being known?"

"Tightness, perhaps."

"And what happens when you're silent? When you hide? What comes up then?"

"Relief, perhaps. Safety."

"And what does that cost you? Choosing silence over speaking? Choosing hiding over being seen?"

"Connection. Intimacy. The marriage itself."

"You said silence lets you hide. Perform. Not real. But what happens when you're always performing?"

I was quiet.

"Dev?"

"I can't say."

"Think about it. That's your homework. What happens when you're always performing?"

I stepped out into the evening. The air was cool, with the scent of rain and damp earth filling my nostrils. My footsteps echoed on the pavement.

PAPERWORK AND PROMISES

I sat, pulled out my phone, and checked it. "Distracted?" Claire asked. "Work email. Sorry."

"You're always checking your phone when you come in."

"Am I?"

"Yes. Every session. What are you avoiding?" I looked at her.

"Then put the phone away. And tell me what happened next."

We got married in March at Hackney Town Hall.

Hackney Town Hall was built with red brick and pale stone. It looked official from the pavement. Inside, the registry office was smaller than I'd expected, more intimate than grand. The ceilings were high, with ornate but faded plasterwork.

Wooden floors that creaked underfoot, each step a quiet announcement. Large windows overlooked a small courtyard where a single plane tree grew, its leaves filtering the March light. The room felt formal but not cold, official but not impersonal.

A small ceremony. Janani's parents, my own, who had flown in from Chennai. A handful of friends. The registrar read the standard vows. We said "I do." Signed the register.

Janani wore the pale green saree from the night we met. I wore the suit I had bought for job interviews years ago, tears in her mother's eyes.

Later, we dined at a Tamil restaurant in Tooting. The eatery was on a busy high street, squeezed between a newsagent and a halal butcher, its presence a small piece of South India transplanted to South London. Inside, the walls were adorned with photographs of South Indian temples and film stars, creating a visual map of home.

The aroma of sambar and dosai filled the air, the smell of roasted lentils and fermented rice batter, of coconut chutney and curry leaves, familiar. My throat tightened before I knew why. Two tables pushed together. Cutlery clattered. Someone kept refilling my father's glass.

Janani's father gave a brief speech on compatibility and commitment. My father said, "Take care of each other."

It wasn't the wedding either of us had imagined as children. No mehendi, sangeet, three-day celebration.

* * *

THE DOCUMENTS SAT in a folder on our kitchen table, each page a small weight.

Janani had arranged them weeks earlier. I touched the top sheet and felt how much of us it was asking for.

The portal asked if our relationship was genuine.

I clicked *Yes* and waited for the page to change, aware of how easily certainty fit inside a box.

* * *

WE MOVED into our first flat together — a one-bedroom in Bethnal Green, the same area where Janani had been living, but on a different street, in a different building. A fresh start.

Moving day was chaotic. Boxes were everywhere. Furniture that didn't fit through doorways. A sofa that took three tries to get up the stairs. Janani is directing, and I am following instructions.

By evening, we had assembled the bed, made the kitchen functional, and unpacked and arranged the books on the shelves. We ordered pizza and sat on the floor surrounded by boxes, eating with our hands because we hadn't yet unpacked the plates.

"This is ours," Janani said, looking around. "It is."

"No more your place or my place. Our place."

I looked at her. She was already folding boxes flat, deciding what stayed.

"Thank you," I said.

"For what?"

"For this. For choosing this. For choosing me." She smiled.

We finished the pizza. Started unpacking. Put away clothes, arrange books, and hang photos. Made the space ours.

I woke to the sound of her making coffee. The aroma of filter coffee, how my mother used to make it, and how Janani had learned to prepare it for me. I got up and headed to the kitchen. She was standing at the stove, watching the coffee filter drip through, her hair still messy from sleep.

"Morning," she said. "Morning."

She poured me a cup and handed it to me. I took it, sipped it. "How did you know?"

"Know what?"

"How I like my coffee."

"I watched. I paid attention. I learned."

I watched her pour it without asking. My chest loosened a fraction.

"Thank you."

"You're welcome."

We stood there, drinking coffee, watching the morning light filter through the kitchen window.

* * *

A LETTER ARRIVED.

*Your application requires further assessment. You have been sched-
uled for an interview at the Home Office on 14 April at 10:00 AM.
Both the applicant and the sponsor must attend.*

The envelope felt heavy in my hands, the paper thick and official.
"It's normal," Janani said, though her voice was tight. "Priya and her
husband had to do this, too. They ask questions."

"I know."

"They'll interview us separately. Ask about daily routines. What
time do you wake up? What side of the bed do I sleep on? Your
favourite food. What we argue about."

I stared at the letter.

* * *

THE HOME OFFICE building in Croydon was brutalist grey, austere
and impersonal. The room reduced everything to procedure.

My palms were damp before anyone asked a question.

Small windowless room. Recording device on the table.

This interview is to evaluate the authenticity of your relationship
with Mrs Janani Krishnan. Please respond honestly. Inconsistencies
could lead to the rejection of your application.

I nodded, as if sincerity could be demonstrated on request.

He opened a folder. "How did you meet? What was she wearing?
What side of the bed does she sleep on? What do you argue about?"

He didn't look up when he asked. I answered anyway.

I answered. My palms were damp. "Why did you marry her?"

"Because she stayed. Because she kept coming back. Because I
wanted her there when the door shut."

More notes.

"Interview concluded. Please wait outside."

Janani emerged, looking drained. She sank into the chair beside
me. "How was it?"

"Clinical. They asked what we had for breakfast this morning."

"What did you say?"

"Toast. Marmite for you, butter and honey for me. Indian tea for both."

I exhaled.

"Good." She took my hand, her grip firm.

* * *

THE DECISION ARRIVED.

Plain envelope. Home Office logo.

I stood in the hallway, clutching the envelope. The paper felt weighty and official. I could smell the ink through it, sharp and chemical. My hands trembled slightly as I tore it open. The letter inside was crisp, with the Home Office logo embossed and raised beneath my fingertips.

We are pleased to inform you that your application for a UK Spouse Visa has been approved. Your visa remains valid for 30 months from the date of this letter.

Relief arrived first; understanding came later.

I read it twice before handing it to Janani, as if the words might change if I let go too soon.

"Thirty months. Then we extend for another thirty, you apply for ILR, citizenship."

"I know."

"But we're on it together now."

"Yeah. Together."

She pulled me into a hug. We stood in the kitchen of our Bethnal Green flat. The room was narrow, with a window overlooking a small garden shared with the neighbours—a rectangle of green that felt like a luxury in London.

Mismatched furniture from charity shops and IKEA, each piece telling a story. Photos on the fridge captured our life—friends, family, meaningful moments. Her books, stacked everywhere, formed a library reflecting her interests and passions. Our home wasn't built on costly renovations but on life's accumulation and meaningful things.

Outside, a bus passed by, its engine rumbling, its passengers visible through the windows, each a story, a life. Someone shouted something unintelligible, the sound echoing through the open window.

A bus rattled past. Someone shouted outside. Janani didn't flinch.

"We should celebrate," Janani said. "Dinner somewhere nice?"

"Or we could order takeaway and watch something terrible on Netflix."

She laughed.

* * *

THAT NIGHT, lying in bed, "I'm glad you're here. Properly here. Not on a visa that could vanish."

"Me too."

"Though technically, you're still on a visa."

"True. But this one's different. This one has a path. Five years to ILR. Six years to citizenship. There's an endpoint."

"Six years is a long time."

"I'm not going anywhere." She looked at me. "Promise."

She kissed me. Then settled against my shoulder, her breathing evening out as she drifted toward sleep.

I stayed awake longer, listening to the distant sound of traffic, the occasional siren.

* * *

OUR PARENTS ORGANISED a traditional ceremony at Shri Siddhi Vinayagar Temple in Harrow. The temple was fragrant with jasmine and incense. Janani appeared in a red Kanchipuram silk saree, with gold zari work that caught the light.

Her friends filled the small temple hall, second-generation Tamil girls who'd grown up in London.

The priest began. Sanskrit, I didn't understand. Rituals I'd seen at relatives' weddings but never thought would be mine.

Then came the thaali. The sacred pendant was tied on a yellow thread around the bride's neck.

I held it, the yellow thread with the gold pendant catching the light. Janani leaned close and whispered,

"Last chance to run. After this, you're religiously and legally stuck with me. I'm going to make you watch terrible reality TV. I steal blankets. I can't parallel park."

I smiled, working to maintain some dignity in front of a hundred witnesses and kept my eyes on the knot.

"What's so funny, Dev?" someone called from the back.

The crowd was chuckling now. My mother looked mortified. My father's expression was neutral.

Janani faced the crowd with perfect innocence.

The priest, who'd been waiting with infinite patience, finally raised his voice: "Now! You must tie it now! The muhurtham time is passing!"

I wiped my eyes, took a breath, and somehow managed to steady my shaking hands.

The nadaswaram and thavil erupted into a swift rhythm. I tied the first knot. Then Janani's aunt stepped forward to tie the second. Her mother tied the third.

Then we circled the sacred fire together. Seven steps, seven promises.

Janani's hand in mine. "Done."

"Stuck," she replied, grinning.

The crowd erupted in applause and ululation from the aunties.

My parents watched from the side. My father's face was neutral, but I saw him nod once.

Tears in Janani's mother's eyes. Her father squeezed her shoulder.

Later, my father pulled me aside. "Relatives are unhappy. They wanted to be there. But you're married now." He looked at Janani, laughing with her friends.

My mother hugged Janani afterwards. Janani hugged her back.

* * *

HER PARENTS TOOK us to dinner afterwards, at an Indian restaurant on Brick Lane. Her father ordered beer.

May you learn to compromise, because you'll need to.

My parents sat opposite Janani's parents, both groups navigating the careful formalities of a first meeting. However, the Tamil connection helped. They discussed leaving, cooking, and raising children in places that weren't quite home. The formality eased.

Janani reached for my hand under the table. Not for show.

* * *

I PAUSED.

"The marriage. There was an emotional connection. Real connection.

But then... I'm not sure. I started focusing on other things."

"What things?"

"The paperwork. The visa stuff. The practical things."

"Easier than what?"

I was quiet. "Easier than... being here. Noticing what Janani needed."

"What happens in your body as you think about being present? About noticing what she needed?"

"I don't know. Maybe... tightness."

"Good. You're noticing. That tightness, what do you think it's telling you?"

"I can't say."

"Think about it. What were you doing when you focused on the practical things? What were you avoiding?"

"Paper is obedient," I said. "Feelings aren't."

The visa renewals. The paperwork."

"Safer than what?"

"I don't know. Maybe... safer than being seen. Than being vulnerable."

"And what did you lose while you were busy being correct?"

I thought about it. "The connection. The intimacy."

"But there was a connection. You said that. Real connection."

"Yes. There was. But I stopped tending to it. I let the practical stuff take over. Not because there wasn't emotion."

Claire was quiet.

"I was protecting myself. From something."

"And why did you withdraw?"

I was quiet. Looked at the window. "Dev?"

I shook my head. The room felt smaller, the air more oppressing. Outside, rain had begun, its sound against the window a steady rhythm. And I wondered: what would happen if I stopped performing? If I ceased shifting between versions of myself?

"We'll come back to that. Next week."

TENDING

I walked in, sat, and looked at the plant on Claire's windowsill, a small green thing in a terracotta pot.

"You're looking at my plant," Claire said. "Sorry."

"Why?"

"It reminded me of home."

"Tell me about it."

* * *

MY PARENTS FLEW BACK to Chennai.

At the airport, my mother hugged Janani.

She turned to me.

They disappeared through security, my father's careful walk, my mother's silk saree catching the airport lights.

* * *

THE APPROVAL EMAIL came at 9:14 a.m. I reread it twice before I told her.

In April, I handed in my notice. My manager didn't ask why. He just nodded and asked about the handover.

One evening in May, we stood in the small garden behind our flat.

She had tied the vine to the fence with twine. The knots were neat.

"It's blooming," she said, touching one petal with her fingertip.

"Mm," I said. I didn't know what to do with my hands.

I pulled her close.

*　*　*

SATURDAY MORNINGS AT BOROUGH MARKET. The market was a sensory feast: the smell of fresh bread from the bakery, the sharp tang of cheese from the cheesemonger, the earthy scent of root vegetables, the metallic tang of fish on ice.

Janani moved quickly, pausing only when certain. She squeezed tomatoes once, then picked the same-sized ones without checking again, along with an aubergine and coriander bundle. I followed, carrying bags, watching her negotiate with vendors, her Tamil accent softening when speaking to the Kerala spice seller.

She'd find the one vendor selling Kerala spices, and she argued gently about curry leaves. I nodded as if I understood what she meant, about the freshness of their cardamom, the authenticity of their black pepper, while I pretended to grasp the difference.

"You're humouring me."

"I'm learning from you."

"Liar."

She'd kiss me anyway.

I started leaving notes. Post-its on her laptop before I left for work.

Your presentation will be brilliant. Remember, you're smarter than everyone in that meeting.

She collected them. I found them later, pressed between the pages of her planner.

"You're a romantic," she accused one evening, discovering a new one stuck to the bathroom mirror.

"Only for you."

"Good answer."

She pulled me into the shower with her, clothed.

On Valentine's Day, I took her to Dishoom. Not because it was Valentine's. Because she'd mentioned wanting to try it weeks earlier.

Tears in her eyes when she realised. "It's dinner."

I watched her face change when she recognised the place.

* * *

ONE RAINY THURSDAY, I came home drenched. Janani took one look at me and started laughing.

"You look like a drowned rat."

"A handsome drowned rat."

She handed me a towel, still grinning.

"I didn't forget. I lent it to someone at the Tube station."

"Dev." She shook her head.

"The one person who needed an umbrella more than I did."

She stepped closer, took the towel from my hands, and started drying my hair herself.

"You're impossible, you know that?"

"You married me anyway."

"I did." She stood on her toes and kissed me, soft and unhurried. "Second biggest," I murmured against her mouth.

She laughed, bright and open. "You love my terrible logic."

"I love you despite your terrible logic." She pulled back enough to look at me.

"Liar."

"Fine. I'd nurse you back to health. But I'd complain the entire time."

"I'd expect nothing less."

She pushed me toward the bathroom.

Twenty minutes later, I emerged warm and dry. She was curled on the sofa with two steaming mugs.

"Better?"

"Much." I sat beside her. Took the mug. "What do you think?"

I took a sip.

"Correct. Because that's what you need when you're cold and wet.

Not weak British tea. Actual tea."

"You're a tea snob."

"Absolutely. And proud of it."

We sat with the rain ticking the window. Her laptop stayed closed.

She set down her mug.

"I'm working to be more here."

"I know. I notice. They notice too."

"Do they?"

"Anjali told me last week you asked about her maths project. Not ' How's school?' asked about the project specifically."

"It's not that remarkable."

"It is, actually."

I reached for her hand. She leaned into me.

"I know. You tell me every time."

"And you still try every time."

"Because then you make it for me."

Quiet for a moment.

"We're disgustingly happy, aren't we?"

"Mental."

"Good." She took my hand.

* * *

WE DISCOVERED that Janani was pregnant on a Tuesday in March. She had been feeling unwell for a week—tired, nauseous, and not quite herself. She took a test that morning and called me at work.

"Can you come home? I need to talk to you."

I left immediately. Found her in the bathroom, sitting on the edge of the bathtub, holding the test.

"Are you sure?"

"I took two. Both positive."

I sat next to her, took her hand, and looked at the test. Two lines. Positive. "How do you feel?"

"Scared, excited, terrified, happy. All of it."

"Me too."

"Are you ready for this?"

"I'm uncertain. Are you?"

"I'm uncertain too. But I want it. I want this."

I pulled her close, held her, felt her breathing, felt her heart beating. "We can do this."

"Can we?"

"We can. Together."

* * *

ANJALI WAS BORN on a Tuesday in October. Three weeks early.

The midwife placed her on Janani's chest, tiny and wrinkled, impossibly real.

She looked at us with dark, unfocused eyes. Then yawned. "She's perfect," Janani whispered.

I touched Anjali's impossibly small hand. Her fingers curled around mine.

"Hello. I'm your Appa."

Sleepless nights and quiet moments. Anjali was sleeping on my chest at 2 AM. Her first steps at eleven months. Her first word: "Amma." Her second: "No."

"She's strong-willed." Janani's mother said during a video call. "Like both of us." Janani squeezed my hand.

* * *

BY THE TIME Anjali turned two, she'd developed opinions about all of

"No nap." She announced one afternoon. Standing in her cot. "Anj, you need to sleep."

"No nap. Play."

Janani stood in the doorway. Arms crossed. Trying not to laugh. "How is this from me?"

"The stubborn certainty that sleep is optional?" Fair point.

Anjali had her own vocabulary now. "Baba" for bottle. "More" delivered as a command, not a request.

She'd toddle after me to my home office. Bang on the door.

One evening, I was on a video call with my team in Bangalore. Anjali, who'd been playing in the corner, her toys scattered around her, decided this was the perfect moment to show off her newfound walking skills.

She toddled into the frame. Stark naked. Holding a banana as a microphone.

"Appa! Appa!" she announced to my baffled colleagues. I grabbed her, trying to maintain professionalism. "Technical difficulties named Anjali?" someone laughed. "Something like that."

I muted the call. Wrestled a nappy onto a very uncooperative toddler.

Then returned to the meeting with her on my lap. "She wanted to say hello."

Anjali waved at the screen.

My colleagues waved back. Clearly entertained.

After we hung up, Janani appeared in the doorway. Trying not to laugh.

"Your daughter introduced herself to my entire team. Whilst naked.

Holding a banana."

"Oh god." She covered her mouth. Shoulders shaking. "Eventually."

"That's parenting, Dev. Sometimes your two-year-old makes a guest appearance during important meetings."

"I'm rolling. I'm rolling." She kissed my forehead. "Am I?"

"You are. And honestly? Your colleagues probably needed a laugh.

Work calls are so serious."

One evening, Janani and I sat on the sofa after Anjali's bedtime. Exhausted but content.

"She's brilliant."

"She is."

"And exhausting."

"Also true."

Janani was quiet for a moment. "Really?"

"Anjali shouldn't be alone. I want her to have a sibling. Someone who shares this strange immigrant-kid-in-London experience with her." She smiled.

"I think we barely survived one."

"We more than survived. We're good at this."

"You're good at this. I'm learning."

"You're learning well." She took my hand.

"I say yes. Let's do it. Let's be mental together." She laughed and kissed me.

Janani took the test — two pink lines. The routine had become familiar, Sunday mornings at Borough Market.

She showed me the stick whilst I was making breakfast. Anjali was in her high chair.

"We're having another baby." Janani grinned.

I pulled her into a hug. Be careful with the pregnancy test between us.

"Baby?" Anjali asked.

"Yes, Anj. You're going to be a big sister." She considered this.

"Our baby." Janani corrected. "My baby." Anjali insisted.

It was going to be interesting.

* * *

PREM WAS BORN on a grey March morning. The labour was faster than with Anjali.

Janani held my hand through her contractions, breathing through the pain with the focus of someone who'd done this before and knew exactly what was coming. Her grip was firm, almost painful. But I didn't pull away. I held on. I was there. For her, for us, for this moment.

When Prem arrived, he didn't cry. He blinked at the lights, assessing the situation and deciding whether this world was worth the noise. He was small, smaller than Anjali had been, but perfect— ten fingers, ten toes, and a full head of dark hair.

I held him. For the first time. His weight in my arms, his warmth against my chest.

Anjali met him. Two years old now.

She stood by the hospital bed, peering at the bundle in Janani's arms. Her expression was cautious, curious, wary—unsure of what to make of this.

"That's your brother."

"He's small."

"Babies are small. You were this small once."

"Was I?" Sceptical.

"Yes. And now you're big. Soon, Prem will be big too."

She reached out. Touched his hand. Prem's fingers curled around hers.

"He likes me."

"Of course he does. You're his big sister."

"I'll teach him things."

"You will."

"Dragons. And reading." Her gaze found mine. "He does."

"Good. My toys are mine. But I'll share sometimes. If he asks nicely."

"He's calm." The midwife said. Placing him on Janani's chest.

Janani laughed. Exhausted and relieved.

I touched his tiny hand. His fingers curled around mine, the grip light, almost tentative. Not urgent as Anjali's had been.

"Hello. I'm your Appa. Your sister's been waiting for you." We brought him home. Anjali met us at the door.

"My baby! My baby!"

She followed us into the living room. Watching as we set the car seat down. Prem blinked at his new surroundings.

"Can I hold him?" Already reaching. "Easy, Anj. Be easy with him."

She sat on the sofa. We gently placed Prem in her lap, our movements calm and deliberate.

"Hi, baby. I'm your big sister. I'm going to teach you all of it. Dragons and books and sharing. But not my favourite toys."

Prem looked at her. Then yawned. Then fell asleep in her lap. "He likes me!"

"He does. Very much."

She sat there for almost an hour, holding her sleeping brother and whispering to him about all the things she intended to teach him — about the park, ice cream.

"And if anyone was mean to you at school, I'll tell them off. Because I'm your big sister and that's my job."

I watched them. Janani was beside me.

"She's going to be a great big sister," Janani whispered. "She already is."

Sunday mornings. Pancakes and chaos. Bedtime stories. Dragons versus diggers. Anjali was asking impossible questions. Prem was stating facts with quiet precision.

Janani whispered from the doorway one evening. "This is parenting," I whispered back.

Both kids were asleep by eight. Janani and I sank onto the sofa, exhausted, happy.

"They're wonderful."

"They are."

"We made good humans."

"We did."

She leaned against me. Outside, London hummed.

* * *

SUNDAY MORNINGS TURNED into a ritual of pancakes and chaos. Anjali demanded more syrup, Prem banged his spoon in his high chair, and Janani and I took turns flipping pancakes, laughing over burns and celebrating successes.

After breakfast, we walked to the small park, Anjali on her scooter, Prem in his pushchair, Janani and I behind holding hands. The park, a green patch with a playground, was enough. Anjali ran to the swings, Prem to the slide, while Janani and I sat on a bench, watching and talking about everything and nothing.

One Sunday, Anjali found the vine in our garden. She was four, and Prem was two. They had been playing in the garden while Janani and I watched from the kitchen window.

Anjali paused in front of it, stretched up, and lightly touched a pink flower, just as she had seen Janani do. Prem toddled over, his small hand reaching for the same flower.

They stood there together, two small children in front of the plant, their hands gentle, their focus entire. Janani and I watched from the window, not interfering.

"This is nice," Janani said one Sunday. "What? The park?"

"This. Us. The kids. Sunday mornings. The routine of it. The normalcy."

I looked at her. "It is nice," I said.

"I never thought I'd have this. A family, a routine, a life that feels... settled."

"Did you want it? Before?"

"I didn't know. I wanted a different life. A bigger one. A more exciting one. But this, this is what I wanted. This is what I needed."

I squeezed her hand. "Me too."

We sat there, watching our children play, holding hands.

* * *

ONE SATURDAY AFTERNOON, I took Anjali and Prem for a walk along the canal near our house. The towpath was narrow, the water still, reflecting the grey London sky.

Anjali ran ahead, stopping every few paces to point at something: a duck, a boat, a tree branch hanging over the water. Prem held my hand, his small fingers wrapped around mine, his steps careful on the uneven path.

"Look, Appa," Anjali called. "A bird."

I looked. A heron stood still at the water's edge, its long neck curved, its grey feathers merging with the water. Anjali watched it, her eyes wide, her body motionless. Prem tugged at my hand.

"Bird," he said. "Yes. A heron."

"What's it doing?"

"Waiting. Watching for fish."

Anjali took a step closer. The heron didn't move. It stood there, patient and focused, present in a way I wasn't. My phone buzzed. My eyes went there before I decided, this walk, these children.

"Appa, are you listening?" Anjali asked.

I looked at her. Her face was turned toward me, expectant, waiting for my attention.

"Yes. I'm listening."

"I said the bird is beautiful."

"It is."

"Do you think it has a family?" I paused.

"I'm not sure. Maybe."

"I think it does. I think it has babies somewhere. And it's getting food for them."

I looked at the heron. "Maybe you're right."

Anjali smiled. She ran ahead again, calling for Prem to follow. "Appa, can we feed the ducks?"

"We don't have any food for them."

"But we could get some. From the shop." I looked at him.

"Maybe next time."

His face fell slightly. But he nodded.

We walked on. Anjali ahead, pointing at things. Prem beside me, his hand in mine. The canal beside us was motionless.

"Appa, look," Anjali called.

I looked. A swan glided past, its white feathers stark against the pewter water.

"What kind is it?" Prem asked.

I didn't answer. My phone buzzed. Work email. I pulled it out and checked the screen.

"Appa?" Prem's hand tightened in mine. "Just a minute." I typed a quick reply and sent it.

Anjali had moved ahead. She was pointing at something else, but I couldn't see what.

"Appa, are you listening?" Prem's voice was small. I looked up. Put the phone away.

He didn't answer. Just kept walking, his hand still in mine, but looser now.

* * *

I WASHED THE RICE TWICE, then a third time, until the water mostly ran clear. I tilted the bowl carefully, watching the last cloudy swirl disappear down the drain before setting the rice aside.

The kitchen was narrow. A single window above the counter looked out onto the neighbouring building's brick wall. In the late afternoon, light filtered in at an angle, catching dust in the air. I wiped the counter once more, although it was already clean, then reached for the saucepan.

The children's shoes lay near the door, one pair neatly aligned while the other was kicked off unevenly. A school bag leaned against the wall, unzipped, with a worksheet slipping halfway out. I nudged it back inside with my foot.

On the hob, oil warmed gradually. I added mustard seeds and waited. When they started to pop, I stepped back instinctively, the sharp sound filling the quiet room. Curry leaves followed, then chopped onions. The aroma spread quickly, familiar, filling the flat.

I checked the microwave clock, still twenty minutes.

From the living room, the gentle hum of the washing machine drifted in. Its rhythm was steady and predictable. I folded a dish towel along its existing crease and hung it back on the oven door handle.

My phone lay face down on the counter. I didn't pick it up.

I moved through the motions leisurely, adding lentils, measuring water, rinsing the chopping board. Steam curled up, slightly fogging the window. I wiped it away with the edge of my sleeve, leaving a faint arc where the glass cleared.

A key turned in the lock.

I didn't look up right away. The door opened, then closed. Shoes were set down carefully this time.

"I'm home," Janani said from the hallway.

"In the kitchen," I replied.

She stepped in, loosened her scarf, and paused for a moment by the door, watching the pot. I stirred, carefully scraping the bottom to prevent anything from sticking.

"Smells good," she said.

I nodded.

She reached for a glass, filled it with water, drank, then left it by the sink. The glass left a ring of moisture on the counter. I noticed it and didn't wipe it away.

The washing machine clicked and went quiet.

I lowered the heat, covered the pot, and stepped back. For a moment, we stood side by side without speaking, the room warm and filled with the aroma of food and steam.

I reached for the plates.

* * *

WHEN PREM TURNED ONE, we bought a house.

Three-bedroom terraced house in Walthamstow, close to good schools and within walking distance of the Tube. The Victorian home features brickwork the colour of London clay, with tall, narrow windows that let in the northern light.

A small back garden, barely twenty feet by ten, but it was ours— a rectangle of opportunity where we could plant things, where the children could play, and where we could sit on summer evenings. The mortgage was enormous—eye-watering. Thirty years of payments that would carry us into our sixties, a commitment that felt both frightening and essential.

"We're doing this," Janani said when we signed the papers, her hand shaking slightly.

"We're insane," I said.

"Insane. But also: we're rooted now. We can't pick up and leave anymore."

"Did you want to leave?"

She paused, pen still in hand. "No. But I liked knowing I could. I liked having the option. Now we're committed. Thirty-year mortgage. Two kids in local schools."

Moving day was chaos: boxes everywhere, the kids underfoot, both sets of parents working to help, only to create more work. But by evening, we had beds assembled and the kitchen functional, and we sat on the floor eating takeaway pizza while Anjali and Prem ran circles around the space.

The next morning, our neighbour knocked — Mrs. Okonkwo from number 47, Nigerian, in her sixties, wearing a headwrap the colour of sunset.

"You're Indian," she announced. "Yes. Tamil, from the south of India."

"Good. Not Gujarati. The Patels, three doors down, only eat vegetarian. Makes it hard to share food." She thrust a covered dish at me.

"Thank you."

"Not kind. Strategic. You have two small children. I have four grandchildren who visit every weekend. They need other children to exhaust themselves with." She peered past me.

"My parents. They're helping us move in."

"Good. Tell them I said hello. And tell your wife the jollof is better than anything she'll find in a restaurant."

I stood in the doorway, holding the dish, watching her walk down the street.

"Who was that?" Janani asked from inside. "Our neighbour. She brought us jollof rice."

"That's nice."

"She said it's strategic. She wants our kids to play with her grandchildren."

Janani laughed.

* * *

I STOPPED. Looked at Claire.

"You've been describing a happy period. A good marriage. Children.

What changed?" I was quiet. "Dev?"

"It just... stopped."

"Stopped how? Tell me about that. About things stopping."

"I can't say."

"What happens in your body right now, as you say 'I'm not sure'?"

"Nothing. I... go blank."

"What's happening right now?" I blinked.

"Where?"

"I don't know. Somewhere else. Not here."

"What happens when you're not here?"

I looked at my hands.

* * *

FIVE YEARS into the marriage

But then things began to drift apart. Gradually. So gradually, I didn't notice.

February. Janani had a one-on-one with Sarah.

She'd been promoted to Director. Sitting across from Sarah's desk and discussing new responsibilities, she was interrupted when Sarah leaned forward.

"The good ones never ask you to be smaller. They expect it." Janani stared at her.

I've seen you diminish over the past year. Your ideas remain brilliant, but you're holding back. And I'm not referring to here. I mean at home.

Janani looked down at her hands. Laptop closed. Notebook shut. "The Paris project."

"Among other things."

"The visa situation…changed it all "

"I know. But that ended months ago. And you're still saying no to things. Still leaving early."

Janani walked back to her desk. Sat down. Stared at the spreadsheet she'd been working on.

School pickup schedule. Violin lessons. Doctor's appointments. All colour-coded.

She closed the spreadsheet.

* * *

Summer

Prem's violin recital.

Janani had marked it in the calendar weeks ago and cleared her schedule.

Told me three separate times.

The morning of the recital, my manager called. There was an emergency meeting: a production outage and a client escalation.

"I can't miss this." I was already pulling on my shoes. "Prem's recital is at four."

"I'll try to make it. But if the call runs long…"

"You're not going to make it. You never make it. Every time there's a choice between your job and our children, you choose your job."

"That's not fair. I'm the primary earner..."

"I'm a director now. I earn almost as much as you. Don't hide behind money."

"Then what do you want me to do? Tell my manager I can't help because my son has a violin recital. That's not how it works in tech."

"No. That's not how it works for you in tech. Somehow, I manage to keep my work commitments and still be there for my children. Somehow, Sarah on my team manages it. Somehow every working mother I know manages it."

"Janani..."

Go. Head to your meeting. Resolve your crisis. Be the hero. I'll take Prem to his recital. I'll sit alone in the audience, watching him search the crowd for you. I'll tell him you had an emergency.

Janani went to the recital.

Prem played beautifully. Kept glancing at the door. Afterwards: "Where was Dad?"

"Work emergency, sweetheart."

"He always has work emergencies." Janani had nothing to say to that.

* * *

THAT NIGHT, after the children were asleep, Janani sat in the garden.

The vine I had planted years ago, with a few pink flowers against the grey fence. She'd wrapped it in burlap each autumn and watered it methodically. She checked on it every few days and tended to it. How she'd cared for everything — children, the house, the marriage.

I'd said it reminded me of home when I planted it.

She'd asked: What about this? This house, these children, me, isn't this home?

I'd looked at the plant. Not at her. Not at the question.

She sat there for a long time. The garden was silent, with London's distant noise muffled by the fence. The October air was chilly. She ought to have gone inside. Should have put on a coat. But she stayed, sitting on the garden bench, gazing at those blooms — the pink flowers that shouldn't exist in London.

She moved slowly, her shoulders rounded, her steps careful. Not tired. Something deeper than sleep could mend it. The weight of carrying everything: school schedules, violin lessons, work deadlines. The weight of being the one who noticed, the one who worked at it.

For years, she'd left notes. She'd asked questions. She'd started conversations. She'd planted the vine. She'd tended it. She'd shown me.

"Look what we can grow, what we can build."

I was there physically. I came home. Ate. Helped with bedtime. And still she kept looking past me, as if I'd stepped out of frame.

She rubbed her thumb over the edge of her phone case. Once. Again. She picked up Prem's practice book from the table, then put it down in the wrong place without correcting it.

When they realised their parents wouldn't stay together, Anjali asked questions, Prem went quiet, and both learned that love wasn't enough. That effort alone wasn't enough.

She went to the kitchen and didn't turn on the light. She kept shrinking to fit into a space that was shrinking every day.

She opened her laptop at the kitchen table. The search bar filled itself: 'separation agreement UK'. She stared at it, then hit enter.

Three PDFs. She opened the first, scrolled once, stopped at a heading, and covered her mouth with her hand. Tea cooling beside her, untouched. The words on the screen, legal language, formal, cold. She shut the laptop without saving anything.

The house remained quiet. Upstairs, it echoed with its own sounds: the heating clicking on, a floorboard settling. The children were in their rooms, the vine outside blooming in the dark, a plant she'd tended.

She poured the cold tea down the sink, washed the mug, and placed it on the drying rack. The same routine, same motions, same careful, methodical way of doing things. Even now. Even when everything was changing.

Got into bed. Lay awake until morning, listening to the sounds of the house: the heating clicking on, children breathing in their sleep, distant traffic.

* * *

CHILDREN WERE ASLEEP AFTER SUPPER. Janani leaned against the kitchen counter, barefoot, watching me dry the last plate longer than necessary.

"You're stalling," she said.

"I'm finishing."

"You finished already."

She crossed the room and took the towel from my hands, dropping it onto the chair. I didn't protest. I rarely did with her.

She kissed me then—not urgently, not playfully. A kiss that assumed its place, as if it belonged there. When she pulled back, her forehead rested against mine.

"Come sit," she said.

We sat on the sofa, legs fitting together effortlessly, years of shared habit guiding us. Her hand slipped under my shirt, warm against my back, familiar enough to calm something restless in me.

I turned toward her slowly, studying her face—the small lines at the corners of her eyes, the way her expression softened when she noticed me looking.

"This," she said quietly, "is my favourite version of us."

I knew what she meant. Not the milestones. Not the plans. This —tired, present, unguarded.

She kissed me again, deeper now, her hand steady at my waist. For a moment, everything else fell away: work, ambition, the persistent pull of elsewhere.

Later, lying beside her with her back against my chest and her breathing steady, I thought—this is what staying feels like.

The thought frightened me with its clarity.

* * *

THERE WAS A DAY THAT WORKED.

Nothing set it apart at the time. No planning. No sense of occasion. The children were restless in the morning, then inexplicably calm by afternoon. We decided, late, to take the train out of the city.

Janani packed swiftly. Sandwiches wrapped in foil. Water bottles we forgot to drink from. She laughed when we missed our stop and didn't try to turn it into a lesson.

We walked, ate, and sat on the grass while the children ran ahead, inventing rules that kept changing every few minutes. Janani leaned back and closed her eyes, the sun catching her face in a way that made her look younger than she usually allowed herself to.

"Don't think," she said, without opening her eyes.

I didn't.

That evening, tired in the simple way that follows movement and air, we put the children to bed and ate quietly. Nothing needed review. Nothing needed fixing.

If someone had asked me then what I wanted, I would have said this.

I wouldn't have known what to do with the answer.

* * *

I PAUSED.

"Janani's attempts to reconnect. Her care. The garden. I..."

I stopped and looked at my hands.

"What do you think you did?"

I looked away. "I just... let it happen. Accepted it. But didn't fight for

it."

Claire waited.

I was quiet. "I didn't notice what she was doing until it was too late."

I paused.

"What happens in your body as you think about not reciprocating?

About not noticing?"

"Heaviness. Sadness."

"Good. You're noticing. You're feeling. That's different from before."

I thought about it. "There were moments when we connected, like when Prerna stayed with us. We talked about it. We worked through it. But those moments were rare. Most of the time, I just… wasn't really there."

"And what did that cost you? Not being present? Not being engaged?"

"Her. The marriage. All of it." Claire was quiet for a long moment.

"It's heavy. Sad. That I didn't see it before."

"What are you seeing now?"

"I'm seeing what I did. What I didn't do."

"What does that feel like?"

I stepped out into the afternoon. The air smelled of rain and exhaust fumes, the sky a dull grey. My footsteps were silent on the pavement.

PART V
THE DRIFT

Where nothing is demanded, and everything is lost.

YEARS WITHOUT LEAVING

$\mathcal{N}$othing in those years felt unstable.

That was the problem.

The days organised themselves with mornings dedicated to work, and children's routines revolving around drop-offs, pick-ups, and simple evening plans. Janani kept lists for groceries, school events, and birthdays, while I paid bills on time and booked holidays early to ensure good seats and arranged repairs before they became urgent.

We were competent.

At night, after the children had gone to sleep, we sat together on the sofa, legs touching, the television on low. Sometimes we spoke. Often, we didn't. Silence between us didn't feel like an absence then.

Years passed without leaving.

That's how it felt at the time—not as if time was passing, but as if repetition was settling into place. The children grew in stages, and I only noticed when clothes no longer fit or shoes pinched. Janani cut her hair shorter a year ago and didn't ask for my opinion.

We hosted friends—other couples with similar lives. Conversations revolved around the same topics: schools, work, rising costs, plans made far enough ahead to seem responsible, but not so distant as to become dreams. Everyone complained mildly. No one sounded unhappy.

Janani was good at this life. Better than I was.

$$* * *$$

SHE REMEMBERED DETAILS, like the names of teachers, which child needed reassurance before bed, and which needed space. When something went wrong, she addressed it directly; when it went well, she didn't draw attention to it.

I admired that about her. I relied on it more than I admitted.

There were moments—rare, fleeting—when the thought arose that something else might have been possible. Not another life. Just a different version of this one. The idea never lingered long. Indulgent. Easily dismissed.

$$* * *$$

ON WEEKENDS, we took the children to the park. Janani sat on the bench, watching them climb, run, fall, and recover. I stood nearby, ready to intervene, often unnecessarily. She smiled when she caught me hovering.

"They're fine," she said.

Sometimes, late at night, she asked about work with attention.

"You've been quiet," she said once.

"I'm just tired."

She nodded and said nothing.

There were opportunities during those years. Invitations. Conversations that could have become something else. I didn't pursue them. I didn't entirely ignore them either. I kept them contained, like documents stored in a folder I never opened.

Janani never asked to see that folder. She trusted what she could observe.

We travelled occasionally, choosing holidays for convenience rather than discovery. Places that promised ease. Hotels where the children slept well. Restaurants that didn't require explanation. Janani read in the evenings while I checked emails I didn't need to respond to.

One night, she reached for my hand as we walked back to the room.

"This is nice," she said. Not enthusiastic. Certain.

I agreed. I meant it.

Years without leaving.

It wasn't dissatisfaction that crept in; it was something quieter—a feeling that decisions had already been made, and I was now living in their aftermath. The lack of choice started to feel heavier than conflict ever had.

Janani noticed changes before I did.

* * *

ONE NIGHT, she spoke without prompting.

"I thought marriage would be steadier," she said. "Not safer. Just steadier."

I waited. She rarely said things like this without intention.

"I thought it would mean choosing again," she continued. "Not every day. But often enough to notice."

I told her I had chosen her.

"I know," she said. "I'm not questioning that." She paused. "I'm saying I thought we'd keep choosing."

I remember nodding and hearing it as reassurance rather than a warning.

Later, I would understand how much she had already explained.

* * *

"YOU'RE HERE," she said once, "but you're somewhere else."

I wanted to argue. Instead, I asked where she thought I was.

She didn't answer immediately. When she did, she spoke carefully.

"I don't think it's a place," she said. "I think it's time."

That stayed with me longer than I let on.

Nothing ended then. Nothing was broken. We carried on. The children grew. The calendar was filled. Work rewarded consistency. From the outside, there was no reason to question anything.

But I began to realise that I hadn't repeatedly chosen this life. I had chosen it once, and then stayed because leaving would have required explanation.

That distinction mattered more than I was ready to admit.

On a typical evening—one I wouldn't usually recall—Janani was at the sink washing dishes as I dried. We moved in quiet, familiar rhythm. Eventually, she paused and glanced at me.

"Are you happy?" she asked.

The question wasn't sudden. It had been approaching for years.

"Yes," I said, quickly enough to sound rehearsed.

She studied my face, not unkindly.

"That wasn't what I asked," she said.

I didn't know how to answer without undoing something.

Later, lying in bed with my back to her, I listened to her breathing even out. I watched the dark gradually shift towards morning and thought—not for the first time—that stability had become a form of concealment.

I stayed anyway.

* * *

THE ENVELOPE WAS THICK. Official.

I placed it on the table and stared at it before opening it. Inside were forms—names, dates, declarations. Boxes that required precision.

Janani filled them out quickly.

I watched her handwriting, neat and consistent.

"You're good at this," I said.

She smiled without looking up. "Someone has to be."

Later, when the children ran through the flat, I was counting rooms, exits, and responsibilities.

I knew where everything was.

I didn't know how to sit still.

COMING APART

I was early and sat in the waiting room. When Claire opened the door, I was already standing.

"You're early again."

"I needed to be here."

"Why?"

"Because this is the hard part. The part I've been avoiding."

"The separation."

"Yes."

"Then let's do it. Tell me what happened."

* * *

ABOUT A YEAR BEFORE WE SEPARATED, Amir noticed. We were at the pub on a Friday evening, our usual routine, but I was quiet, distant, and even my laughter sounded delayed, as if it had to travel through something to reach my mouth.

"You alright, mate?"

"Fine. Just tired."

"You've been tired for months. That's not tired. That's something else."

"I'm fine, Amir. Really."

"You're not. I can see it. You're disappearing, becoming someone else."

"I'm uncertain what you mean."

"Yes, you do. Your accent changes mid-sentence. You're not here, somewhere else, and I'm not sure where."

"I'm fine."

"Stop saying that. You're not fine. I'm worried, Janani's worried, everyone's worried, but you won't talk about it, won't let anyone in."

"I don't need help."

"Everyone needs help sometimes. That's what friends are for, what I'm here for: to help, be here, be actually here."

"I know. And I appreciate it. But I'm fine." He studied me, the way you research the weather when you're deciding whether it's going to break.

"Alright. But if you need anything, if you need to talk, if you need help, I'm here, always. That's what friends do: they show up."

"I know. Thank you." But I didn't call, and even as I said thank you.

* * *

THE CHILDREN WERE ASLEEP. The dishwasher hummed in the kitchen, steady and mechanical.

Janani sat at the dining table with her laptop open. She closed it when I came in.

"You're still up," I said.

"Yes."

I poured water and drank it standing, scrolling through my phone.

"I need to ask you something," she said.

I looked up. "Now?"

"Yes."

I sat across from her. Folded my hands.

212

"Do you notice when your voice changes?" she asked.

"What do you mean?"

"When you talk," she said. "Sometimes it sounds like you're presenting."

"That's just work."

"It's not only at work."

I leaned back. "Is there something specific?"

"No," she said. "That's the problem."

I checked the time. "It's late."

"That's what we always say."

I exhaled. "Janani, I don't understand what you're asking."

"I'm asking if you feel present."

"I'm here," I said.

She nodded.

"I miss you," she said.

"I'm right here."

"That's not what I meant."

"I don't want to fight," I said.

"I'm not fighting."

"Then what is this?"

I didn't get an answer.

"We're both tired," I said. "Let's not make this bigger."

"Yes," she said.

I rinsed my glass, set it in the rack, and kissed her forehead.

Nothing had happened. I went to bed knowing that wasn't true.

* * *

JANANI WOKE before the rest of the house. Anjali and Prem grew up, and their voices changed, their questions more complex, their needs more specific.

I know these details because she told me later and because I can picture them: the quiet before the day begins, the small pocket of time when a person can still hear their own thoughts.

The ceiling fan turned. Dev slept facing the edge of the bed, one hand tucked under the pillow, just as he always slept. And Dev was me, but also the version of me she shared her life with, the one she watched from the other side of the mattress.

She slipped out. In the kitchen, she filled the kettle and set it on the stove.

The flame caught.

London morning, pale light filtering through the windows. Across the street, curtains drawn, lives folded inward.

She opened her laptop at the dining table. The screen illuminated the room. The email had been sitting there for three weeks. A former colleague. A university teaching role.

We thought of you.

She'd read it on the train, standing, phone in one hand, pole in the other. Her hands had been steady, but inside, a shift had happened.

She'd told herself she would respond that evening. Then a deadline, Dev stayed late, laundry, groceries, exhaustion—life filling every gap until there was no gap left for choice.

The kettle whistled. She poured water and set the mug aside. When she returned to the laptop, she didn't reread the email. She placed her fingers on the keyboard, ready to type, respond, and say yes.

She closed the laptop.

She drank her tea standing by the sink. A door opened upstairs, a floorboard creaked, the house waking in stages.

Dev entered the kitchen, rubbing his eyes. "Morning."

"Morning."

He reached for a cup. She shifted aside, the gentle physical yield that had become a habit. Later, she responded to the email.

Thank you for thinking of me. Yes. I would be interested.

No explanation. No apology. No qualifiers.

She read it once. Her finger hovered over the trackpad.

She thought of the seminar room from years ago: tables scarred with initials, a whiteboard that never quite erased cleanly.

She clicked send.

The confirmation flashed, then vanished.

* * *

SUNDAY AFTERNOON. The children were with Janani's parents. The house was silent. The kind of silence that should feel like relief, but instead feels like a test.

Janani was preparing lunch. I was on my laptop, finishing work from Friday, telling myself it would only take a few minutes, saying the same to myself I always did.

"Can you set the table?"

"In a minute."

"Dev, the food's getting cold."

"Sorry, almost done."

I arrived at the table twenty minutes after she'd called. The food was cold.

"I asked you to set the table."

"I was working."

"On a Sunday."

"I needed to finish it."

She stood. Cleared her plate. "I apologised."

"You said you were finishing. That's not the same as sorry."

"You're right. I'm sorry. I should have stopped."

She went upstairs.

I sat at the table with cold curry.

* * *

THE PROMOTIONS OCCURRED within six months of each other. This was earlier—years earlier—when the children were younger, and when we still believed that momentum was the same as stability.

Mine first: Senior Engineer, with increased responsibilities, travel, and a higher salary. Janani cooked dinner to celebrate. I talked about my new role and the team.

215

Then hers. Director of Digital Strategy. A title she had worked towards for years. More meetings, longer hours.

She told me over dinner. "They offered me Director."

"That's amazing."

"Fifteen percent raise. My own budget. Real authority."

"You deserve it. You've been doing the work anyway." She paused.

"We'll make it work. We could use the extra income. "Dev."

I stopped, but stopping then was surface-level, the kind of stop that looks like listening while the mind keeps moving.

"I told you I got promoted to Director. And your first thought is how it helps with our mortgage."

I opened my mouth. Closed it, the reflex of retreat.

"You immediately went to logistics. To see how it helps us financially."

"You're right. I'm sorry. Congratulations, really."

She smiled slightly, and the slightness, I didn't understand yet.

We cleared the table together, loaded the dishwasher, and said goodnight.

* * *

MY TRAVEL BEGAN. Edinburgh, Manchester, Birmingham. Consecutive weeks. Hotels that looked the same, expense reports that blurred together.

I'd come home exhausted, bags under my eyes. Laptop still warm from the train, the heat of work carrying into the house like a smell.

"How was it?"

"Productive. Exhausting. The kids?"

"Fine. Prem's fighting bedtime. Anjali has a school project on Friday."

"I can pick that up tomorrow."

"I already got it. Craft drawer."

Each time she said, 'I already got it,' I felt a wave of relief, though it should have been gratitude or shame.

* * *

ONE EVENING, I arrived home late. The house was quiet. Janani was already in bed. I checked on the children. Anjali was asleep, her book still open on her pillow, the pages bent where her hand had slipped away.

"Appa," he said. His voice was small in the dark room. "You should be asleep."

"I was waiting for you."

I sat on the edge of his bed. The room was dim, lit only by the nightlight.

"What's wrong?"

"Nothing. I just wanted you to read me a story."

I looked at the book on his nightstand. A picture book about a dragon and a princess: we'd read it before.

"It's late, Prem. You should sleep."

"Please? Just one story."

I picked up the book, opened it, and started reading. The words came automatically.

I read the words. My voice was steady. Professional.

Prem listened, his eyes on the pictures, his small body still, trusting that my voice meant I was there.

I finished the story, closed the book, and set it on the nightstand.

"Goodnight, Prem."

"Goodnight, Appa."

I kissed his forehead, turned off the light, and left the room.

I walked downstairs, sat on the sofa, opened my laptop, and checked my email.

The house was still.

One Friday evening, I came home at nine. Janani sat in the dark living room, laptop closed beside her.

"Kids asleep?"

"Hours ago."

"Sorry, I'm late. The deployment took longer than expected."

"Dev. What's Prem's teacher's name?"

I paused.

"Miss Harrison. She's been his teacher since September. It's February."

"I'm sorry. I've been swamped."

"I know. You're always swamped."

She stood and walked to the bookshelf. She pulled out her old planner and opened it. Post-its fell out, yellow squares covered in my handwriting.

You're brilliant. Remember, you're smarter than everyone in that meeting.

She let them scatter on the floor between us.

"I kept every single one. Two hundred and forty-seven." She knelt. Picked one up. Read it without inflexion.

"Running late. Don't wait up"

"Three years ago. That was the last one." She stood, still holding it.

The Post-its lay scattered across the floor. Yellow squares. She picked up her laptop. Left me standing there.

I slept on the sofa that night, the house feeling suddenly larger, as if distance had been built into the walls.

* * *

ANJALI'S SCHOOL had an application deadline.

A selective secondary school. One of the best in London. She'd been working toward it for two years—extra tutoring, mock exams, evenings bent over practice papers. Her grades were strong. Her teacher had written a recommendation.

The application required a parent interview.

Both parents. Mandatory.

Janani had marked it in the calendar months ago. She told me about it every week. Sent reminders. Added it to the shared calendar. Texted me again that morning.

> *The interview is at three. Don't forget.*
> *I won't.*

The day of the interview, I had a client meeting. Important. High stakes. A major contract. I'd scheduled it weeks earlier—before I knew about the interview. Or maybe I'd known and forgotten. Or perhaps I'd known and chosen not to remember.

I called the client. They couldn't move it. The meeting was critical. The contract was worth millions. My manager was attending. The CEO was attending. I couldn't miss it.

I called Janani.

"I can't make the interview," I said.

She was quiet. Then, carefully: "Dev, it's mandatory. Both parents. They won't accept the application otherwise."

"I know. But this meeting—this client—it's critical. I can't reschedule."

"So you're choosing work over Anjali's school application."

"I'm not choosing. I don't have a choice."

"You always have a choice," she said. "You're choosing work."

"Can't you reschedule the interview?"

"I already tried. They said no. The deadline is today. If we miss this, the application is rejected. No appeals."

"Can't we apply somewhere else?"

"We can. But this is the school she wanted. The one she's been working toward. The one her teacher recommended. The one that would have been best for her."

"I'm sorry," I said. "I really am. But I can't miss this meeting."

A pause. Then: "Fine. I'll go alone. I'll explain. I'll see if they'll make an exception."

She hung up.

I went to the meeting. Sat through it. Nodded at the right

moments. Spoke when required and made the correct arguments. We secured the contract.

When I got home, Janani was in the living room. Anjali was already in bed.

"How did it go?" I asked.

She looked at me—not angry, not tired. Just emptied of hope.

"They wouldn't make an exception," she said. Both parents are mandatory. The application was rejected."

"What?"

"The application was rejected, Dev."

"But—can't we apply to another school?"

"We can. But not this one. Not the one she wanted. Not the one she prepared for. That door is closed."

"I didn't realise—"

"You didn't realise?" She said it evenly. "I told you. I reminded you. I put it on the calendar. I texted you. You didn't realise—or you didn't hold it in your mind long enough to matter."

I said nothing.

"Anjali asked where you were," she continued. "I told her you had a work meeting. She nodded. That was it. No questions. No tears. Just… acceptance. As if she already understood how these things work."

"I'll make it up to her," I said. "I'll help her apply elsewhere."

"It's not about other schools," Janani said. "It's about being there when it mattered."

I went upstairs. Anjali was asleep, her face turned toward the wall. Tear tracks marked her cheeks. I sat on the edge of the bed and watched her breathe, the weight of what I'd taken from her settling slowly, heavily, into my chest.

The next morning, I found Janani in the kitchen before the children woke. She was making tea.

"I'm sorry," I said. "I didn't realise how important it was."

"You didn't realise," she repeated. No anger. Just a fact.

"Let me fix it. Let me help her with the next applications."

"I don't want fixing," she said. "I want you to show up. To

remember. To be there when it counts. But you don't. You can't. Or you won't."

"I'll do better."

"You've said that before."

She finished her tea, rinsed the mug, and left the room.

* * *

PREM HAD BEEN STRUGGLING.

Reading. Writing. Keeping pace in class. His teacher had noticed. Janani had noticed. I had seen too—and done nothing. I hadn't said anything. Hadn't asked questions and hadn't made time.

Janani made the appointment. A developmental assessment. Someone who could look at the whole picture, who could tell us what was happening and how to help him.

She told me about it more than once, and she put it on the calendar. Added reminders. Texted me. Called me the day before.

"The appointment is tomorrow at two," she said. "The specialist needs both parents. It's important. Please don't forget."

"I won't."

On the day of the appointment, a server went down.

Critical failure. System-wide. Clients affected. I called my team. No one else could handle it. Everyone was already stretched. The problem was mine.

I called Janani.

"I can't make it," I said. "There's a work emergency."

She didn't respond immediately.

"Dev," she said finally. "This is important. The specialist needs both parents. It's policy. They won't do the assessment otherwise."

"I know. But the system is down. I can't leave."

"So you're choosing work over getting your son help."

"I'm not choosing. I don't have a choice."

"You always have a choice," she said. "You're choosing work."

"Can you reschedule?"

"I already tried. The next appointment is in six months."

She let the number sit between us.

"Six months," she said. "That's six more months of him struggling. Six more months of falling behind. Six more months of thinking he's stupid or broken or not trying hard enough."

"I'm sorry," I said. "I really am. But I can't miss this. The client is losing money. I have to fix it."

Another pause.

"Fine," she said. "I'll go alone. I'll see if they'll make an exception."

She hung up.

I fixed the server. Restored the system. Saved the client.

When I got home, Prem was already asleep. Janani was in the living room, reading. She didn't look up.

"How did it go?" I asked.

"They wouldn't make an exception," she said. Both parents are mandatory. Policy."

My stomach tightened.

"The appointment was cancelled. The next available is in six months."

"Six months?"

"Yes," she said. "Six months."

She looked at me then—not angry, not raised voice. Just tired.

"That's how long he'll wait. That's how long he'll struggle. All because you didn't show up."

"I didn't realise—"

"You didn't realise?" she said. "I told you. I put it on the calendar. I reminded you. You didn't realise—or you didn't hold it long enough to matter."

I said nothing.

"Prem asked where you were," she continued. "I told him you had to work. He nodded. That was it. No questions. Just… acceptance."

"I'll help him," I said. "I'll work with him at home."

"It's not about homework," she said. "It's about getting him the help he needs. The help that could change how he sees himself. And now he has to wait."

I went upstairs. Prem was asleep, his face turned toward the wall. Tear tracks marked his cheeks. I sat on the edge of the bed and watched him breathe.

Six months.

Six months of waiting.

Six months of struggle.

All because I didn't show up.

The next morning, Janani was in the kitchen before the children woke. She was making tea.

"I'm taking the kids to my parents' this weekend," she said. "You can use the time to catch up on work."

"That's not fair."

She met my eyes. "Prove it."

She left the room.

* * *

ONE EVENING, I caught myself mid-sentence.

I'd been discussing Anjali's school with her. Then my phone rang. It was work. Halfway through explaining the situation, I switched to a British corporate voice.

She noticed.

After I hung up, she was watching me. "You changed."

"Changed what?"

"Your voice. Your whole demeanour. Mid-sentence, you pulled away."

"I was being professional. For the call."

"No. It's not a professional voice. You do it all the time. One moment you're one person, the next you're someone else."

I laughed it off.

"Not like this. Do you even notice when you do it?" I opened my mouth. Closed it.

* * *

ONE FRIDAY EVENING, Janani suggested we go out.

"There's a new restaurant in Islington. We could get a babysitter. Us.

Like we used to."

I looked at my laptop.

"It's Friday, Dev. One evening. Three hours. That's all I'm asking."

"I know. But this project is important. The client's been waiting."

"What about letting me down? What about letting us down?"

"It's not the same thing."

"Isn't it?" She was quiet for a moment. I couldn't remember.

"I can't recall."

"Six months ago. My birthday. And you checked your phone three times during dinner."

"I'm sorry. I'll make it up to you."

"You always say that. But you never do." She stood.

"Janani, wait."

But she was already walking away.

* * *

THE FOLLOWING WEEK, I worked through the weekend, Saturday and Sunday, both days. The children asked me to play, but I said later. Janani asked me to help with lunch.

On Monday morning, I left for work before the children woke. I came home after they'd gone to bed. On Tuesday, the same. On Wednesday, the same. By Thursday, I'd forgotten what day it was.

Janani talked to me. Asked questions, waited for answers. But I was too tired. Too focused.

"Dev, can we talk?"

"Not now. I'm working."

"When then?"

"Later. I'll be done soon."

* * *

ONE TUESDAY AFTERNOON, I had a work meeting with an important client—high stakes.

I was confidently presenting a technical solution, clear and articulate. After five minutes of speaking, I couldn't remember a single word.

The words kept coming. My hands moved, gesturing at the screen.

The client nodded.

The presentation continued. The client nodded. Asked questions. I answered. The answers came automatically.

The meeting ended. People congratulated me.

I smiled, said thank you, shook hands, then walked back to my desk. I sat down, stared at my screen, and for a moment, I wasn't sure if I had been there at all.

* * *

JANANI STARTED ASKING QUESTIONS. "Are you alright?"

Then: "You seem distant."

And finally, direct: "Where do you go? It's as if you're watching yourself from outside."

"I'm tired."

Her voice had a British inflexion, and she offered a reassuring smile, as if she were trying to speak in a tone she thought might reach me. "That's not an answer."

"It's all I have."

One night, after a fierce week, she found me standing in the bathroom at 2 AM and staring at my reflection.

"Dev?"

I didn't recognise the face in the mirror. Brown skin. Grey at the temples. Lines around the eyes.

It looked like me. But no recognition looking at it. "Who am I?"

"What?"

Janani came closer.

"When I'm not at work, with the kids... when it's me... who is that?" She touched my arm.

I was quiet. "I'm uncertain anymore." She pulled me into a hug.

*　*　*

ONE EVENING, after the kids were asleep.

"You're not here. You haven't been here for months. Maybe years."

"I'm right here."

"No. You're performing here. It's different."

"I'm not sure how to be anything else."

"Then we need to figure that out. Because I can't be married to someone who's playing the role of husband."

*　*　*

JANANI DIDN'T TRY to speak to me. She prepared breakfast, got the children ready, left for work, returned home, cooked dinner, and put the children to bed.

One evening, I arrived home late. The house was quiet. The children were asleep. Janani was in the living room, reading. She didn't look up when I entered, didn't ask about my day, didn't try to talk.

I stood there for a moment.

She turned a page. Didn't look up. "I'm home."

"I can see that." Her voice was flat.

I went upstairs. Got ready for bed. Lay down. Stared at the ceiling.

*　*　*

TWO WEEKS before she asked for a separation, Janani worked one last time.

She came into my study. I was working. Laptop open. Phone nearby. "Dev, can we talk? Please, for ten minutes."

I looked up. Saw her face, the exhaustion, the giving up. "I'm in the middle of work."

"It can wait. This can't."

I closed my laptop. Turned to face her. "What is it?"

She sat on the edge of the desk. Studied me, working to see me, to find me.

"I need you to be here. Here. Not performing, not disappearing. Here.

With me, us."

"I am here."

"No, you're not. You're somewhere else. Somewhere I can't reach."

"I'm not sure how to be anything else."

"Then learn. Go to therapy. Talk to someone. Figure it out. But do something because I can't do this anymore. I can't keep trying to reach someone who isn't there. I can't keep carrying all of it alone."

"I'll try."

"You've said that before."

"I know. But this time, I mean it."

"Do you?" She studied me, working to see if I meant it. "Yes. I do."

She remained silent for a long moment. Then she stood. "Alright. I'll give you one more chance. But this is it—the last one. If you don't change, if you don't show up, if you don't be here, I'm done. I'm leaving."

"I understand."

"Do you? Because I'm uncertain you do. I'm uncertain you understand what you're losing. What you're breaking."

She left the room.

And I didn't do anything. I didn't call a therapist, didn't make an appointment, didn't try to change, didn't try to be present, didn't try to be real. I went back to work, disappeared again, let her down again, broke her heart again.

* * *

SATURDAY AFTERNOON.

The children were at their parents' house for the weekend. The house was still.

I was in my study, working. Laptop open. Code on the screen. The familiar escape, the familiar refuge, the familiar way to not be here.

Janani appeared in the doorway. She'd been silent all morning, moving through the house like a ghost, as if she were already gone, as if she had already left.

"Dev, we need to talk."

I looked up. Saw her face. The exhaustion. The giving up. The end. "I think we should separate."

The words hung in the air between us. Heavy. Final. Real.

I closed my laptop. The screen went dark. I could see my reflection on it: tired, confused, lost—the man who'd vanished from his own life.

"How do you want to do this?"

"I'll find a flat. The children stay with you during the week. I'm on weekends. We can work out a schedule."

"You're sure?"

"I'm sure. We've tried for years. I'm exhausted, Dev. I can't keep reaching for someone who isn't there."

I wanted to argue. To promise I would change. To beg for another chance. To say the words that would make her stay, that would make her believe, that would make her hope one more time.

But I'd made those promises before. I'd said those words. I'd broken them—every time.

"Alright."

"That's it? ' Alright? '

"What do you want me to say? That I'll change? I've said that before.

It didn't work."

"I want you to fight. Once. To show me this matters to you."

But I couldn't speak. The words wouldn't come. They were there, in my throat, but they wouldn't form. I was vanishing even as she was asking me to be here, to fight, to choose her, to choose us, to choose this.

She sat back down. "Do you know what I'm most afraid of? Not being alone. I can handle being alone. I'm afraid of what this will do to the children. Of having to explain that their parents won't be together any longer. Of watching their faces change when they realise we're dismantling the life we built."

She looked back at me. "But I'm more scared of staying. I keep shrinking to fit into a space that gets smaller every day. And I can't do that any longer. I'm too tired. Too exhausted from carrying all of it. The schedules, emotional weight, constant effort to reach someone who isn't there."

"I'm here."

"Are you?" Her voice was soft. "Because I don't believe you are. I think you're somewhere else. Somewhere I can't reach. And I've been trying for years. And I'm finished trying."

She stood up. "I'll start looking for places next week."

"Janani."

She stopped at the doorway.

"I'm sorry. For all of it. For not being able to be who you needed me to be."

She was quiet. Then: "I know."

* * *

I PAUSED.

"The separation, one final argument, Janani leaving, and I began to fall apart."

"Why didn't you fight for the marriage?" Claire asked. I was quiet. "I couldn't. I wasn't sure how."

"What happens in your body as you think about not fighting? About not knowing how?"

"Heaviness. Emptiness."

"What do you think you were doing? When you didn't fight?"

"I don't know. Maybe... I was so far gone, I didn't even know what was happening."

"What does 'so far gone' mean?"

"I couldn't see what was happening."

"What couldn't you see?"

I looked at my hands. The silence stretched. "I was disappearing. I wasn't there to fight."

"And what does that mean? Being gone? Not being there?"

I was quiet. "I was dissociating, leaving my body. I wasn't here." She paused, observing me more closely than earlier.

I walked out into the evening.

WHAT I DIDN'T CHOOSE

*C*laire waited. Five minutes. Ten.

"What's happening?" she asked finally, her voice gentle, not pushing.

"I'm uncertain if I can do this." The words came out smaller than I intended, my voice catching slightly.

"Do what?"

"Talk about what came after. The emptiness. The nothing." My throat felt tight, the words scraping against something raw.

"You don't have to. But if you can, it might help."

I was quiet, the weight of what I hadn't said pressing against my chest.

Then I began.

* * *

THE QUESTION CAME from the school office.

Which parent should they call if there is an issue during the day?

I answered without thinking.

"Janani," I said.

The word settled into the space between us. The administrator repeated it, confirming. I nodded.

Janani avoided eye contact with me. She expressed her thanks to the woman and then turned away, already heading towards the door.

Outside, she said, "You could have corrected that."

"I didn't think—"

"That's exactly it," she said.

I didn't argue. The answer had already been given. Out loud. To someone else.

* * *

THE CHILDREN WERE AT HER PARENTS' house that Saturday morning in late October. The flat was quiet—too quiet. Every sound seemed amplified: the refrigerator humming, the heating clicking on, my own breathing.

Janani sat opposite me, folding her hands on the table. Steady. Decided. Morning light filtered through the window, weak and ashen. I could smell her coffee, still warm, strong with cardamom. My laptop was open in front of me, code on the screen—a refuge I wasn't using, a prop for disappearing.

"I want a separation," she said.

"What?"

"A legal separation. Leading to divorce."

The words entered the room like blunt objects. I heard them as dialogue, as if quotation marks had formed around them. Words other people used. Other marriages.

"You can't be serious."

"I am. I've thought about this for months."

"Months?" I said. "You didn't say anything?"

"What was there to say? That I was miserable? You knew that. That our marriage was hollow? You knew that too."

I closed my laptop. The screen went dark, and in it I saw my reflection—tired, confused, unrecognizable.

"Every marriage has difficult phases," I said. "We have two children."

"Dev, we've been living like roommates for two years," she said. "The only time we talk is to coordinate childcare."

"We talk."

"When was the last time you asked me how I was?" she said. "Not work. Not errands. Me."

I couldn't answer. I couldn't remember.

"I've been working," I said. "Trying to keep us financially stable."

"And I haven't?" Her voice rose but stayed controlled. "I worked full-time, raised two children, made every compromise—and you accepted it as if it were my role."

"I never asked you to give anything up."

She stood and walked to the window, not pacing—measuring space.

"Move to Paris? Can't. Your visa is tied here. Change jobs? Can't. We need stability for immigration. Even having a life outside this marriage—can't. I needed to sponsor your right to stay. To turn our relationship into paperwork."

"The visa—"

"No," she said. "The visa was the constraint. The problem is you never fought it. You let me disappear. You let me become the person who made your life possible."

She turned back to me. "Do you know what that felt like? Watching you stay silent while I drowned?"

"I cared," I said. The words sounded hollow.

"When was the last time you chose me?" she asked.

I searched my memory and found nothing recent enough to matter.

"You can't answer," she said. "Because you haven't. Not in years."

"I can't do this anymore," she continued. "I waited for you to fight for us. To see me. To be a partner instead of just... here."

"I'm trying."

233

"Are you? You stopped asking about my day. You stopped showing up. You're here physically, Dev. But you're not here."

"I know," I said. "I'm sorry."

"Sorry isn't enough," she said. "This wasn't an accident. This was years of choosing not to see me."

"That's not fair."

She turned sharply. "Excuse me?"

"I worked. I provided. I kept us stable."

"You disappeared into your laptop," she said. "That's not providing. That's hiding."

"I was trapped," I said. "Every decision was weighed against the risk of losing everything—the job, the visa, our life. I didn't have the luxury of risk."

"You weren't trapped," she said. "You were comfortable."

She stood by the window again, her voice quieter now.

"I'm not angry anymore," she said. "I'm exhausted. Tired of being the only one who notices. The only one who fights."

"I tried," I said, hearing how weak it sounded.

"No," she said. "You managed. You handled logistics. But you didn't see me. And that's not enough."

We sat in silence.

"What about the children?" I asked.

"They'll have both parents," she said. "We'll be civil. Better than this." She paused. "I'll need to find a flat. A month or two."

"I'll move out," I said. "You and the kids stay."

She looked at me.

"This is your home," I added. "You made it one. I just lived in it."

She studied me for a long moment.

Then she nodded.

* * *

WE REMAINED in the same room after separation. Divorce proceedings to follow once I find a place.

234

The children were still at her parents' house. We had two hours before collection. Neither of us moved.

Janani settled on the sofa. I took the chair across from her—the coffee table between us.

She looked at her phone, put it down, looked at it again as the screen lit up and went dark repeatedly, a nervous way of avoiding looking at me, at the gap between us that had grown so wide it seemed unbridgeable.

Her hands trembled slightly, and I longed to reach out, to soothe them, to offer some comfort, but I didn't, because I'd lost the right to comfort her, lost the right to touch her, lost the right to be the person who made things better.

"Do you need the car?"

"No. You can take it." She nodded.

Silence. The radiator clicked. The neighbour's dog barked. Traffic droned outside.

I could smell the washing powder on her clothes across the sofa. "We should probably decide on the schedule. For the children who do mornings, who do evenings."

"We can work that out."

"I'll make a spreadsheet." I nodded, and I heard myself nodding, as if agreement could stand in for presence, as if logistics could make this bearable.

She stood and moved to the kitchen, her steps purposeful and controlled, as if she were holding herself together by sheer will. She poured water she didn't intend to drink, the glass clinking against the counter, the sound sharp in the silence.

She returned, sat in a different spot on the sofa, creating distance between us—physical space reflecting the emotional gap that had widened over the years, turning into a chasm neither of us knew how to bridge.

"I should go pick them up."

"I'll come with you."

"No need. I can manage."

"I know. But they'll want to see us both."

She looked at me. "They'll want to see us together. Happy. But we're not that anymore, are we?"

"We're still their parents."

"Yes. But not together. And they'll notice." She stood. "You can come. But let's not pretend. Let's be honest with them. As honest as we can be."

* * *

WE TOLD THE CHILDREN TOGETHER. Sat them down on the sofa—Anjali on one side, Prem on the other.

Janani and I are in the middle, trying to explain something we barely understood ourselves, and even as I said it was, we were there, in that moment, trying.

"Your mum and I have decided to live in different places for a while," I said.

"Why?" Anjali asked.

"Because we need some space. To figure things out."

"Are you getting a divorce?" Prem asked.

Janani looked at me. I looked at her. Neither of us had said the word yet. Neither of us had made it real.

"We don't know yet," Janani said. "We're going to try living apart first. See how that feels."

"Will we still see you?" Anjali asked, looking at me.

"Of course. Every week. I'll pick you up from school. We'll have dinner. We'll do all the things we always do."

"But you won't live here."

"No. Not for now."

Tears in Anjali's eyes as her small face crumples, the weight of understanding settling on her shoulders. Prem's face also crumples, his lower lip trembling.

Trembling, his small body shook with uncontrollable sobs. Janani pulled them both close, held them, and whispered to them, her voice steady even as I saw her tears, her pain, and her heart breaking.

I remained, watching, my hands empty, useless, hanging by my sides, as if I'd broken something that couldn't be fixed, as if I'd shattered the one thing that mattered—the one thing I should have protected—and now I could only stand there, helpless, watching the damage I'd caused.

"It's going to be okay," Janani said. "We're still a family. We're going to live in different places."

But I could see in their faces that they didn't believe her.

* * *

THREE DAYS LATER, Prem asked the question.

I'd picked them up from school. Anjali went straight to her room.

But Prem lingered in the kitchen, watching me make tea.

"Appa?"

"Yes, Prem."

He was quiet for a moment, his small hands gripping the edge of the table. "Do you still love Mummy?"

The question caught me off guard. I set the kettle down. Turned to face him.

"Yes. I still love Mummy. Just... differently now."

"What does that mean? Different?"

I knelt. Eye level. His dark eyes searched mine, waiting for an answer that would make sense, that would fix everything.

"It means... we love each other, but we can't live together anymore. Like friends who love each other but need to be in different places."

He nodded. Processed this. Then: "Will you leave us too?"

My throat tightened. "No, Prem. Never. I will always be your Appa. I will always be here. That won't change."

"Promise?"

"Promise."

He crawled into my lap. Eight years old, but still small enough.

I held him. Felt his breathing, the weight of him against my chest, the trust he was still willing to give.

"It's not your fault," I said. "None of this is your fault."

"I know," he said. But I could hear the question in his voice.

The doubt. The fear that maybe, somehow, it was.

I held him tighter. Wished I could protect him from this. From the questions, the uncertainty, and the weight of adult decisions made without his consent.

"I love you, Prem. And Anjali. More than anything. That never changes, no matter where I live."

He nodded against my shoulder. Stayed there for a long moment.

Then he wriggled free, slid off my lap, and went upstairs to join his sister.

I remained kneeling on the kitchen floor. The kettle clicked off.

Steam rose, then disappeared. And I understood, in that moment, the weight of what I'd broken. Not just the marriage. Not just the partnership. But the certainty my children had taken for granted— that their parents would always be together, that home was a fixed point, that love meant always.

I'd shattered that. And no amount of promises could fully repair it.

* * *

THE FIRST WEEK without the children, I didn't know what to do with myself. The house felt too quiet. Too empty. I'd wander from room to room, searching for something to do, something to fill the silence.

I couldn't focus. My mind kept drifting to the children. Were they okay? Were they happy? Did they miss me? Did they hate me?

I called them every night. Anjali would answer, her voice cautious and controlled. She'd tell me about school, her day, or nothing at all.

Prem would sometimes come to the phone, sometimes not. When he did, his voice was small, quiet.

"I miss you," I'd say.

"I miss you too," they'd say.

But the words came out flat. Something we said because we were supposed to, not because we meant it.

The first weekend they returned, I worked too hard. I prepared elaborate meals they didn't want, and planned activities they weren't interested in. I made everything perfect, but they still left on Sunday evening without looking back.

"You don't have to try so hard," Anjali said on Sunday evening, before they left.

"I want to make it good for you."

"It's good. You're here."

But I wasn't sure it was.

* * *

ONE SUNDAY AFTERNOON, Anjali needed help with her homework.

She was working on a family tree project. A simple assignment— Draw your family, write names, and where they came from.

She'd spread her papers across the kitchen table. Coloured pencils scattered. Her handwriting is careful and deliberate.

"Appa, where was your Appa born?"

I was on my laptop. Checking emails and responding to messages.

The work never stopped, not even on weekends.

"Neyveli," I said, not looking up.

"And your Amma?"

"Same. Neyveli."

"And where is that?"

"South India. Tamil Nadu."

I heard her pencil scratching. Then silence.

"Appa?"

"Yes, Anj."

"Can you help me? I don't know how to spell Tamil Nadu."

I looked up. She was watching me, waiting. Her dark eyes, so much like Janani's, focused on me.

I closed my laptop. Moved to the table. Sat beside her.

"T-A-M-I-L- N-A-D-U."

She wrote it carefully. "And what does it mean? Where are you from?"

"Where I grew up. Where my family comes from."

"And do you miss it?"

The question surprised me. "Sometimes. But London is home now. You're here. Amma's here."

She nodded. Continued drawing. I watched her work. She'd drawn a tree. Branches spreading. Names in boxes. Her handwriting was careful, thoughtful.

"Appa?"

"Yes?"

"Are we still a family? Even though you and Mummy don't live together?"

My throat tightened. "Yes, Anj. We're still a family. Just... a different kind."

"Like a broken family?"

"No. Not broken. Different. Some families have parents who live in different houses. But they're still a family."

She looked at me. Really looked. Her eyes searching mine, looking for truth, for certainty, for something to hold onto.

"Okay," she said. But I could hear the doubt. The question. The fear that "different" might be another word for "broken."

She went back to her drawing. I stayed beside her, watching and wanting to help, to explain, to fix it. But knowing I couldn't. Not really. Not in a way that would make it make sense.

My phone buzzed—work email. I felt the pull, the need to check, to respond, to do something that made sense, that I could control.

I ignored it. Stayed at the table. Watched my daughter draw her family tree. A family that looked different now. A family I'd changed.

She finished. Set down her pencil. "Done."

"It looks good," I said.

"Thanks." She gathered her papers and put them in her school bag.

I stayed at the table. My phone buzzed again. Again. I ignored it.

Stayed there, in the kitchen, in the moment, trying to be present and trying to be here.

But my mind kept drifting. To work. To emails. To everything else. Everything except this moment. This child. This attempt to be present that I kept failing.

I'd come back to the table. But I wasn't really here. Not fully. Not the way she needed.

* * *

THE CITIZENSHIP.

Plain envelope. Home Office logo. The letter I'd been waiting for since landing in London eight years earlier arrived.

I sat at the kitchen table in my new flat, the wood grain visible beneath the cheap laminate, with scratches and water rings marking its surface.

I called Janani. She deserved to know.

"It came. The citizenship. The letter arrived today."

My hands trembled slightly as I opened it, the paper crinkling loudly in the silence of my flat, and I held my breath, waiting for the verdict that would decide whether I could stay or had to leave, whether eight years of my life had been enough to earn the right to remain.

"Congratulations." Her voice was careful, measured, distant. "Thank you for everything. For sponsoring me, for all the paperwork you helped with. This wouldn't have happened without you." The words sounded flat, as if I were reading from a script.

"You would have figured it out. You're resourceful."

Silence stretched between us. The phone felt heavy in my hand, the plastic warm from being held too long.

"How are the kids?"

"Fine. Anjali's asking when you're coming for dinner. She misses you."

"Wednesday. It's my night with them. I'll bring pizza. Their favourite kind."

"Wednesday. Yes. I'll let them know."

More silence. The sound of her breathing. Of my own. Of all the things we weren't saying.

"I'm sorry. For all of it, stopping, letting you do everything whilst I just... existed. For forgetting who you were whilst I was working to figure out who I could become."

Her voice was thick when she spoke. "I'm sorry too. For giving up, not fighting harder, letting the resentment build until there was nothing left."

"Do you think we could have fixed it?"

"No. We broke a long time ago, Dev. We didn't admit it until now."

"I know."

"I should go. The kids are home soon."

"Okay. See you on Wednesday."

"Wednesday."

She hung up.

I remained in my flat. Citizenship letter on the table. The thing I'd been working towards for eight years—permission to stay permanently.

* * *

ONE EVENING, I found myself at the same Pret a Manger where Janani and I had met for coffee during our early days of dating. I'd stopped going there after we got married, choosing places closer to work instead. But that evening, I walked past it, saw the familiar tables, the same layout, and went inside.

Ordered my usual—chicken sandwich and coffee. Sat at one of the high tables near the window, the very spot where we'd sat that first Thursday afternoon.

I watched couples at other tables. Easy conversation. Shared meals. I'd had that. Once. And I'd lost it.

I finished my sandwich. Threw away the wrapper.

I walked home, taking the longer route past the places we'd been together. The café where we had our first proper date, the park where we strolled with Anjali when she was a baby, and the street where we first lived after getting married.

By the time I reached my flat, the evening had turned to night.

London's lights spread out below me.

I played Tamil music, filling the flat with familiar melodies- the language of home, childhood, a life left behind. I made tea, savouring the warmth of the cup and steam rising. I sat on the floor, as the sofa still felt unfamiliar and burdened by others' lives, choices, and furniture. I needed a space that was mine, even if it was just the floor, this moment, this music, this tea, and this small space I claimed as my own.

The children came every other weekend. I'd try to make it normal, with pizza dinners, parks, movies. But I could see them watching me, noticing the quiet and absence of their mother, and how the flat didn't feel like a home. "Where's Mummy?" Anjali asked once. Standing in the doorway of the bedroom that only held my things. "At her flat. With Prem."

"When are we all going to be together again?" I had no answer for that.

On weeks when they weren't around, I'd ring my parents. Brief chats. They'd inquire about work, and I'd reply that everything was fine. My mother would ask about the children, and I'd tell her they were well, growing, and happy.

What else could I say?

I'd stopped calling Janani except when I needed to coordinate pickup times or schedule changes, the bare minimum of necessary information.

* * *

THE ENVELOPE CAME in the post on a Tuesday.

It was thicker than everything else that morning. Council tax reminders. School newsletters. A bank statement I didn't open.

This one was heavy. Stiff with finality.

I stood in the hallway holding it for a long time. Keys still in my hand. The flat was quiet. No children, background radio, rushed mornings.

The hum of the refrigerator and the faint sound of water moving through pipes in someone else's flat.

I opened the envelope at the kitchen counter.

The words were exactly what the solicitor said they would be: transparent, impersonal, and efficient. We had agreed on everything already.

I signed where I was supposed to, initialled the margins, and dated the last page.

My handwriting looked steadier than my hands.

I left the papers on the counter and made tea. The kettle clicked off.

Steam rose. I poured the water and forgot the teabag.

I sat at the table with a mug of hot water and the divorce papers between my hands.

I didn't take them down.

That evening, I stepped into the bedroom.

Her side of the wardrobe was empty. Not half-empty. Empty.

I stood there for a long time. Looking at the space. The hangers were gone too. Not clothes. Everything. Like she'd never existed in this space.

I opened the drawer on my side, found a shirt I'd been looking for weeks. It had been tangled with her things. Now it was alone, folded, waiting.

I took off my wedding ring. Held it in my palm. Light. Gold. A circle.

Nothing more.

I opened the drawer. Set it inside. Closed the drawer.

I reached for it without thinking. Felt the bare skin—the absence.

* * *

I PAUSED.

244

"That's how it was. The period after separation. Sleepless nights. Mechanical workdays. The sense of being unmoored." Claire waited.

"I didn't even know what was happening."

"But you're here now."

Claire waited. Let the silence sit. Then: "What is emptiness?"

"I don't know. The absence of feeling?"

"Is it?"

I was quiet. "I can't say."

"What would it mean if it wasn't?"

"And what's the difference? Between disappearing and stopping feeling?"

I thought about it. "I'm not sure. Maybe... I didn't disappear. I was still there. Physically. But I stopped feeling."

"What does that mean? Physically but not emotionally?"

* * *

THE FOLLOWING WEEK, I sat in Claire's office. The same chair, the same view, but I sat straighter, my shoulders less tense.

"How are you?" she asked.

"I've been thinking about what you said. About the difference between disappearing and stopping feeling."

"And?"

"I think I understand it now. I was still there. Physically. But I stopped feeling."

Claire nodded. "And where did that show up most clearly? Where did you notice it?"

I thought about it. "With the children. Anjali and Prem. I changed nappies. I fed them. I played with them."

"Tell me about that. About being with them physically but not being present."

"I'd be reading them a bedtime story, but my mind would be at work. I'd be playing with them, but I'd be thinking about deadlines, about meetings, about everything except them."

"What happens in your body as you think about that? About being with them but not being present?"

"Heaviness. Sadness. Like I was failing them. Like I was letting them down."

"And what do you think you were teaching them? By being there but not being present?"

"That work mattered more than they did. That being present didn't matter. That disappearance was normal."

Claire was quiet. "And what were you doing with your voice? With your accent? With the way you spoke to them?"

I paused. "I was speaking in a way that was professional, distant, and removed. Not the way I spoke to them when they were babies." My hands were cold, the warmth having left them.

"And why do you think you did that?"

"I'd done it for so long that I didn't know how to turn it off. Even with my own children. Even at home." The words tasted bitter, as old coffee left too long.

"And what did that cost them?"

I was quiet. Everything. Their father, his presence, his real voice, his authentic self. Outside, a siren wailed in the distance, its sound fading as it moved away.

"They didn't get me. They got a version of me, a professional version, a shifted version."

"And what do you want to do about that now?"

"I want to be present. To show up. To be there. Not just physically. Emotionally. To speak to them in my real voice. To be the father they deserve. The father I want to be."

Claire nodded. "What would that look like? Being present for them?"

"I don't know. Maybe... speaking in my real voice. Not the corporate version."

Outside, rain had started, a fine mist that makes everything look blurred at the edges. I stood under the awning, watching the water bead on the pavement.

PART VI
WHAT REMAINS

Where choosing becomes possible

THE UNMAKING

I walked in, sat, and looked at my hands.

"Dev?"

"I'm fine."

"You're not fine. Your hands are shaking."

I looked at them. "I didn't notice."

"What happened this week?"

"Nothing. Everything. I just… stopped."

"Stopped what?"

"Eating. Calling people. Functioning."

* * *

JANANI MOVED out on a Saturday in March.

Two suitcases by the door. The moving van idled outside, exhaust mixing with the cold morning air.

We told the children the night before. Anjali was ten. Prem was eight.

Anjali stood in the doorway, arms crossed. Her school jumper still had a stain from lunch the day before.

"Why are you leaving?"

249

Janani knelt so they were eye level. "I'll see you all the time. Every week."

"Are you and Daddy getting divorced?"

Janani looked at me. I nodded. "Yes."

Prem said nothing. He pressed his forehead to the window, watching the van.

The driver knocked. Janani stood, brushed off her knees, and looked around the hallway as if memorising it—the hooks, the shoes, the ordinary evidence of daily life.

After the van pulled away, the three of us sat in the living room.

Anjali's eyes filled. Prem held her hand.

"Is it my fault?"

"No."

"But we won't all be together anymore."

"No," I said. "We won't."

She buried her face in my shoulder. Prem sat rigid beside her, gripping her hand as if anchoring her.

* * *

THE DIVORCE DID NOT ARRIVE as a rupture. It assembled itself.

Through emails that stayed polite. Conversations that repeated themselves. Decisions deferred until they became irreversible.

Janani moved through the flat carefully, as if sound required permission. Papers were signed. Evenings rearranged. Our shared life is separated into columns.

Eventually, the divorce was finalised.

* * *

THE FIRST WEEKS alone with the children were chaotic.

Anjali needed to be at school by 8:30. Prem was required to practice the violin before nine. I had work calls at nine. The arithmetic never worked.

I burned breakfast. Forgot lunches. Sent Prem to school twice in one week with mismatched socks. The second time, he didn't mention it. He looked down at his feet, then back up, deciding it wasn't worth asking.

"Where's Mum?" he asked one morning, eating cereal straight from the box.

"Her flat."

"When's she coming back?"

"Friday after school."

He nodded. Then said, "Dad, why do we have so many spoons but only one that's the right size for cereal?"

I opened the drawer. He was right.

"That's strange," he said, and poured more cereal, milk dripping onto his shirt before I noticed.

At night, after they slept, I sat in the living room with the television low. It filled the space but didn't reach me. Time passed. I watched it do so.

* * *

IN APRIL, we filed for divorce.

The solicitor's office was in Holborn. Neutral colours. Beige walls. Grey carpet that absorbed sound. A desk with spreadsheets that would determine our future.

Custody. Assets. Child support. Boxes to tick.

"Shared custody?" the solicitor asked.

"Fifty-fifty," Janani said.

"Agreed."

"The house?"

"I'll keep it," I said. "Buy out Janani's share."

"I'm renting," Janani said. "Nearby."

The solicitor explained the process—conditional order, waiting period, final order—the bureaucracy of undoing a life.

"Any chance of reconciliation?"

Janani and I looked at each other.

"No," we said.

* * *

MY MOTHER CALLED on a Sunday afternoon.

The children were with Janani. The house was quiet. I'd been working. Or pretending to work. Sitting at my laptop, staring at the screen, not really seeing anything.

The phone rang. I almost didn't answer. But it was my mother.

I hadn't spoken to her in weeks.

"Dev?"

Her voice. Warm. Familiar. The voice of home, of Neyveli, of everything I'd left behind.

"Amma. How are you?"

"I'm fine. Your father is fine. How are you?"

"Fine."

Silence. The kind that meant she knew I was lying. My mother could hear it in my voice. The flatness. The absence.

"Dev, what's wrong?"

"Nothing, Amma. Just tired. Work is busy."

"And Janani? The children? How are they?"

I paused. Wondered what to say. How to explain. How to make it make sense in Tamil, in the language of home, in the context of a culture where divorce was still whispered about, still something that happened to other families.

"They're fine. Anjali is ten now. Prem is eight."

"And Janani?"

"She's... fine. She's moved out. We're separated."

The silence stretched. I could hear her breathing. The sound of the fan in Neyveli. The distant sound of the street outside.

"Separated?"

"Yes."

"Divorce?"

"We're... working through it."

"Dev, what happened?"

What could I say? That I'd stopped showing up? That I'd disappeared? That I'd worked myself into a fog, a state where I couldn't be present, couldn't be here?

"It's complicated, Amma. We grew apart."

"But you have children. Two children. How can you grow apart when you have children together?"

I had no answer. Or too many answers. None that would make sense to her.

To a woman who'd stayed with my father for forty years, who'd made it work, who'd shown up, who'd been present, who'd never disappeared, never stopped feeling, never stopped choosing.

"It's different here, Amma. In London. Things are different."

"Different how? Love is love. Family is family. That doesn't change because of where you live."

I closed my eyes. Felt the weight of her words. The truth in them. The judgment. The disappointment.

"I know, Amma."

"When are you coming home? To Neyveli?"

"I don't know. Work is busy. The children..."

"The children need their father. And you need your family. Your home."

"I know."

"Come home, Dev, just for a week. Your father and I miss you. We want to see the children."

"I'll try, Amma. I'll see."

"Don't see. Come. Family matters. More than work. More than everything."

"I know."

"Do you? Because sometimes I wonder. Sometimes I think you've forgotten what matters."

The words stung. Because they were true. I had forgotten. Or not forgotten. Just... stopped choosing. Stopped showing up. Stopped being present.

"I'll come, Amma. Soon."

"Good. We'll be waiting."

We said goodbye. I hung up. Sat there in the quiet house.

Listening to the silence. The absence.

My mother was right. I'd forgotten what mattered. Or I'd stopped choosing it and stopped showing up for it. Stopped being present for it. Family. Home. The people who mattered.

I'd left them behind. Not just geographically. Not just physically. But emotionally. I'd disappeared, even from myself.

The phone sat on the table. Silent. Heavy. A reminder of what

I'd left behind what I'd stopped choosing, what I'd stopped showing up for.

* * *

WE SETTLED INTO A RHYTHM. Week on, week off. Transitions on Sunday afternoons.

Weeks with the children were structured: early mornings, school drop-offs, work calls, homework, dinner, baths, bedtime stories. I learned through failure—meal prep, alarms, shared calendars, buffers for late trains and sick days.

Sometimes Janani texted, *"Prem forgot his music book."*

Sometimes I texted, *"Anjali's PE kit is still here."*

We became efficient. Civil. Two managers handing over responsibility on schedule.

Weeks without the children were quieter.

The house felt larger. The stairs are louder. The refrigerator is accusatory in its constancy.

* * *

THE ENVELOPE ARRIVED ON A TUESDAY.

Plain white. Official crest.

"Final Order."

Ten years of marriage reduced to a single page. I filed it away where paperwork belongs. I didn't frame it or destroy it. I treated it like what it had become: documentation.

* * *

THE CHILDREN ADJUSTED FASTER than I expected.

They stopped asking when we'd all be together. They packed their bags on Sundays without reminders. They learned which clothes belonged in which house.

"Do you like it better this way?" I asked Anjali once.

We were making pasta—the one meal I could cook reliably.

"You and Mum don't fight anymore," she said. "That's better."

"Are we happier?"

"I don't know," she said. "But you're not pretending."

* * *

I WAS FORTY-FIVE. Divorced. A parent half the time.

Still in the same house in Walthamstow, because it was where the children lived. The same street. The same rooms, empty every other week.

* * *

I WITHDREW WITHOUT NOTICING.

Missed calls accumulated. Invitations declined. Eventually, they stopped coming.

I ate poorly. Stopped shopping. Let takeaway containers pile up.

I functioned. That was all.

With the children, I performed competence—packed lunches, asked the right questions, and kept the machine running.

Inside it, I shut down.

* * *

ONE SATURDAY, while the children were with Janani, I opened the fridge.

Expired milk. Wilted vegetables. Food gone bad.

I threw everything away. Cleaned the shelves. Wiped the counters.

I picked up toys in the living room, placed them in boxes, then left them there, unlabeled.

The disorder wasn't physical. It was me.

I sat on the floor among the toys, then stood and put them back. Leaving the mess visible felt more honest.

* * *

AMIR NOTICED.

He'd been there since Dubai. The one who explained systems without condescension. The one who made foreign places survivable.

Now he called.

"You haven't been to the pub in weeks."

"Busy."

"With what?"

"Work. Kids. Life."

A pause. "If you need anything…"

"I know."

He hung up. I stayed where I was.

* * *

ONE EVENING, the doorbell rang.

"I made curry," Amir said. "Too much."

He walked in, set the food down, and looked around.

"You're not doing well."

"I'm managing."

"Managing isn't living."

We ate in silence. The food was warm, spiced, grounding.

"How are the kids?"

"They're okay."

"And you?"

256

"I'm fine."

He stayed. Talked. Listened.

When he left, he hugged me.

"Call me," he said. "Anytime."

* * *

"I HIT BOTTOM," I said. "Stopped eating properly. Stopped calling people. Amir saw it."

"And that's when he intervened," Claire said.

"Yes."

"What do you feel when you think about him seeing you?"

"Relief," I said. "And fear."

"Fear of what?"

"Being seen."

She nodded. "And now?"

"I'm starting to see myself."

I stood, walked to the door, then turned back.

"Thank you," I said.

"For what?"

"For not letting me disappear."

FRAGMENTATION

$\mathcal{I}$ walked into Claire's office, sat, said nothing, and waited for her to begin.

"You've been quiet," Claire said. "What's happening?"

"I'm seeing it now. All of it. The patterns. The damage. I can't unsee it."

"What happens in your body as you see it?"

"Heaviness. Pain. As if I'm splintering."

"Tell me about splintering."

"It doesn't feel like progress. It feels like destruction."

"What's the difference between splintering and seeing what was always there?"

I thought about it. "Seeing is awareness. Splintering is what it feels like while it happens."

I looked at my hands. "I'm already changing. I'm here. I'm talking."

* * *

THE FIRST THREE months of therapy were brutal.

Week three. I sat in the same chair, with the same view of the window, but something had shifted. I was noticing things: how my shoulders tensed when I walked in, how I automatically straightened my posture, how my voice prepared itself before I even opened my mouth.

Claire noticed too. "What are you noticing?"

"My shoulders. They tense. My voice. It prepares itself. Before I even sit down."

"What does that feel like?"

"Exhausting. I can't turn it off."

"You don't need to turn it off. You need to understand why it happens—what triggers it."

I opened my notebook. I'd written down the homework assignment, every instance of switching, every moment I'd noticed myself becoming someone else. The pages were filled, more than I'd expected.

"Read me one."

I flipped through the pages and found one from last Tuesday. "Work meeting. Helen walked in, senior partner. My voice changed immediately, more formal, more British, as if I were trying to match her accent."

"Did you notice it in the moment?"

"No. After about an hour, reviewing my notes, I realised my voice had been different, and I hadn't noticed."

She nodded. Made a note. "What did you notice, exactly?"

"That I'd shifted into performance and didn't know I was doing it until after."

"How do I stop it?"

"You don't. Not yet. First you learn to catch it. Then you learn to pause. Then you learn to choose. That takes time."

She leaned forward. "You need to learn what it feels like in your body right before the switch. There's a signal. A tightening. A shift in your breathing. We're going to help you notice it."

"I'm not sure I can."

"You can. But it takes practice, like learning a language. At first, you translate everything. Then it becomes automatic. This is the reverse—making the automatic visible again."

I closed my notebook. "It feels as if I'm coming undone. As if there's no real me underneath, just versions."

* * *

WEEK EIGHT.

"Something happened—school pickup," I said. "Anjali's teacher came over. Started talking about her maths scores."

"What happened?"

"My shoulders went up. My voice got higher. More eager to please. I caught it. Mid-sentence."

"What did you do?"

"I stopped. Took a breath. Let my shoulders drop. Then I continued, but slower. In my actual voice."

Claire leaned forward. "How did that feel?"

"Terrifying. Like I was doing it wrong. Like she'd notice."

"For speaking in your actual voice?"

I nodded. "Yeah. Like my real voice is wrong."

"It kept you safe before," Claire said.

"What would it mean if it were safe to be you?"

"I can't say."

* * *

MONTH FOUR OF THERAPY.

"I had an episode. Work call with a client. His voice was sharp, demanding things we couldn't deliver. The tone made everything feel wrong—made me feel small."

"What happened?"

"My voice disappeared. Not physically, but I couldn't access it. My accent flattened. Everything went corporate, perfect, professional. I was watching it happen like I was outside my body— floating above myself, disconnected."

261

"I couldn't stop it even though I was watching it. I couldn't make myself here."

"Did you try the grounding?"

"After the call ended. I looked for five things I could see, starting with my feet on the floor. It took ten minutes to come back."

Claire was quiet. "What happened just now?"

"I noticed it while it was happening."

"And before?"

"I wouldn't have noticed until days later. Maybe not at all."

She nodded. "What's different?"

"I'm more aware."

* * *

SIX MONTHS IN. A work meeting.

Helen walked in. Senior partner. British accent. The kind that made me feel scrutinised. My shoulders tensed, my breath shortened, my voice prepared itself.

I recognised the signal—the tightening in my chest, the bracing. My mind is searching for the right words, the correct version of myself.

I stopped mid-sentence. Put my feet flat on the floor. Felt the ground beneath me. Noticed the table, the pen, the window, the chair. In, out. In, out.

Then I continued, slower, in my real voice—the one with hints of Tamil Nadu, years in Dubai, and a decade in London blended. Not the polished version. Not the performance.

Helen noticed. "You sound different today."

"Do I?"

"More you. It's less like you're reading from a script."

I smiled—really smiled, not the polite work smile. Thank you.

She looked at me. "You seem more present."

"I am. I'm working to be."

"Good. It suits you."

* * *

ONE EVENING, between sessions, I practised the grounding techniques at home. The flat was quiet. The children were with Janani.

I sat on the floor, back against the sofa, breathing steadily.

Five things I could see: the lamp on my desk, the book on the floor, the window, the chair, and my hands.

I opened my eyes and looked properly—shadows from the lamp, the curl of the book's pages, streetlights reflected in the window, wood grain through varnish, the lines and scars in my hands.

Four things I could touch: my shirt fabric, the desk wood, the paper of the book, and the cold windowpane.

Three things I could hear: traffic outside, the refrigerator hum, my own breathing.

Claire had said: Your body needs to learn that you're here, now. Present.

I did it every day—in the morning before work, in the evening before bed, and when I felt myself starting to drift.

Sometimes it worked. Sometimes I still floated above myself. But even then, it helped.

* * *

ONE SATURDAY MORNING, about six months into therapy, Anjali came into my room while I was doing the exercise.

I was sitting on the floor, back against the bed, eyes closed.

"What are you doing?"

I opened my eyes. "Practising."

"Practising what?"

"A technique Dr Claire taught me. For when I feel disconnected."

She sat beside me, cross-legged. "Can I try?"

"Sure. Close your eyes. Let's start with four things you can touch."

She closed her eyes. "My pyjamas, the carpet, my hair, my hands."

"Good. Three things you can hear."

"Your breathing. The heater. An aeroplane."

"Two things you can smell."

"Breakfast. Your shampoo."

"One thing you can taste."

She stuck out her tongue. "Nothing. Maybe toothpaste."

I laughed. "Perfect."

"Did it help?" she asked. "Do you feel more… here?"

I thought about it. "Yes. Actually, I do."

"Then I'll do it too when I'm scared," she said. "Will you remind me?"

"Of course."

She hugged me quickly. "You're better, Appa. More here. I like it."

"I'm glad."

"Me too," she said. "Because before, sometimes it felt like you were somewhere else even when you were in the room."

* * *

MONTH FIFTEEN. A session about choices.

I sat in the same chair, the same view. Different now—able to see the patterns.

"I keep going back to the marriage," I said. "What if I'd fought harder? Gone to therapy earlier? Noticed sooner?"

"What do you think would have changed?" Claire asked.

"Maybe we'd still be together. Or maybe I'd only have delayed the inevitable."

"And the choices," she said. "Not calling home and working late. Not showing up. What was underneath them?"

I was quiet. "Attempts at control. Controlling by avoiding. If I stayed busy, I didn't have to feel. If I worked late, I didn't have to be present. If I didn't call, I didn't have to remember what I'd left behind."

"Understanding doesn't excuse it," I said. "It explains it."

"And what does understanding allow?"

"Change," I said. "That's where it begins."

* * *

EIGHTEEN MONTHS INTO THERAPY, Dr Claire asked, "Who are you, Dev?"

"I'm someone who learned to survive by becoming whoever was needed."

"What else comes up?"

"Someone who destroyed his marriage by never being there. Who let his wife carry everything? Who chose work over connection? Safety over vulnerability."

"What happens when you think about dissociation?"

"It made it easier to drift without noticing. But I still made choices. I still chose to work late, to avoid conversations, to withdraw."

Claire was quiet. "And now?"

"I don't want to disappear from my own life anymore."

"It's not too late," I said. "I can still choose to be present."

* * *

BY THE SECOND year of therapy, I'd made changes.

I quit the fintech job. I started consulting—nonprofits, refugee organisations, small businesses that mattered. Work that felt authentic rather than performed.

The children noticed.

"You seem more like yourself, Dad," Anjali said one evening. She was taller now. Eleven.

"Do you know what that means?" I asked. "More like myself?"

"Yeah," she said. "Before, you were always trying to be what we needed. Now you're just… you."

I pulled her into a hug. "Thank you."

"You're our dad," she said. "That's how it works."

* * *

ANJALI'S SCHOOL had a presentation day. Parents invited. She'd been working on it for weeks. A project about migration. About her family. About her grandparents in Neyveli, her parents in London, the journey between.

She'd told me about it and asked if I was coming.

"Of course," I'd said.

The day before, work called. A client meeting. Important. High stakes. They needed me there.

"I can't," I said.

"Dev, this is a major contract. We need you."

"I committed to my daughter's school presentation."

"Can't you reschedule?"

"No."

The word came out clear. Certain. I'd said it before I'd even thought about it. Before I'd considered the consequences, the cost, the possibility of losing the client.

"Are you sure?"

"Yes. I'm sure."

I hung up. Called Anjali's school and confirmed the time. Made sure I could be there.

The next morning, I arrived early. Found a seat in the back. Watched the other presentations. Listened. Really listened. Not thinking about work, about emails, about everything else. Just here. Present.

Then it was Anjali's turn.

She walked to the front. Nervous. Eleven years old, but still small in front of the room. She looked at me. I smiled. Nodded. You can do this.

She began. Her voice is unmistakable. Confident. She talked about Neyveli.

About the bougainvillea in her grandmother's garden. About the journey to London. About having two homes. Two languages. Two

worlds.

"My Appa came from Neyveli," she said. "He came to London to build a life. And he did. And now we're here. And we're a family. And that's enough."

Her words. Simple. Clear. True.

She finished. The room clapped. She looked at me. Smiled. Relieved. Proud.

Afterwards, I went up to her. Hugged her.

"You were brilliant," I said. "Really brilliant."

"You came."

"Of course I came. I said I would."

"But usually work..." She stopped. Didn't finish the sentence. Didn't need to.

"Not this time," I said. "You're more important. This was more important."

She looked at me. Really looked. As if seeing me for the first time. As if recognising something new, something different, something she'd been waiting for.

"Thanks, Appa."

"You're welcome."

We walked out together. Her hand in mine. The way it used to be. The way I'd forgotten it could be.

My phone buzzed. Work. Again. Multiple messages. The client was upset. Wanted to reschedule. Wanted to know if I was available tomorrow.

I read them. Felt the pull, the need to respond, to fix it, to make it right. The old pattern. The old response.

I put my phone away. Looked at my daughter. At her face, bright with pride. The way she was walking, taller, more confident.

"Do you want to get ice cream?" I asked.

"Really? Right now?"

"Yes. Right now. Just us."

She smiled. "Yes. Let's go."

We walked to the ice cream shop. Talked about her presentation. About Neyveli. About her grandmother. About the bougainvillea.

"Do you miss it?" she asked. "Neyveli?"

"Sometimes. But London is home. You're here. Your mum is here.

That's enough."

"Is it? Really?"

"Yes. Really."

We ate our ice cream. Sat on a bench. Watched the city go by.

My phone buzzed. Again. I ignored it. Stayed there. Present. Here. With my daughter. In this moment. It was enough. This. This moment. This child. This choice to be present.

It was more than enough.

* * *

THAT EVENING, after we'd returned home, Anjali asked about the Tamil words in her presentation.

"How do you say 'home' in Tamil?" she asked.

"Veedu," I said.

"Veedu." She tried the word. The sounds are unfamiliar to her tongue. "And 'family'?"

"Kudumbam."

"Kudumbam." She tried it again. "What about 'I love you'?"

"Naan unnai kaadhalikkiren."

"That's long."

"Yes. But it's clear. Direct. No ambiguity."

She smiled. "Say it again."

"Naan unnai kaadhalikkiren."

"Naan unnai..." She paused. "I can't remember the rest."

"Kaadhalikkiren."

"Kaadhalikkiren."

"Good. Very good."

"Will you teach me more? Tamil words?"

"Of course. What do you want to learn?"

"Everything. Words for things I know. Things I don't know. Words my grandmother uses. Words you used to use."

"I'll teach you. We can do it together. You and Prem both."

"And will you speak Tamil with us? Sometimes?"

I paused. Thought about it. About the language of home, of childhood, of my mother. About sharing it with my children. About reconnecting with something I'd put aside, something I'd forgotten, something I'd stopped choosing.

"Yes. I'll speak Tamil with you. Sometimes. When we're alone. When you want to practice."

"Good. Because I want to talk to Paati properly. In Tamil. Like you do."

"Like I used to do."

"You still can."

"Yes. I still can. I just... stopped. Forgot. Got busy."

"Well, now you can remember. With us."

"Yes. Now I can remember."

We sat there together. She was with her notebook, writing down words. I'm teaching her. The sounds of Tamil fill the room.

The language of home, of my mother, of Neyveli, of everything I'd left it behind, but it was still mine, still part of me, still something I could share, could teach, could pass on.

"What about 'father'?" she asked.

"Appa."

"Appa." She smiled. "I already know that one."

"Yes. You already know that one."

She wrote it down. Then: "And 'mother'?"

"Amma."

"Amma." She wrote it. Looked at the words on her page. "So many words. So many things to learn."

"Yes. But we have time. We can learn together."

"Okay. Appa?"

"Yes?"

"Thanks for teaching me. For remembering. For being here."

"I'm glad to be here. Really."

"Me too. I'm glad you're here, too. Really here. Not just physically."

Her words. Simple. Clear. True.

I was really here. Not just physically. But present. Engaged. Connected.

Teaching my daughter Tamil. The language of home. The language of my mother. The language of Neyveli. The language of everything I'd left behind but was still mine, still part of me, still something I could share.

"Let's do this again tomorrow," she said.

"Yes. Tomorrow. And the day after. And the day after that."

"Okay. Deal."

"Deal."

We shook hands. Laughed. Then she went upstairs to her room. To her life. Her world.

I stayed in the kitchen. Looking at the words she'd written.

The Tamil words. The words of home. The words I was teaching her. Passing on. "Veedu" -Home. "Kudumbam"- Family.

"Naan unnai kaadhalikkiren"- I love you.

The words mattered. The language mattered. The connection mattered.

I was remembering. Reconnecting. Choosing again. Choosing to be present. Choosing to share. Choosing to be here.

Really here.

* * *

I PAUSED.

"That's how it was," I said. "The therapy. Learning to see myself. Learning to be present."

"What are you seeing now?" Claire asked.

270

"I'm here. I'm present. But I still don't know if it's enough."

"Enough for what?"

I didn't answer.

"Not being enough for someone else and being enough for your-self," Claire said. "We'll continue. Next week, we'll talk about what comes next."

I walked out into the London afternoon. The air smelled of exhaust and damp earth. The sky was a uniform grey.

LEARNING TO TEND

"Two years into therapy, I walked into Claire's office and settled into the familiar chair.

"How are you?" she asked.

"Better. Present. More aware."

"You've done the work. You've changed."

"I have."

"You're ready. For what comes next. The work continues, but now you're ready to live it."

"Thank you. For all of it."

"You're welcome. Keep coming. Weekly. For as long as you need. But you're ready."

* * *

THE CONSULTING WORK found its rhythm. I helped eight nonprofits, mainly refugee organisations, navigating visas and documentation-boring but familiar. Endless forms, multiplying documents, interviews to prove worth, months of waiting, and the fear that a missing paper, misunderstood question, or policy change could end it all.

I'd sit with people who'd fled war, persecution, and violence, helping them fill out forms that asked to quantify their trauma and justify their existence. I saw in their eyes the same fear I'd carried: being sent back, losing the life you built, or being told you didn't belong.

Then, one Tuesday afternoon, my email pinged.

I was working from home, reviewing a grant application for a refugee resettlement charity, spreadsheets open, the numbers beginning to blur.

The notification appeared in the corner of my screen. I clicked without thinking.

The name made me stop breathing. Maya Krishnan.

The room fell silent. The traffic outside faded. My hands stilled on the keyboard.

I clicked it open.

Hi Dev,

I understand this might come as a surprise. Prerna mentioned you're now in London and that you and Janani have separated. I'm also in London now, relocating here permanently to expand our operations and establish our UK base.

I'd love to see you. Not to dwell on the past, but to catch up and see how you're doing.

Are you available this week? Coffee? Lunch?

Maya

I read it, reread it, read it a third time, slower, as if the words might rearrange themselves into something comprehensible.

Maya, here in London.

Fourteen years since Dubai, since we'd last spoken, since I'd watched her walk away with her back straight and her eyes fixed ahead, not looking back.

I pushed my chair away from the desk, rose, moved to the window, gazed out at the wet London street below, puddles reflecting the street-lamps in fragmented light.

Prerna, of course. She'd moved to London a year after I did and worked in fintech. We met for coffee every few months. I'd mentioned the divorce in passing, in a casual conversation, as a fact.

I hadn't considered that Maya would know. Hadn't thought she'd reach out.

I went back to my desk.

Typed:

Hi Maya.

Yes, I'm in London. Coffee would be good. This week works. Name a time and place.

Dev

I pressed send before I could delete it again. She replied within an hour.

Thursday, 3 PM. The coffee shop in Clerkenwell. The one with the outdoor seating. You'll know it.

I closed the email. Opened it again. Closed it.
The name sat there in my inbox. Maya Krishnan. Thursday.

* * *

THURSDAY CAME, and I'd spent two days unable to concentrate. Work piled up, emails unanswered. I'd stare at my screen, Maya's name floating in my mind.

The coffee shop was exactly as she'd described: Clerkenwell, with outdoor seating despite the October chill. The tables outside were mostly empty. A few smokers huddled in corners, coats pulled tightly around them.

I arrived ten minutes early, ordered a flat white, found a table at the back where I could see the door, and sat with my back against the wall, an old habit.

The coffee arrived, too hot. I held the cup, let it burn my palms. Then the door opened.

She walked in.

Fourteen years, yet her manner remained the same: shoulders back, confident stride, eyes scanning the room, taking everything in, assessing, calculating—just as she always had, as she moved through Dubai, through boardrooms.

Her hair was shorter, black, and sharply cut. She wore a black coat that looked expensive, tailored to her frame, and carried a leather bag that was structured, not slouchy — a statement piece. Everything about her was deliberate, from her choices to her every detail.

She saw me. Stopped. Then smiled.

Not the bright, challenging smile from Dubai that made every-thing else fade. Softer. More measured. But still Maya. Still, the woman who had built companies. Still, the woman who had risked everything. Still, the woman who had walked away.

She crossed the room. Pulled out the chair across from me without asking and settled into it as if she owned the space.

Fourteen years. And she still moved that way. Still sat that way. Still studied me that way.

"Dev."

Her voice. The same. Irish accent still there, but softer. I rose. We didn't hug, just remained.

"You look good."

"You too."

She caught the waiter's eye. Raised a finger. "Espresso, please."

We settled into our chairs. She unbuttoned her coat but didn't take it off.

"Prerna said you're divorced."

"Separated. I divorced a couple of years ago. Final."

She nodded. Looked down at her hands. "I'm sorry. That must have been hard."

"It was."

"You're in therapy?"

"Yes."

The espresso arrived. She held the cup but didn't drink. Warmed her hands around it.

I've been in London for six months now. Moving headquarters here.

Building a life.

How is it?

It's quiet and different. She examined her hands before looking up at me. Dubai was noisy. Everything felt urgent, critical, and life-or-death. Here, it's calmer, quieter, slower, and more settled. I'm unsure how to be at ease.

She turned to face me.

Fourteen years, Dev. I've thought about you over the years, wondered what happened to you, where you went, if you were happy, and whether you'd found what you were searching for.

She paused, put the espresso down untouched. Her hand trembled slightly. She noticed, pulled it back, and put it in her lap.

When Prerna told me about your divorce, I was at a loss for what to do. Part of me thought maybe I shouldn't, perhaps it's been too long, we're different people now, and it's too late.

Silence. The kind that stretches, the kind that makes you aware of every breath, every heartbeat, every moment passing.

But I'd always wonder then. What if we'd tried? What if we'd been different people? Older. More settled. What if we'd been brave enough? What if we'd been ready?

She looked away, out the window at the October light, grey and flat, back at me.

I'm asking you to consider something. I'm not good at putting myself out there, you know that. I'm good at building companies and taking risks, but this? This is different. This is harder.

"Maya."

"I know you're in therapy. I know you need time. But I'm here. In London. For good. And I'm asking if you'd consider... us. If we could try again. Now that we're different. Now that we're both alone."

She picked up the espresso. Her hand trembled slightly. She set it down again.

"I don't need an answer now. But I need to know. Because I can't keep wondering."

"How long?"

"A month. That's enough time. Enough to think. To decide." She paused.

"I'll be here. Same place. Same time. Four weeks from today. If you come, we'll talk. If you don't... I'll know."

She rose. Put money on the table. More than the espresso cost. "I hope you come."

I remained there. The table was empty except for my cooling coffee and her untouched espresso. The money she'd left.

I watched the cup. Still warm.

* * *

MAYA'S WORDS. I can't stop wondering. Her hand was trembling on the cup. The untouched espresso. They lingered with me. I'd wake up thinking about them, go to sleep thinking about them.

One evening, my phone rang. It was Janani. "Dev, can we meet? I need to talk to you."

"Are the kids okay?"

"They're fine. Can you meet tomorrow? That café in Hackney. Near the canal. One o'clock?"

"Yes."

I hung up.

* * *

THE HACKNEY CAFÉ was small and intimate, like a secret, with warm lighting on wooden tables. Windows overlooked the canal, reflecting grey, muted sky—creating a peaceful, monochrome palette. Everything was soft and muted, as if the city was holding its breath, creating an atmosphere that makes you lower your voice and want to stay.

Janani was already there when I arrived, sitting by the window with a cup of tea. She looked different—her hair was shorter, and she wore a dark green jumper I'd never seen before. She seemed settled, comfortable, as if she'd found her place or built something.

I ordered a coffee and sat opposite her. The table was small, and our knees nearly touched. I could smell her perfume, the same one she had always worn, the same scent I had forgotten I remembered.

"Thanks for coming."

"Of course."

"I left because I was withering. I had to prove I could build a life on my own terms. And I did." She studied me, seeing me for the first time,

working to decide if I was real, if I was here, if I was the person she'd left or someone new.

She paused. The silence stretched, a hush that makes you aware of every breath, every heartbeat, every moment passing.

"I've built a good life on my own. Everything I wanted, I've created. The job, flat, routines, peace, quiet. The space to be myself. To not shrink, disappear, carry everything alone." Her words were laconic, precise, each one measured.

She looked out at the canal, back at me.

"But I've been thinking about you, about us, about whether there's space in the life I've built for someone who's here now. Not the person you were, the person who disappeared, the person who let me carry everything. But someone who's actually here, someone who's engaged."

I waited. Because I wasn't sure what to say, I wasn't sure if I was that person, and I wasn't sure if I could be—the weight of the question pressed against my chest.

"I've decided I want to find out. But only if it fits. Only if it adds, not takes from it. I'm not going back to making myself smaller or to carrying everything. I've proven I can do it alone. Now I'm choosing to see if we can do it together. Differently."

She paused, looked out at the canal, the water, the grey light.

"If we attempt this and you disappear again, I'm walking away— no second chances, explanations, or attempting again. I'll walk away, and I won't look back. Because I've learned that I can, that I don't need you."

I took a breath. "I take responsibility for disappearing. I own that. But you've built everything. How am I going to make it any better? What am I filling in?"

She was quiet.

"I didn't fight when you asked for separation. What makes you think I'll live up to your expectations now?"

"I'm not asking you to live on eggshells."

"That's what it feels like."

* * *

WE BEGAN MEETING REGULARLY- JUST CONVERSATIONS, coffee, walks- not dates or romantic efforts. We talked about children, work, life, learning to be together without expectations or pressure. Initially cautious, guarded, and protective of ourselves, weeach waited for disappointment, for things to fall apart, and for the pattern to repeat.

One Tuesday, we met for coffee. I arrived early and sat at a table by the window, watching the canal, the water, the grey light, and the city moving. Life was ongoing. My palms were damp. I checked my phone three times, although I knew she wasn't late. This felt different —significant, as if it truly mattered.

Janani arrived, sat down, and ordered tea. We talked about the children, work, and nothing else. Yet it felt careful and guarded, as if we were both holding back, protecting ourselves, waiting.

"This is hard," I said. "What is?"

"This. Being here. With you. Working to rebuild, to trust, to hope."

"I know."

"Are you scared?"

"Terrified."

"Me too."

"But we're here. We're working at it."

"It is."

We remained there in the silence.

* * *

ONE SATURDAY, we took the children to the park. Anjali and Prem ran ahead, playing, laughing, being children. Janani and I walked behind, watching them, talking about nothing, about everything.

"They seem happier," Janani said. "Do they?"

"Yeah. They've noticed you're different. More here. More engaged."

"I'm working at it."

"I know. And they see it. I see it."

We settled on a bench. Watched the children play. The sun was out, rare for October. The park was full of families, of children, of life.

"This is nice," I said. "What? The park?"

"This. Being here. With you. With them. Not having to perform. Not having to be perfect. Just being."

She studied me, seeing something she hadn't seen before, seeing me for the first time in years.

"It is nice," she said.

* * *

281

SHE EXAMINED HER HANDS. "I came here with my terms, my conditions, what I need. I didn't ask what you need. Or if you even want this."

"I've learned to live on my own, too. I've built something that works.

Reconciliation is hard."

"So what do you want, Dev?"

"I know I love you. But I'm terrified of disappointing you again."

"Then maybe this isn't about my terms or your terms. Maybe we

Both need to figure out if there's a version of us that works. Not the old us. Something new."

"So we're dating."

"We're seeing if this works. For both of us."

* * *

WE AGREED TO TRY AGAIN, but gradually—no moving back in, no cohabitation. Just dating properly.

"Six months," Janani said. "Dinners. Conversations. Intentional time. If we both still want this after six months, we'll talk about next steps."

"That's fair."

The café around us kept moving—cups clinking, voices rising and falling—while we sat there negotiating a future that still felt like a question.

"And I need something from you, Dev," she said. "Specific. Not a promise. A commitment."

I looked at her—careful, guarded, but open enough to risk this.

"Okay," I said. "I'll do the work. I'll show up. I'll be here. Really here."

She nodded, but I could see the doubt: *I've heard this before.*

I hesitated, then said it anyway. "And it has to work both ways. Respect, trust, commitment. From both of us."

"What are you asking for?" she asked.

"That you're in it," I said. "Not testing me and not waiting for me to fail. Actually, choosing this too. I can't do it if I'm walking on eggshells."

"I'm here," she said. "I'm the one who suggested we try."

"I know. I'm grateful. I need to know this isn't only a trial I'm taking."

She held my gaze for a long moment.

"You're right," she said finally. "It has to work both ways."

Then she added, quietly, "But I need to see it from you first. I need to see you show up. Then I'll match it."

"That's fair," I said.

And it wasn't entirely fair. But it was honest.

"I understand," I said. "You have reasons to be guarded. I'll do it. I'll show you. And I hope it becomes something you can trust."

She studied me as if recalibrating.

"Okay," she said. "I'll try too. I'll try to trust it. I'll try to match it. But I need to see you first."

"I will," I said.

We sat in the silence for a moment, letting the terms settle.

"This is hard," I said.

"Yes," she said. "It is."

We finished our drinks, paid, and walked to the Tube side by side. Not touching. Just together.

At the turnstiles, we stopped—our usual parting spot.

"Thank you," I said. "For trying."

"Thank you for showing up," she said. "For actually being here."

"I'll see you on Tuesday?"

"Yes. Tuesday."

She went through first. I watched her disappear down the stairs, then turned to my own gate.

It was a beginning. Small. Fragile. Uncertain.

But it was a beginning.

* * *

EACH WEEK FEATURED SMALL GESTURES, conversations, and moments of connection. We met for dinner on Tuesdays, coffee on Saturdays, and took the children to the park, museums, and the cinema. We learned to be in each other's presence again without expectations or pressure to be perfect.

Small gestures began to matter. I'd bring her a strong, no-sugar coffee on Saturday mornings. She'd remember things I mentioned, like books or movies, and bring them up casually, showing she cared.

One Thursday, I was working late when Janani texted to check in. Nothing urgent, just checking. I called her, said I was fine and working. She asked if I'd eaten; I hadn't. She offered to bring food, and I declined, but she insisted. She arrived at my office with homemade, simple food. It mattered—the gesture, her care, and her presence.

"You didn't have to do this."

"I know. But I wanted to. I wanted to show up, to be here."

"Thank you."

"You're welcome."

She stayed for a bit. Watched me eat. Asked about my work. Listened. Listened. The way she used to, how I'd forgotten she could, how I'd forgotten I needed.

"This is nice," she said. "What? The food?"

"This. Being here. With you. Showing up."

"I know what you mean."

"Do you? Because I'm not sure you do. I'm not sure you understand how much it matters."

"I'm learning."

"Good. Keep learning, showing up, being here."

* * *

ONE TUESDAY, we visited an intimate Islington restaurant that felt like a secret. We ordered wine, shared starters, and talked about children, work, and life—easy, natural conversation, as if reminding ourselves how to be together.

"This is nice," Janani said. "What? The restaurant?"

"This. Being here. With you. Not having to be anything. Just being."

"I know what you mean."

"Do you? Because I'm uncertain you do. I'm uncertain you understand how hard it was, how lonely, how exhausting."

"I'm working to understand."

"I know. And I see that. I see you working at it. I see you doing the work. I see you actually being here."

"Does it?"

"Yes. It does. Because before, you weren't working at it, you weren't here, you weren't engaged. Now you are, you're working at it, you're here. And that matters. That makes all the difference."

I looked at her. This woman who'd left me, who'd saved herself, who'd built a life without me. This woman was choosing to try again, to trust again, to hope again.

"Thank you," I said. "For what?"

"For giving me another chance. For seeing the work. For believing I can change."

"I'm not giving you a chance. I'm choosing to see if we can build something new. Something different. Something that works for both of us."

"And if it doesn't?"

"Then we walk away. No second chances. No attempting again. We walk away, and we don't look back."

I nodded, understood, and accepted.

* * *

TWO MONTHS IN, we almost gave up.

It was a Tuesday. We'd had dinner. The conversation had been stiff, cautious, guarded, as if we were both holding back, both protecting ourselves, both waiting for the other to let us down.

"This isn't working," Janani said. "What isn't?"

"This, us, working at it. It's too hard, it's too much. I can't do this anymore."

"What do you mean?"

"I mean, I'm tired. I'm exhausted. I'm working so hard to trust, to hope, to believe. But it's not working. I'm still waiting for you to disappear. I'm still waiting for you to let me down. I'm still waiting for the pattern to repeat."

"I'm not going to disappear. I'm not going to let you down. I'm not going to repeat the pattern."

"How do I know that? How do I trust that? How do I believe that?"

"I can't promise certainty. But I'm here. I'm working at it. I'm doing the work. I'm actually here. I'm showing up."

"But for how long? How long until you get tired? How long until you disappear again? How long until I'm carrying everything alone again?"

"I'm not sure. But I'm here now. I'm actually here now. I'm showing up now. And I'll keep showing up. I'll keep being here. I'll keep doing the work."

"But what if it's not enough? What if I can't trust? What if I can't hope? What if I can't believe?"

"Then we'll figure it out together. We'll take it one day at a time, one conversation at a time, one moment at a time. We'll build trust, we'll build hope, we'll build belief, slowly, carefully, together."

She was quiet. Her gaze stayed on me, working to see if I meant it, attempting to believe, striving to hope.

Her hands were still, but her voice wavered slightly. "Me too."

"What if we fail again?"

"Then we'll have worked at it, done the work, shown up, been here."

"Is it?"

"I think so. I hope so."

She reached across the table. Took my hand. Squeezed it. "Okay. Let's keep working at it. One day at a time, conversation at a time, moment at a time."

"Okay."

* * *

REACHED FOR HER INSTINCTIVELY. It wasn't theatrical, just a familiar gesture—my hand moving towards her arm as she stood beside me in the kitchen, close enough that the old sense of space remained intact.

She noticed.

She didn't step back. She didn't tense up. She shifted her weight, picked up her mug, and moved it from one hand to the other, creating a slight, deliberate pause.

"I'm going to stand over here," she said.

Not defensive. Not apologetic. As if stating where a chair belonged.

I let my hand fall. The space between us widened by inches, not more. Enough.

She returned to her task, carefully rinsing the cup and placing it upside down on the rack. She always dried her hands before touching anything else. That was new. Or maybe it wasn't. I only noticed it now.

Later, when we sat at the table, she chose the chair opposite me rather than the one beside me. The difference was subtle but clear. Opposite me, she could look directly at me without leaning in.

I realised then that this was how she did it.

Not by refusing contact outright. Not by explaining herself again. But by adjusting the choreography—where she stood, where she sat, how long she lingered before responding.

When the conversation drifted towards the familiar, she gently steered it away, like guiding a child from a busy road without emphasising the danger.

"You don't need to tell me that," she said once, when I started to explain myself.

It wasn't dismissal. It was containment.

Later still, when I left, she didn't follow me to the door. She stayed where she was, one hand resting on the back of the chair she'd chosen, watching me collect my coat.

"Text me when you get home," she said.

Outside, I understood what she was doing.

She wasn't punishing me. She wasn't closing the door. She was training the space between us to hold.

It was the most intimate thing she had done since we separated.

* * *

"You stay in therapy. Weekly. I can't do this if you're not doing that work."

"I'm already seeing Dr Claire. I'll keep going." She nodded.

"Janani."

Her head turned toward me.

"Despite everything, I'm still the same Dev who was stunned by you at that community event. Your looks, voice, demeanour."

Her eyes filled with tears.

* * *

That evening, I called Maya.

She picked up on the second ring. "Dev?"

The phone felt heavy in my hand. I was sitting in my flat. Lights off. The streetlamp outside cast orange light through the window.

"I'm reconciling with Janani. We're going to try again." Silence.

Traffic outside. The hum of the refrigerator. My own breathing. "I wanted to tell you. Before the four weeks."

More silence. Then a breath. Not quite a sigh. Something heavier. "Thank you for telling me."

I could hear her shifting. A chair creaks. The sound of her setting something down. A glass, maybe. Or her phone switching hands.

"I'm sorry."

"Don't be."

Her voice was steady, but there was something beneath it—something I recognised from fourteen years ago. The way she'd sounded when she told me to go to Janani. Her shoulders dropped slightly, yet her words remained gracious.

"I'm happy for you. I am."

"Maya."

"No, I mean it. You need to make it work this time. Both of you."

I heard her stand. Footsteps. Hardwood floor. Then softer. Carpet.

She was moving through her flat whilst we talked. "Are you sure? About her?"

"Yes."

"Then that's what matters."

A pause. I could hear her breathing, slow and controlled, the way she breathed when she was keeping something in.

"We would have been a disaster, you know. Even now. Even older. I'm still the person who works sixteen-hour days. Who travels three weeks a month. Who built a company instead of a life?"

"Maya."

"And you're still the person who needs roots. Who needs someone who's there? Who can't be a weekend thing between flights to Singapore and San Francisco?"

She laughed. But it wasn't bitter. Tired.

"I knew that when I sent the email. But I had to ask. Had to know for sure. Otherwise, I'd spend the next fourteen years wondering again." The sound of a door opening. Closing. She'd stepped outside. I could hear the wind. London wind. The same wind that was outside my window.

"Where are you?"

"Balcony. Needed air."

Silence. The wind. The city is humming below us—Miles apart but hearing the same sounds.

"Take care of yourself, Dev. And take care of her."

"I will."

"Make it work this time. Fight for it. Don't let her disappear."

"I won't."

"Good."

Another pause. Longer this time. "I should go."

"Maya."

"It's fine. Really. I'm glad you called. I'm glad you're attempting again. And I'm glad I asked."

She hung up.

I remained in the dark. Phone still against my ear. Listening to the dial tone until it clicked off.

The orange streetlamp light lit the floor. My hands trembled, shaking as I looked at them. They'd held her hand fourteen years ago but let go, choosing safety and fear over love.

I set the phone down, stood, and looked out at London from the window—Maya's city, seen from her balcony miles away—same town, night, and wind, but different lives, choices, and futures.

I wondered if she was the same Maya from fourteen years ago. She kept her back straight, didn't look back or show weakness, nor let anyone see her break. I asked if she was okay and alone. Maybe she wondered what might have been, whether she had made a mistake, or whether I had.

I hoped she was okay, that she would find someone, that she would be happy, that she would build the life she wanted and deserved — the life I couldn't give her, the life I'd been too afraid to try for.

I remained for a long time.

* * *

THE FIRST DINNER was on a Thursday evening.

A small restaurant in Hackney. Tables are close together. Warm lighting. The noise of other diners creates a buffer, a distance from the silence between us. I arrived first. Found a table. Sat. Waited.

She arrived ten minutes later. Apologized. Traffic.

"It's fine," I said. "I've only been here a few minutes."

She sat across from me. The table is small. Our knees are almost touching. I could smell her perfume. The same one she'd always worn. The same one I'd forgotten, I remembered.

"How are the children?" I asked.

"Good. Anjali's enjoying school. Prem's violin lessons are going well."

"Good. That's good."

We ordered. Wine. Food. Safe choices. Things we'd ordered before. Familiar territory.

"How's work?" she asked.

"Good. Busy. The consulting work is going well."

"And therapy?"

I paused. Wondered how much to say. How much was too much? How much was not enough?

"It's... helpful. Hard. But helpful."

"Good. I'm glad."

"Thank you. For... for everything. For getting me help. Even after..."

"You don't have to thank me. It wasn't... I didn't do it for you. I did it for the children. For them to have their father. Really have him."

"I know. But still. Thank you."

She nodded. Looked away. Then back at me. "You look different."

"How?"

"I don't know. Less... tense. More... present. Like you're actually here, not just physically here."

"I'm working at it. Being present. Being here."

"I can see that. It's good. It suits you."

The food arrived. We ate. Talked. Carefully. Navigating new territory. Building something new. Something different.

"How's the teaching?" I asked.

"Good. I'm enjoying it. The students are engaged. They ask good questions."

"What are you teaching?"

"Postcolonial literature. Rushdie. Roy. Things that matter. Things that connect."

"You sound different when you talk about it."

"Do I?"

"Yes. Lighter. Like you're doing it because you want to, not because you have to."

She smiled. "I am. It feels... right. Like I'm using my education, my knowledge, my passion. Not just my skills."

"That's good. You deserve that. To do something you love."

"Thank you."

We finished eating. Drank our wine. Talked. Carefully. Cautiously. Building something new, something fragile, something we were both trying to protect, to nurture, to see if it could grow.

"Should we go?" she asked.

"Yes."

I paid. We walked to the Tube together. Side by side. Not touching and not holding hands. Just... together. In the same space. Moving in the same direction.

At the turnstiles, we stopped. Our usual parting spot. The place where we'd said goodbye, where we'd gone our separate ways, where we'd been going our separate ways for months.

"Thank you," she said. "For dinner. For... for showing up."

"Thank you for coming. For... for giving me a chance."

"We'll see."

"Yes. We'll see."

She went through the turnstile. I watched her go. Down the stairs. Out of sight. I stood there for a moment. Then I went through my own turnstile. Walked to my platform. Waited for my train. It had been careful. Cautious. Tentative.

But it had been real. We'd been present. We'd been here. Really here. Not just physically. But emotionally. Engaged. Connected.

It was a beginning. Small. Fragile. Uncertain.

But it was a beginning.

* * *

MONTH FOUR. She taught an evening seminar at the university. She'd mentioned it casually. Postcolonial literature. Adult learners. Something she was attempting.

"Can I come? Sit in the back?"

She looked surprised. "You want to?"

"I want to see you teach."

So I settled in the back row of a classroom in Bloomsbury. Watched Janani come alive.

Twenty adults. Mostly immigrants. Discussing Rushdie and Roy. She asked questions that made them think. Listened with intent.

Drew connections they hadn't seen.

Afterwards, she introduced me to a few students. "This is Dev. He's... we're seeing each other."

She stumbled on the label. We both laughed.

Walking back to the Tube. "You didn't have to come."

"I wanted to. You're brilliant at this."

"It's part-time. Two courses. Nothing major."

"It's nothing. You're good at it. You care about it."

THREE WEEKS INTO MONTH FOUR, I made a mistake.

I'd forgotten. A dinner we'd planned. A small restaurant. Thursday evening. I'd said I'd be there. I'd confirmed it and texted about it that morning. Then work happened. A client emergency. A system crash. Critical. Needed me there. I'd handled it. Fixed it. Called the client. Explained. Resolved.

Then I looked at my phone. Five missed calls. Three texts.

All from Janani.

Blimey. It was eight thirty. We'd planned to meet at seven. I'd forgotten entirely.

I called her. "Janani. I'm so sorry. I forgot. Work happened.

A client emergency. I... I should have called. I should have let you know."

Silence. The kind that meant she was disappointed. Not angry. Disappointed. That was worse.

"It's okay," she said. But I could hear it in her voice. The resignation. The "here we go again." The expectation of disappointment.

"No, it's not okay. I'm sorry. I should have called. I should have texted. I should have remembered."

"You're at work?"

"Yes. But I can leave. Now. Come to the restaurant. Or meet you somewhere. Wherever you are."

"I'm already home. I waited. For an hour. Then I came home."

"Janani, I'm sorry. Really. This was... it was a mistake. A real mistake. Not an excuse. Not a justification. A mistake. And I'm sorry."

"I know. But... Dev, we've been doing this for four months. Four months of being careful, of showing up, of trying. And you... You forgot."

"I know. And I'm sorry. I can't... I can't make excuses. I can't justify it. I just... I forgot. And I'm sorry."

Silence. Then: "What would you have done before? In the old days? If this had happened?"

I thought about it. "I would have called and made an excuse. The said work was more important. Justified it. Made it seem like it wasn't my fault."

"And now?"

"Now... I'm calling to acknowledge the mistake—apologising, really apologising, and not making excuses or justifying it, just acknowledging. Apologizing. Trying to make it right."

"How?"

"I don't know. But I want to try. I want to make it right."

"Come over to my flat. If you want, we can order something. Talk. If you want."

"Yes. I want to. If you'll let me."

"Yes. Come over."

I left work. Took the Tube. Walked to her flat. Knocked on the door.

She opened it. Still dressed. Ready for dinner. Her face guarded. Careful. But not closed. Not shut.

"I'm sorry," I said. Again.

"I know. Come in."

I came in. We ordered food. Sat. Talked. Carefully. Cautiously.

"This was a test, wasn't it?" I asked.

"What?"

"You asked what I would have done before. This was a test. To see if I'd changed. If I'd handled it differently."

She looked at me. Really looked. "Yes. In a way. I needed to know. If you'd changed, suppose you'd handle it differently, if you'd... if you'd really be here even when it's tough. Even when it's inconvenient."

"And? Did I pass?"

"You didn't forget on purpose. You didn't prioritise work on purpose. You made a mistake. A real mistake. And you acknowledged it. Apologized. Really apologised. Tried to make it right."

"Is that passing?"

"It's... It's a start. It's better than before. Better than excuses. Better than justification. Better than 'work is more important.'"

"But?"

"But I still waited. For an hour. Alone. Wondering if you'd show up. Wondering if you'd remember. Wondering if this would be different. And it wasn't. Not completely."

"I know. And I'm sorry. I can't... I can't undo that. I can't make it, so you didn't wait. I can only... I can only try to do better. Try to remember. Try to show up. Even when it's hard."

"Even when it's inconvenient?"

"Yes. Especially when it's inconvenient."

She looked at me. Studied me. As if seeing me for the first time. As if recognising something new, something different, something she'd been waiting for.

"Okay," she said. "Okay. We'll see."

"Yes. We'll see."

We ate. Talked. Carefully. Building something new. Something fragile. Something we were both trying to protect, to nurture, to see if it could grow.

It wasn't perfect. It wasn't enough. Not yet. But it was a start. It was different. It was better.

And maybe, just maybe, that was enough.

* * *

AMIR INVITED US TO DINNER. The routine was established: we met regularly for coffee, walks, and conversations. The children had stopped asking about gatherings—they'd adjusted, and we were adjusting.

When he called, "Both of you. Properly. I want to see if you lot are making this work or pretending for the kids."

We went to his flat in Shoreditch. He'd cooked curry, rice, and too much of everything.

His girlfriend, Sarah, was there. American. Worked in tech. She and Janani bonded over shared frustration with startup culture.

Dinner was easy. Janani and Sarah talked about work. Amir and I discussed football. Normal evening.

* * *

AMIR and I went to the pub, like we used to, before everything— separation, divorce, therapy, reconciliation. We sat at our usual table, ordered pints, and talked about work and life.

Everything. About nothing.

"You seem different," Amir said. "How?"

"More here. More engaged. More you. Less... performative. Less like you're working to be someone else."

"I'm working at it."

"And how's that going?"

"It's hard. But it's worth it."

"Good. Because the person I knew, the person I became friends with, that person was real. And I missed him. I missed you."

"I missed you, too. I didn't realise how much until I started therapy."

"And Janani? How's that going?"

"It's going. We're working at it. We're making progress."

"Good. Because she's good for you, she always was. You needed to be good for her, too."

"I know. And I'm working at it."

"That's all anyone can ask for. The working at it, showing up, actually being here. The being here."

AFTER DINNER, Amir pulled me aside to the kitchen whilst the women talked in the living room.

"You seem better."

He was loading the dishwasher. Plates clinking.

"Yeah, about that..." He paused. Plate in hand. "I'm glad Janani got you sorted. That was brilliant of her."

"What do you mean?"

He kept loading dishes. Didn't look at me. "Getting you to Dr Claire.

That whole intervention. Took guts." Intervention. Not referral. Not a suggestion. "What intervention?"

He stopped. Turned. "You don't know?"

I stared at him.

"Shit." He set the plate down. "I thought you knew. I thought she'd told you by now."

"Told me what?"

He closed the dishwasher. Leaned against the counter.

"Janani came to me. Said she'd noticed something was wrong. The way you'd switch accents mid-sentence, blank stares, and disappear. She couldn't sleep."

I stared at him.

"She'd talked to her friend, Dr Claire, and got a professional opinion. Then came to me, asked if I could get you to see her because you wouldn't go if it came from Janani. Had to come from a friend."

"So the card. The intervention. That was orchestrated?"

"Yeah. Janani set it up. Claire agreed to see you as a favour to her. The whole thing was planned."

I settled at the kitchen table. "Your voice changed."

"I can't define what I am."

"She watched you fragment for years. Then, it gets worse after the divorce. And instead of walking away completely, she got you help. Even though you were separated."

He settled across from me.

"That's not control, mate. That's love."

I heard Janani laugh in the other room, easy and unguarded, the way she used to laugh.

"Does she know you know?"

"No. And I wasn't supposed to tell you. But you lot are attempting again. You should know."

He rose. "Be grateful. Not everyone gets a second chance. And not everyone has an ex-wife who cares enough to get them help even after everything fell apart."

He left me sitting there. Went back to the living room.

* * *

THAT NIGHT, after leaving Amir's, we walked to the Tube. The October air was cold and the city silent, making conversations seem louder and everything feel more significant.

Did you have a good time? Yeah. Amir himself.

She laughed. "He is."

We reached the turnstiles, our usual parting spot, the place where we said goodbye, the place where we went our separate ways, the place where we'd been going our separate ways for months. But tonight was different.

I said her name. "Janani."

She turned. Her expression was careful, guarded, waiting, expecting something, knowing what was coming.

Thank you. For Dr Claire. For getting me help. Even after everything. Her expression tightened. "Amir told you."

"He did."

"I'm sorry. I know I should have said something. But I didn't know how to bring it up. And then we started dating again, and it felt weird to..."

Don't apologise. You saved my life. Literally, you saw what was happening. And instead of walking away, you did something about it. You got me help. You saved me. Even after everything, after I'd let you down.

Her eyes filled with tears. But she didn't cry. She maintained eye contact, seeing something, working to believe.

I couldn't let you break. You're the children's father. And I still..." She paused, looked away briefly, then looked back at me. "I still cared. Even when I shouldn't have, even when it would have been easier to walk away, but I couldn't."

I pulled her into a hug, right there at the Tube station. Commuters flowed around us, people walking past, the city moving, life continuing, but in that moment, everything stopped.

"Thank you."

* * *

WE SAT in Janani's flat on a Sunday evening. The children were with her parents for the weekend, and the flat was still — a stillness that felt peaceful, like home, like we had earned it, like we had built it together.

She'd made tea. Indian. Strong enough to strip paint. I'd learned not to add milk until she said it was ready. I'd learned a lot of things. About her, us, what we could be, and what we were becoming.

We sat in silence for a while.

"I need to tell you something," Janani said. "What?"

"I'm working so hard to trust, to hope, to believe. But I'm scared it won't work. I'm scared you'll disappear again."

"I know."

"Do you?" Her voice was quiet. "Do you know how hard this is?" I was quiet. "I think so. I'm scared too."

"Of what?"

"Of disappointing you. Of not being enough."

She nodded. "We're here, though. We're showing up."

"We are."

"Does it?"

"Yes. Because before, we weren't working at it. We weren't showing up. Now we are."

I looked at her. This woman who'd left me, who'd saved herself, who'd built a life without me, who was choosing to be vulnerable, honest, real, to trust, to hope, and to believe.

"Thank you," I said. "For what?"

"For being vulnerable. For being honest. For trusting me."

"I'm working at it."

"I know. And I see it. And it matters."

She smiled. Not the cautious smile. Not the wary smile. The genuine one, the one that lit up her eyes, that made everything seem possible, that made everything feel right.

* * *

"We said six months. But I already know my answer. What about you?"

I looked at her sitting cross-legged on the sofa, hair tied back, wearing an old t-shirt I thought she'd thrown away. She kept it because she hoped, cared, and never stopped loving me.

Yes. I want this. I want to try. Properly.

She smiled. Not the careful smile. Not the guarded smile. The real one, the one that reached her eyes.

Set down her tea. Then let's do it properly. Let's move back in together. But differently this time.

How?

She studied me, seeing something, working to believe, attempting to trust.

"We keep our own spaces. You keep the house. I keep my flat. But we spend most nights together. We date whilst living together. We build something new instead of working to resurrect what died."

"That works."

"And we're honest. If it's not working, we say so before the resentment builds. Before we stop seeing each other again."

"Agreed."

She moved closer. "We're doing this." She kissed me.

"Don't disappear on me this time."

* * *

THE DECISION TO try again was built gradually, methodically. One conversation at a time. One moment at a time. One gesture at a time.

It was the coffee on Saturday mornings, the food on Thursday evenings, the conversations on Tuesday nights, the walks in the park, the moments of vulnerability, honesty, and trust.

It was the work, the therapy, the showing up, the working at it, the failing, the attempting again.

It was the daily choice, the moment-by-moment choice, the choice to show up, to be here, to work at it, to trust, to choose each other.

* * *

WE TOLD the children the next day.

After almost 18 months of our separation, Anjali was eleven, and Prem was nine. They had watched us date, cautious and intentional, maintaining separate homes. They observed us being careful, deliberate, and independent. They had learned not to hope. They had learned not to expect. They had learned to protect themselves. And they had learned to be cautious, too.

"Your dad and I have something to tell you," Janani said.

Prem looked up from his book. Anjali's eyes narrowed slightly; she'd learned not to hope too quickly, be sceptical, protect herself, wait, observe, avoid getting hopes up, expecting too much, or being disappointed again.

"We're moving back in together." Prem's face lit up. "For real?"

"For real. Different this time. I'm in therapy—your mum's teaching. We're not going back to how it was before. But we're choosing to be a family again, to work at it, to fight, to be here."

"How?" Anjali asked. "How is it different?"

"Because we've both changed, because we've both learned, because we've both done the work, because we're choosing this, not falling into it, because we're being honest about what we need, about what we can give, about what we're willing to do."

"And you'll be here?" Prem asked. "For dinner? For bedtime? For everything?"

"Most of the time, yes. Sometimes I'll have to work late. Sometimes your mum will have to work late. But we'll be here. We'll show up."

"Promise?" Anjali asked. "Promise," Janani said. "Promise," I said.

And I meant it. "When?" Prem asked.

"This month. We'll find a new place, smaller, less stressful, somewhere that's ours together, that doesn't have the weight of the old house or the memories of failing. A fresh beginning."

Anjali had been quiet. Now she spoke. "Are you sure? Because last time it didn't work."

"We're sure," Janani said. "We've both changed—your dad's learning to be present here. I'm learning to ask for what I need. We're not promising perfect. We're promising honesty, to work at it, to show up, to be here, to fight for this, not to disappear, not to let each other down."

She looked directly at me. "I spent years waiting for you to see me. To truly see me. Not the version of me you needed me to be, but the person I actually am.

The person who needs things, who feels things, who has her own interiority that exists completely separate from you. And you're learning to do that now. You're learning to see me, not just observe me."

Anjali looked at us both, working to see if we were telling the truth, if we meant it, if we were different, if we'd changed. "You seem happier. Not pretending."

"We are."

Prem crawled into my lap. Nine, but still small enough. "Does this mean you'll be home for dinner every night?"

Most nights, yes. Good. I missed that.

Prem launched himself at us. Arms around both our necks. "This is good. You're both good."

Janani and I looked at each other over his head.

* * *

We found a smaller place in Leyton. A terraced house on a quiet street, the kind where neighbours knew each other's names, children played in the street, and the pace of life was slower and more measured. Three bedrooms, enough for the children and us, but not so much.

That we could slip away into separate corners. Small garden at the back, overlooked by other houses. The street was lined with cherry trees that would bloom in spring, their pink blossoms forming a canopy of colour. We sold the Walthamstow house because it was too big, too full of memories of failure. This new place was smaller, more manageable.

Moving day was different this time. The children helped by carrying boxes, organising their rooms, and making the space feel like theirs. Janani and I worked together, not in separate corners avoiding each other, but side by side.

That evening, after we had unpacked everything, we sat in the living room. The children were in their rooms, settling in and making the space theirs. Janani and I sat on the sofa, surrounded by boxes.

"This feels different," Janani said. "How?"

"It does. Like we're building something, choosing this, being here."

"We are."

"Are we? Really?"

"Yes. We are. I'm here, choosing this, choosing you, choosing us."

She continued to look at me, trying to see if I meant it, trying to believe it, trying to trust it.

"I believe you," she said. "Thank you."

"Don't thank me. Just be here. Be engaged. Be real."

"I will."

"Promise?"

"Promise." I meant it.

"This feels different," Anjali said, standing in her new room. "How?" I asked.

"It does. Like we're a family again."

I looked at her. This child who'd learned not to hope, who'd learned to protect herself, who'd learned to be careful.

"I am here," I said. "I'm here, I'm actually here."

"I know. I can tell."

On moving day, Amir arrived in a van.

"Heard you're doing something daft like reconciling. Thought you'd need help."

We moved boxes for six hours. At the end, standing in the doorway of the new place: "This suits you better. The big house always felt as if you were working too hard."

"Thanks for everything. For the intervention. For being honest when I couldn't be."

"That's what mates do, innit." He clapped my shoulder. "Don't mess this up again."

* * *

THAT EVENING, after the children were asleep in their new bedrooms, Janani and I lingered in the garden.

The vine came with us. I'd carefully dug it up from the old house and transplanted it here. The soil felt cool against my hands, the roots still delicate and fragile. It sulked for weeks, shedding leaves. But now it was blooming again, pink flowers contrasting with the grey fence.

"My mother checked on her bougainvillea every evening. For fifty years."

Janani reached for my hand.

We remained together in the small garden, the plant blooming, London noise in the background.

* * *

THREE MONTHS AFTER MOVING IN, we were lying in bed on a Sunday morning.

Grey light filters through the curtains. The children are still asleep, and the house is quiet. Janani was reading. I was half-awake, watching her hold the book and turn the pages.

Not looking up from her book: "I've been thinking."

"About?"

"I'm taking you somewhere." I waited.

"Iceland. You and me. Properly away."

"You want to go to Iceland?"

I've wanted to do it for years, ever since I was twenty-five. I once had it all planned: a solo trip, a camper van, the whole Ring Road. Then work got busy, life got busy, and I kept postponing it, waiting for the right moment. She put down her book, her eyes meeting mine. But the right moment never comes. You have to create it.

"When?"

"Next month. Two weeks. My parents will take the kids. We rent a camper van. Drive wherever we want. No schedule. No plan. Just us."

She reached for her phone and pulled up photos. The screen glowed in the dim light. Images of Iceland, mountains, waterfalls, black sand beaches, and volcanic landscapes that looked like another planet.

Softly: "Look at this. Moss-covered lava fields at Þingvellir, where you can stand between two continents—Europe and North America—literally in the gap. She swiped to show Seljalandsfoss, where you can walk behind the waterfall, feeling the sound, mist, and power up close."

Her face, more than the photos, how her eyes brightened, how she smiled.

"There are hot springs everywhere," she continued. "Natural pools. Geothermal water. Warmth from the earth itself. And at night in summer, the sun barely sets. Golden hour that lasts forever. Light that makes everything beautiful."

"You've clearly thought about this."

"I have. For a long time." She set the phone down. "I want to see beautiful things with you, Dev. Not because we're escaping. Because we're choosing to."

The old version of me would find reasons to say no: too expensive, too impractical, what if work needed me.

"Okay."

"Okay?"

"Yes. Let's go to Iceland. Two weeks. Camper van. No plan." She smiled. "Really?"

"Really. I want to stand between continents with you. I want to walk behind a waterfall and get soaked. I want two weeks where nothing matters except what we choose to do that day."

She kissed me.

Then she was already reaching for her laptop, pulling up rental sites, flight schedules, maps.

There's this one waterfall. And black sand beaches. And puffins. Did you know Iceland has puffins?

She planned our adventure, her excitement palpable, her hands moving as she talked, her eyes bright with possibility.

* * *

WE LANDED IN REYKJAVIK.

The airport was small. Modern. The air was cold. Different from London's damp, chilly. This was sharp. Clean. A cold that made you feel alive.

We picked up the white, small, and functional camper van.

Janani drove first. She'd never driven on the right side of the road before, but she learned quickly and confidently, the way she did everything, head-on.

We drove out of Reykjavik. The Ring Road stretched ahead. Mountains in the distance. Volcanic landscapes. Beauty that made you forget to breathe.

We stopped at Þingvellir first. The place where you could stand between continents, where Europe and North America met, where you could be in two places at once.

I stood there, one foot on Europe, one foot on North America, standing in the gap, standing between, like me, like us, between worlds, between who we were and who we were becoming.

Janani took my hand. We remained together in the gap, between continents, between worlds, between who we were and who we were becoming.

We drove on, stopped at waterfalls, walked behind Seljalandsfoss, got soaked, laughed, laughter that comes from deep inside.

We found hot springs, natural pools, geothermal water, and the warmth from the earth itself. We sat in the water, the cold air above, warm water below, the contrast made everything feel more real, more immediate, more alive.

At night, we parked the camper van, cooked simple meals, and sat outside, watching the sun not set. The golden hour seemed to last forever, with light that made everything beautiful—light that made you remember why you were alive.

We talked. About everything, about nothing, about who we were, about who we were becoming, about what we wanted, about what mattered.

On our last day, we settled on a black-sand beach. The days had blurred together. Too fast. Too slow. Just right. Time that felt like forever and no time at all. The waves crashed, the wind blew, and the sky was grey. But everything felt beautiful. Everything felt right. Everything felt real.

"I'm glad we did this," Janani said. "Me too."

"I want to do more of this. More choosing, actually being here, being engaged. More being real."

"Me too."

She took my hand. We stood there on the black sand beach in Iceland.

* * *

ONE YEAR later

My mother called.

The bougainvillea is blooming beautifully this year.

Her voice was warm, familiar, the voice I'd known my whole life, the voice that had called me home, checked on me, loved me, remembered me.

My father called. Your mother passed last night. Heart attack. Sudden. The words didn't make sense. They were words other people used.

Words that belonged to other families.

I hung up, sat down, stared at the wall. The world went quiet. Janani found me, sat beside me, and held me. Her arms around me,

Warmth against me, presence beside me.

"I'll come with you," she said. "To Neyveli. To the funeral. I'll be there."

"Thank you."

We booked flights, packed bags, told the children, and explained what had happened.

* * *

NEYVELI WAS the same but different. The streets were the same, the houses were the same, the vine was the same. But everything was different. The funeral was three days. Relatives came, neighbours came, people.

Janani stayed with me through everything: the funeral, the grief, the brokenness. She waited, was there, truly present. She held my hand, sat with me, listened. She was there in a way I hadn't been for her, for my mother, for anyone.

On the fourth day, my father and I stood in the mutram. The bougainvillea bloomed magnificently, with pink flowers covering the wall—the same flowers she'd checked on every evening for fifty years.

She checked on it every evening, my father said. For fifty years. Even the day she died. She was gone.

What will you do with it?

Check on it. Every evening. As she did.

We stood in silence, two men who'd never learned how to talk to each other, united by grief.

* * *

THAT EVENING, I found letters she'd written but never sent. One dated two years earlier:

I check on the bougainvillea every evening and think of you. It blooms every year, even when the weather is bad. It reminds me of you, far from home, surviving in a place that should be wrong for you, but blooming anyway. That's enough for a mother.

I sat in her room for a long time. The realisation coming from deep inside, from a place I didn't know existed, from a place that had been holding everything, waiting, missing her.

I'd been too busy running, leaving, choosing other things, other places, other lives—too busy to notice, to see, to understand that she'd been waiting, checking, remembering, loving, and there.

Janani found me. Sat beside me. Held me. Her arms around me, warmth against me, presence beside me.

After a while: "You were loved. Even from a distance. The bougainvillea leaf. A promise that you were remembered, that you were loved, that you

Mattered. Even when you weren't there, even when you were far away, even when you were choosing other things, other places, other lives."

I looked at her through tears. "I never realised."

"You were too busy running to notice who was waiting. But she was.

Always."

"How did you know?"

"Because that's how mothers love."

She'd understood my mother better than I had.

* * *

WHEN WE RETURNED TO LONDON, we went to the garden. Evening light fading. The winter air was cold, a cold that made you feel alive.

My mother checked her garden each evening for decades. She would stand there in the mutram, Neyveli, the place that had been home, that had been hers, that had been ours. She would stand there, check on the bougainvillea, think of me, remember me, love me, care for me.

Janani reached for my hand, her fingers warm against mine, her presence beside me.

We stood there together. The vine was blooming against the fence.

* * *

ONE YEAR later

I watch myself with the children here, engaged. We're making something new. Not perfect, but real.

* * *

310

THE THERAPY SESSIONS CONTINUED. Weekly.

I was different now.

The vine in our garden bloomed. Pink flowers against the muted London sky, their petals vivid against the ashen backdrop.

Janani checked on it every evening, as my mother had.

I watched her touch the leaves, watched her notice new growth. She tended it without needing thanks.

* * *

ONE EVENING IN LATE OCTOBER, I walked home from the Tube station. The air was sharp, a cold that made you feel alive. The sky was shifting from slate to violet, and the streetlamps started to glow, their light softly spreading against the evening.

I walked past the small park near our house—the one where we'd taken the children on Sunday mornings. The swings were vacant now. The slide hushed. The playground was motionless.

I kept walking, past the houses, past the gardens.

Then I saw it, a bougainvillea growing against a fence, pink flowers vivid against the ashen evening.

I stopped, stood there, looked at it, really looked.

The flowers were the same pink as those in Neyveli, the same pink as those my mother had tended, and the same pink as the ones that had bloomed outside our government quarters year after year without anyone guiding them, without anyone asking them to.

I stood there watching it, noticing it.

Then I heard it, a sound muted at first, then swelling, wings, birds, a flock of them flying overhead, their shapes silhouetted against the violet sky.

I looked up and watched them fly in formation, their movements smooth, their bodies moving as one, dispersing and coming together again. Not the perfect synchrony I'd seen in videos, memories, or dreams, but something else: birds finding each other, adjusting, realigning, choosing to move together.

I stood there watching them, really watching, not thinking about work or deadlines or everything else, just watching, just noticing.

The birds flew on, their shapes diminishing against the sky, their sounds ebbing, their presence receding.

I kept watching until they were gone, until the sky was vacant again, until the moment had passed. But something had shifted, something had changed.

I looked back at the vine, the pink flowers.

The evening air was sharp, the sky a deep violet, and the street-lamps radiated their glow. Rain started to fall, initially light, then becoming steady—the kind that drips through your clothes if you stand in it too long.

I didn't rush. I allowed it to fall on my face, my hair, my shoulders. The water was cold against my skin, the scent of wet pavement and damp earth filling my nostrils. I was truly there.

ACKNOWLEDGMENTS

This book would not exist without the stories of countless immigrants who have shared how they live, how they love, and how they endure. To those who have left home: your courage is not always visible, and your loneliness is often unspoken. Yet the act of rebuilding a life elsewhere—of learning to belong in unfamiliar places—is among the quietest and most demanding forms of heroism. This story belongs to you. Not entirely, but in part.

To my family: thank you for your patience, support, and faith during the long hours of writing and rewriting. Your belief sustained me through doubt and reminded me that home is not only a place, but the people who make it.

To my friends: thank you for reading early drafts, asking difficult questions, and standing by the work when it felt uncertain. Your friendship formed the ground on which this book could take shape.

To my beta readers: thank you for your care, honesty, and attention. Your insights have shaped this book in both visible and unseen ways. Your time was a gift.

To the towns and cities that have hosted me: thank you for teaching me that home can be carried—that it is not fixed, but felt.

To the flowers that bloom without asking: thank you for the reminder that beauty needs no permission, and persistence no applause.

And to the reader: thank you for meeting this story with patience and openness. Some journeys are outward. Others unfold quietly within.

To those walking difficult paths: you are not broken, and you are not lost. You are learning—slowly, imperfectly—to bloom where you stand.

ABOUT THE AUTHOR

Durai R is the author of *"The Smile of the Bougainvillea"*. His writing focuses on human interiority and self-reflection, particularly on how ordinary decisions quietly shape the direction of a life. He is drawn to stories of transition—migration, displacement, moments of change that leave lasting emotional traces and lives lived provisionally.

His work explores themes of migration, intimacy, and the understated moral costs of ambition. He is interested in how people come to feel estranged from the lives they once imagined, lives shaped less by fate than by accumulated choices, and lived within emotional and physical spaces they move through without fully inhabiting.

www.ingramcontent.com/pod-product-compliance
Lightning Source LLC
Chambersburg PA
CBHW070551260626
47161CB00002B/567